Praise for LuAnn McLane

He's No Prince

"This is a laugh-out-loud story and one you won't want to put down." —Fresh Fiction

"I loved all the aspects of this story. It was truly a great romance." —*The Romance Studio* (5 stars)

"This is a fun, lighthearted frolic. . . . Fans will enjoy." —The Best Reviews

"Had me smiling like a loon . . . a delightful read." —Book Binge

"LuAnn McLane is a master at creating sensitive love [sto]ries . . . sweet, sinful, and utterly satisfying!" —Romance Novel TV

[Re]dneck Cinderella

"_____" —The Best Reviews

"A pure _____ [t]he queen of Southern, romantic _____ —Manic Readers

"A lighthearted, quic_____ [sou]thern-fried language and man_____ as a frozen fruit pop on a hot, lazy _____ —*San Fran*_____ *Review*

"A hysterical, sexy, highly entertaining read." —Errant Dreams Reviews

"Funny . . . for a lazy day in the sun or for a great pick-me-up." —Night Owl Reviews

A Little Less Talk and a Lot More Action

"Macy and Luke are fabulous lead protagonists. They make this tale work as a deep yet humorous character study with a strong support cast." —*Midwest Book Review*

continued . . .

"[McLane] has a knack for rollicking Southern romances and her newest is no exception."
—*The Cincinnati Enquirer*

"[A] fun and flirty contemporary romance about grabbing that second chance." —Fresh Fiction

Trick My Truck but Don't Mess with My Heart

"[There's] an infectious quality to the writing, and some great humor." —*Publishers Weekly*

"Sweet . . . a real Southern-fried treat." —*Booklist*

"[A] quick-paced, action-packed, romantic romp . . . hilarious." —Romance Designs

Dancing Shoes and Honky-Tonk Blues

"Lighthearted comedy and steamy romance combine to make this a delightful tale of a small town that takes Hollywood by storm." —Romance Junkies

"A hoot a minute. . . . LuAnn McLane shows her talent for tongue-in-cheek prose and situations . . . a winning tale not to be missed." —Romance Reviews Today

"A fun story filled with plenty of laughter, tears, and all-out reading enjoyment." —Fallen Angel Reviews

"A fabulous story. . . . Get ready for a deliriously funny, passion-filled rumba in this book."
—The Romance Readers Connection

"A fun small-town drama starring a delightful . . . lead couple and an eccentric but likable support cast."
—The Best Reviews

"LuAnn McLane makes the pages sizzle. . . . *Dancing Shoes and Honky-Tonk Blues* is one of the better romances out there this month." —Roundtable Reviews

Dark Roots and Cowboy Boots

"An endearing, sexy, romantic romp that sparkles with Southern charm!" —Julia London

"This kudzu-covered love story is as hot as Texas Pete, and more fun than a county fair."
—Karin Gillespie, author of *Dollar Daze*

"A hoot! The pages fly in this sexy, hilarious romp."
—Romance Reviews Today

"Charmingly entertaining . . . a truly pleasurable read."
—*Romantic Times*

Wild Ride

"A collection of sensual, touching stories . . . *Wild Ride* is exactly that—a thrilling, exhilarating, sensual ride. I implore you to jump right in and hold on tight!"
—A Romance Review

"Amusing, lighthearted contemporary romances starring likable protagonists."   —The Best Reviews

"Scintillating romance set against the backdrop of a tropical island paradise takes readers to new heights in this captivating collection of erotic novellas. The three tales are steamy and fast-paced, combining descriptive romance with creative love stories."
—*Romantic Times* (4 stars)

"A solid collection. . . . For readers, it is a ride worth taking with these three couples."
—Romance Reviews Today

Hot Summer Nights

"Bright, sexy, and very entertaining."
New York Times bestselling author Lori Foster

"Spicy."   —A Romance Review

"Superhot summer romance . . . a fun read, especially for fans of baseball and erotica. This one earns four of Cupid's five arrows."   —BellaOnline

"Funny, sexy, steamy . . . will keep you glued to the pages."   —Fallen Angel Reviews

ALSO BY LUANN MCLANE

CONTEMPORARY ROMANCES
He's No Prince Charming
Redneck Cinderella
A Little Less Talk and a Lot More Action
Trick My Truck but Don't Mess with My Heart
Dancing Shoes and Honky-Tonk Blues
Dark Roots and Cowboy Boots

EROTIC ROMANCES
"Hot Whisper" in *Wicked Wonderland* anthology
Driven by Desire
Love, Lust, and Pixie Dust
Hot Summer Nights
Wild Ride
Taking Care of Business

Playing for Keeps

A CRICKET CREEK NOVEL

LuAnn McLane

A SIGNET ECLIPSE BOOK

SIGNET ECLIPSE
Published by New American Library, a division of
Penguin Group (USA) Inc., 375 Hudson Street,
New York, New York 10014, USA
Penguin Group (Canada), 90 Eglinton Avenue East, Suite 700, Toronto,
Ontario M4P 2Y3, Canada (a division of Pearson Penguin Canada Inc.)
Penguin Books Ltd., 80 Strand, London WC2R 0RL, England
Penguin Ireland, 25 St. Stephen's Green, Dublin 2,
Ireland (a division of Penguin Books Ltd.)
Penguin Group (Australia), 250 Camberwell Road, Camberwell, Victoria 3124,
Australia (a division of Pearson Australia Group Pty. Ltd.)
Penguin Books India Pvt. Ltd., 11 Community Centre, Panchsheel Park,
New Delhi - 110 017, India
Penguin Group (NZ), 67 Apollo Drive, Rosedale, North Shore 0632,
New Zealand (a division of Pearson New Zealand Ltd.)
Penguin Books (South Africa) (Pty.) Ltd., 24 Sturdee Avenue,
Rosebank, Johannesburg 2196, South Africa

Penguin Books Ltd., Registered Offices:
80 Strand, London WC2R 0RL, England

First published by Signet Eclipse, an imprint of New American Library,
a division of Penguin Group (USA) Inc.

First Printing, March 2011
10 9 8 7 6 5 4 3 2 1

To Doug

Your unwavering support and encouragement means the world to me. This is our year!

Acknowledgments

I would like to give heartfelt thanks to the editorial staff at New American Library. It takes a team to get a great book on the shelf, and I am grateful to each and every one of you. I especially want to extend a very special thanks to Jesse Feldman for keeping me on track and to Laura Cifelli for challenging me to grow and get better with each book. I truly appreciate your dedication and hard work. And, as always, thanks to my dear agent, Jenny Bent. You have believed in me from the beginning, and I can't thank you enough. Finally, thank you to my readers. Your kind words keep my fingers on the keyboard.

1

Sweet Southern Comfort

WELCOME TO CRICKET CREEK, KENTUCKY, BIRTHPLACE OF NOAH FALCON, Noah read as he drove his red Corvette convertible past the city-limits sign. He had won several awards as a major-league relief pitcher, but this little bit of hometown recognition never failed to bring a smile to his face. Of course, he'd never dreamed he would be returning home to audition for the community theater. His life wasn't exactly going as planned.

Noah's smile faded as he turned onto Main Street. The once-thriving little town was all but deserted, even on a Saturday afternoon. Several of the shops had FOR LEASE signs in the windows, and other storefronts were looking run-down.

He supposed that the sluggish economy had taken its toll on the small river town where the locals earned a living on charter boating and tourism. He guessed that here, like everywhere else, it was difficult for the local stores and restaurants to compete with nearby suburban chains. Some of the antiques shops had survived, and he smiled when he stopped at the red light and spotted Myra's Diner, where he had consumed many a cherry

Coke, double cheeseburger, and giant onion rings with his rowdy teammates after high school baseball games.

As Noah idled there at the light, he remembered Myra Robinson, as feisty as she was tiny, who had somehow managed to keep Noah and his cronies pretty much in line. All she had to do was raise one eyebrow in their direction and they would pipe down ... well, at least for a minute or two. He also recalled Myra's niece, Jessica, who had caused quite a stir when she had shown up on her aunt's doorstep pregnant at sixteen. But free-spirited Myra lived by her own rules. She had taken her niece in and after sweet little Madison was born, she charmed the town with her mop of blond curls and big blue eyes. Noah shook his head thinking that here he was, twenty years later, auditioning for a play that Jessica's daughter wrote. As he passed the diner he did notice that there seemed to be some construction going on inside and hoped it meant that the restaurant remained on solid ground.

"Yes!" Noah shot a celebratory fist into the air when he saw that Grammar's Bakery, home of the best butter cookies on the planet, was still in business. "Thank God for small favors!" he said to the blue sky and then slid his sleek red car into a parking spot directly in front of the bakery. He glanced at his watch. If he was lucky they would still have a few cookies left. He unfolded his jeans-clad legs from the driver's seat and eased his road-weary body to a standing position before stretching. At least nobody in here would poke fun at his cowboy boots or western-cut flannel shirt. It was a bit on the cool side to have the top down, but on a bright, sunshiny day like this Noah couldn't resist. "You can take the boy out of the country ..." he said under his breath and then grinned. Man, it felt good to be back home.

A bell jingled when Noah tugged the door open, and he had to stop in his tracks and take a deep breath of air scented with cinnamon and yeast. "Please tell me you have some butter cookies left."

"I think so." A teenage girl with a pale blond lopsided ponytail glanced up from wiping the counter and gave him a bored smile.

"Sweet. I'll take them all." Since it was Saturday afternoon the shelves were already mostly bare, but he glanced in the glass display case and breathed a sigh of relief when he spotted a couple dozen butter cookies dotted with pastel icing. A fat cinnamon cake topped with mounds of crumble called his name, and so did a flat, crispy elephant ear. Oh, and he needed a loaf of white and a loaf of marble rye . . .

"Well, I'll be a monkey's uncle!" boomed the big voice of Mabel Grammar. She stood there with her hands on her ample hips and grinned while the double doors to the kitchen swung back and forth behind her. "Noah Falcon?"

Noah pushed his mirrored aviators up onto his head and grinned back. "The one and only."

"No truer words were ever spoken." Mabel laughed, causing her double chin to jiggle. "Well, aren't you just a sight for sore eyes?" She dusted floured hands on her apron and ambled out from behind the counter.

"And so are you, Mabel," Noah told her and gave her a big bear hug. "It sure smells good in here." After he stepped back he noticed that the teenager's jaw had dropped.

"Noah, this is Chrissie."

"Uh-uh . . ."

"You mean you're not Chrissie?" Noah asked with a grin.

"No, I mean . . . yes. Really? You're *Noah Falcon*?" She stood up from her slouch and suddenly appeared less bored.

"Yep." Although Noah bestowed his best Dr. Jesse

Drake soap-opera smile upon her, it grated a little that he wasn't worth the time of day until she knew he was famous. He had experienced much of the same after he was no longer a major-league baseball player, and now that he had been booted off *Love in the Afternoon*, his net worth had taken a nosedive once again. His personal life had taken a tumble too. No one wants a has-been, only a *right-now*, and it was beginning to wear on him—but he kept his smile in place and gave her a wink. She was just a kid and meant no harm.

Chrissie's eyes widened. "Dude, my mom was so upset when you got all blown up in that car wreck."

"What?" Mabel took another step back and gave him a once-over. "What's this about a car wreck?"

"On television," Noah explained. He hadn't seen his untimely death coming either, but before he could elaborate Chrissie interrupted with an excited wave of her hands.

"He plays Dr. Jesse Drake on *Love in the Afternoon*."

Mabel slapped her leg. "Oh, that's right. I'm never home in the afternoon to watch."

"You should totally TiVo it."

"Chrissie, honey, I have no idea what in the world you're even talkin' about. I have a tough enough time workin' my remote."

"My mother never misses it," Chrissie gushed. "She said she knew you back in high school. She said you were superhot."

"Thanks . . . I think."

"N-not that you aren't now," Chrissie quickly amended and then blushed. "You know, for an old dude."

"Oh, Chrissie, good one," Mabel said and slapped her leg again.

"What?" Chrissie frowned for a second, and then she said in a rush, "Oh, not *old* . . . old."

"Chrissie, honey, you'd better quit while you're

ahead." Mabel chuckled but then pressed her lips together when Noah gave her a look. "Oh, Noah, I think
you're still cute as a button with those dimples and all."
She reached up and pinched his cheeks.

"You meant ruggedly handsome, right?"

Mabel patted his cheeks. "You betcha. Well, except
you could use a shave."

"That's my sexy soap-opera stubble, I'll have you
know." When he playfully arched one eyebrow and
struck a pose, Chrissie whipped out her cell phone and
snapped a picture. Great—he looked like a total ass-
hat. Plus, he wanted to keep his presence here on the
down low for a while. He would have asked her to de-
lete it, but she seemed so thrilled that he didn't have
the heart.

"Camera didn't break, did it?" Mabel asked Chrissie, who looked at her like she was one taco short of a
combo.

"Miss Mabel!"

"Oh, Noah knows I'm just yanking his chain," she
said with a wink in his direction.

"My mom is gonna freak," Chrissie announced when
she looked at the picture.

Noah laughed. Although his hometown had always
showered him with pride, Noah's friends and family
also made certain that he checked his ego at the door.
What they didn't know was that except when he was
on the baseball field or in front of the camera, his hotshot persona was just that—an act that he wasn't always
comfortable with. He'd much rather be noshing on chili
cheese fries at Myra's Diner than eating sushi at a fancy
restaurant, but if he wanted to continue with his acting
career he had to keep up his over-the-top image.

"Well, now . . ." Mabel waved her hand toward the
glass cases just as the bell above the door tinkled. Noah
turned to see a tall, slender woman enter the bakery.

"Noah, do you see anything that strikes your fancy?" Mabel asked.

"Um ..." Noah opened his mouth to answer but paused when the woman's eyes widened a fraction before she pushed her rimless glasses up and sort of looked down her nose at him. Not understanding what he had done to deserve such a reaction, he tried to coax a smile from her but failed. When she abruptly turned away, Noah studied her profile, thinking that she looked a bit familiar, but he couldn't quite put his finger on it. He was used to getting smiles instead of snubs, and he racked his brain but came up empty.

"Well, hey there, Olivia," Mabel said to the woman and got a warm smile in return. Her brown hair was pulled back into a tight, controlled bun, and from her creased slacks to her ironed oxford shirt everything about her screamed prim and proper. Oh ... but she had a full, sensual mouth that was shiny with pale peach gloss, making Noah fantasize that she was wearing black lace lingerie beneath her neatly pressed pants. He could just imagine her loosening her bun and shaking her hair free ...

"Noah?" Mabel persisted. "Have you decided what you want?"

"Yeah ..." he answered, but cookies were no longer on his mind. "I have."

When he failed to elaborate, Mabel shook her head and turned to Olivia. "What brings you in today?"

"Do you have any butter cookies left?" Olivia asked hopefully. Like her appearance, her voice seemed all business but possessed an unexpected throaty edge along with a hint of the South.

"I believe we do," Mabel answered and then glanced at Chrissie.

"Um, Miss Lawson, I'm afraid that Dr. Jesse Drake, I mean, Noah, um, *Mr. Falcon* already spoke for them."

"Oh," she said in a disappointed tone and glanced down into the glass case.

When she licked her bottom lip Noah heard himself say, "I'll share them with you."

"Thanks ... but no," Olivia replied in a gracious but not overly friendly tone. She smiled, but it was a tight little smile that matched her tight little bun. By rights Noah should have been totally put off.

But he wasn't. Not even a little.

Women young and old usually fawned all over him. He never quite understood it, but he had come to expect it, and Olivia Lawson's snooty attitude intrigued him.

"Put her cookies on my bill," Noah said firmly to Chrissie.

"I appreciate your kind offer." Olivia inclined her head at him and bestowed another tight smile upon him. "Truly. But that won't be necessary."

Noah glanced at Chrissie and then back at Olivia. "I insist." He gave her a megawatt smile that had never failed him.

Until now.

Olivia's chin came up a notch and a delicate eyebrow arched above her glasses. "No ... but *thank you*," she said smoothly but firmly, like Southern Comfort sliding over cracked ice.

Noah realized that Mabel and Chrissie were looking back and forth at them like a tennis match, which caused his competitive nature to rise to the occasion. But he had to wonder why Olivia Lawson had such a bur up her butt anyway. Again, her name sounded familiar and yet he still couldn't place her. Okay, the ball was in his court, so he smacked it. "In fact, you may have them all. I suddenly have a craving for cinnamon cake instead."

"I wouldn't dream of denying you the cookies, Mr. Falcon. I eat them all the time. I'm sure it's been a while since you've had one."

"Sad but true. Ah . . . and as I recall they simply melt in your mouth, don't they?"

Olivia's cheeks turned a pretty shade of pink. "Yes, and I hope you enjoy your treat."

"But I'll be in Cricket Creek for a while, so I can part with them. Chrissie, give Miss Lawson the cookies."

Chrissie stood behind the counter with a white bag and a tissue paper in her hand and eyed them uncertainly until Mabel stepped in. "Oh, for pity's sake! Chrissie, divide the cookies between the two of them. They're on the house."

"Mabel, no!" Olivia fisted her hands on her hips and looked at Noah as if he had just committed a crime, when all he was trying to do was be a nice guy.

What's up with this chick, anyway?

"In fact, I've changed my mind. I'll take the elephant ear. And a carton of chocolate milk." When Chrissie opened her mouth to protest, Olivia pressed her lips together and silenced her with the raise of one hand.

"Okay, Miss Lawson," Chrissie said and bent her head to her task.

"Thank you," Olivia replied more gently, but she appeared a bit flustered. "How is your essay coming along, Chrissie?"

Chrissie sighed with the drama of a teenager. "Okay, I guess. But I won't lie. I hate it."

"Writing a good essay is the key to doing well in college. Just remember to back up your thesis. Rough draft is due on Tuesday."

Chrissie nodded glumly. "I know."

"So, you're a teacher at Cricket Creek High School?" Noah tilted his head in question.

"Yes, English and drama," she answered and then looked at him a bit expectantly. There was something here he wasn't getting and he was dying to know just *what*, but she turned her head, dismissing him. He heard

Mabel chuckle and looked her way, but she tried to disguise her mirth with a cough and then straightened up some loaves of bread.

Noah turned his attention back to Olivia, who accepted the white paper bag along with the carton of milk with a smile. For some reason the image of Miss Prim and Proper eating the big, flat, sticky elephant ear and washing it down with chocolate milk from the carton struck him as funny, but he wisely kept his amusement to himself, something he normally didn't do.

"You know I'm always willing to stay after school and help or you can e-mail me. Don't hesitate. Okay, Chrissie?"

"I won't," Chrissie replied. "Thanks, Miss Lawson."

"You're welcome. See you on Monday," Olivia said and turned to leave.

"Thanks for stopping in, Olivia," Mabel said and was rewarded with another warm smile. Noah, however, got a brief polite nod as she breezed past him, leaving behind a sultry floral scent that was even more enticing than the aroma of baking bread.

Noah watched her walk out the door and then moved to the side and angled his head past a wedding cake in the front display window. He watched Olivia pause and glance at his Corvette, raise her chin, and then sashay across the street. "What? She hates sports cars? Come on, it's an American classic."

"She drives a hybrid," Chrissie explained.

"Figures," Noah mumbled but then watched her until she was out of sight.

"Somebody sure is smitten," Mabel observed in a deep singsong voice.

"Uh . . . ye-ah," Chrissie echoed with a head bop. "Wait. What is 'smitten'?"

Noah turned around to face two smiling women. "I'm not smitten. I'm . . . perplexed."

"I think you mean intrigued," Mabel commented and widened her eyes when Noah gave her a look. She waved her hands in the air as she took a step back. "I'm just sayin'."

"Am I wrong or does the woman dislike me for no apparent reason?" He looked from Mabel to Chrissie.

Chrissie nibbled on the inside of her cheek and wiggled her shoulders back and forth while in thought. She suddenly stopped and pointed at him. "Maybe you knew her, like, you know, when you lived here?"

Noah rubbed his chin. "Olivia Lawson . . . ? Doesn't ring a bell, but then again, I was drafted into baseball when I was eighteen. I've been away for a long time." He shook his head. "And my life before that was pretty much consumed with baseball too," he said, more to himself than to them, but it was true. Everyone thought he lived a charmed life, but it wasn't without cost, lately leading him to behavior he wasn't proud of. He hoped that coming home would heal him in more ways than one. "Mabel, has Olivia lived here all her life?"

"Far as I know. She's around thirty-five or -six and you're what—thirty-eight?"

Noah nodded.

"So you would have gone to high school together," Chrissie said thoughtfully. "I bet Miss Lawson was a total nerd-ball and you were this hot athlete. Like in the movie *She's All That*. She was probably secretly in love with you. My mom said all the girls were."

Mabel rolled her eyes. "Do not egg him on."

"Hmm . . ." he mused and then mumbled, "Olivia Lawson. Olivia . . ." He snapped his fingers. "Livie Lawson?"

Mabel shook her head. "She doesn't go by that anymore, but she was called Livie as a kid."

Chrissie looked at him with interest. "So you do remember her?"

"Oh, yeah." Noah closed his eyes and nodded. "Chrissie, keep a few cookies out for me, but gather the rest of them up and tie the box with a pretty ribbon." He paused and then said, "No, wait—do the same with the cinnamon cake."

"Uh-oh. What did you do? Stand her up for the prom?" Mabel asked.

Noah winced and then raked his fingers through his hair. "Well, no, it's not quite that bad ... but not exactly that good either. It's all coming back to me now."

"Are you going to tell us?" Chrissie asked with a little bounce.

"No. Sorry, Chrissie, but wish me luck, okay?"

"Okay," she replied but gave him a disappointed pout.

"Mabel, do you know where I might find her?"

"As a matter of fact, yes. Remember Jessica Robinson from down at the diner?"

Noah smiled when he pictured the golden blond beauty with amazing amber eyes. "Oh, yeah."

"Well, her daughter, Madison, wrote an award-winning play, and the Cricket Creek Community Theater is putting it on for the summer run."

"I know all about it," Noah replied.

"Really? How?" Mabel asked.

"I'm here to audition for the lead."

Mabel and Chrissie exchanged a look.

"What?" Noah asked.

"Oh, boy." Mabel turned to Chrissie. "Give the man a cookie. He's gonna need it."

2

A Cold Blast from the Past

Olivia stomped into the Cricket Creek Community Center and sat down on a folding chair so hard that the legs tipped sideways. With a little yelp she righted herself and managed to rescue her milk, but her elephant ear fell to the tile floor with a plop. "Oh . . . f-fudge!"

Madison looked up from her script and grinned. "For a second I thought you were going to drop the f-bomb. I should have known better."

"Cursing is a sign of a bad vocabulary," Olivia commented, reaching down for the bag.

"Then at least come up with something more creative than 'fudge.'"

"Duly noted," Olivia agreed as she opened the milk carton and inserted the small straw.

Madison leaned forward and put her elbows on the table. "So, what's got your Hanes Her Way in a wad?"

"How'd you know I wear those?"

Madison scrunched up her nose. "Just a guess. So tell me."

"Noah Falcon," she answered tightly and broke off a piece of elephant ear. "Want some?"

"Thanks." Madison accepted the offer and then tilted

her head to the side, causing her long, curly blond hair to slide over her shoulder. "Wait." Her big blue eyes widened. "How did you know about Noah Falcon? I've been dying to tell you, but I was told to keep it hush-hush."

"Hmm?" Olivia washed down her bite of crunchy goodness and then frowned. "Know what?"

Madison glanced left and right. "Noah Falcon is reading for the male lead," Madison told her in a high-pitched whisper. "Isn't that exciting?"

"What?" Olivia leaned forward. "No way!"

"Yes," Madison said with a smile but then shook her head. "Wait—you didn't mean that in a good way, did you?"

"Not so much . . ."

Her smile faded. "I don't get it. Noah Falcon will bring attention to my play and warm bodies into the seats, Olivia. He's a professional. This is amazing news. I thought you'd be over the moon. The man is famous, not to mention smokin' *hot*." She leaned back and fanned her face.

"Madison, have you seen him act?"

"Well, no, but—"

"He's a baseball player, not an actor." Olivia peered at Madison over her glasses and then removed them. She only needed them for reading but was always forgetting to take them off. "I'm certain that Noah Falcon got the job on *Love in the Afternoon* for his looks, not his talent."

"Um, Olivia . . ." Madison tilted her head with a look of warning, but Olivia was on a roll and wouldn't be shushed.

"Sure, he's eye candy and his mug would look good plastered on a poster," Olivia continued hotly, ignoring Madison's wide eyes and shaking head, "but he would never do your warm and witty play justice."

"We don't really know that," Madison insisted, with

a little eye-roll-slight-nodding gesture. "In fact, I'm sure he's going to be amazing."

Olivia snorted. "Yeah, right, he—" She stopped short when Madison gave her a hard nudge beneath the table. *Oh . . . no.* Olivia's heart started beating in rapid alarm. She swallowed and then mouthed, "He's standing right behind me, isn't he?"

Madison gave her a short, choppy nod.

"Well, now," began a deep, silky voice that added even more heat to Olivia's already hot blush, "maybe, just *maybe*, there's more to me than meets the eye."

Olivia shifted in her seat and slowly turned to see Noah Falcon leaning one shoulder against the door-frame. Scuffed cowboy boots were crossed at the ankles, and a white bakery box with a pretty ribbon dangled from his fingers. "How long have you been standing there eavesdropping?"

"Olivia!" Madison whispered, but Olivia was fixated on Noah.

"Hey . . ." He straightened up and pointed over his shoulder. "The sign out front says that this is the community center. I'm part of the community and the door was open."

Olivia arched one eyebrow. "You haven't been part of this community for a very long time."

"Well, now." His slow grin did funny things to Olivia's stomach. "I'm back." He set the box on the table. "And I come bearing gifts."

"How many times do I have to tell you that I don't want your cookies?" she sputtered, but then she looked at Madison with embarrassment. She needed to get herself under control and present herself as a professional. She inhaled sharply and folded her hands together. Losing her composure was totally out of character for her and she didn't like it one bit. "But thank you for bringing them," she added in a nearly calm manner. Madison, thank goodness, didn't appear upset. In fact, she had a slight grin on her face. Weird . . .

"I thought you might say that." Noah pushed the box closer. "So I didn't bring cookies."

"Oh." Olivia was curious but feigned indifference. She glanced at Madison and couldn't understand why she looked like she had just won the lottery. Noah Falcon was the devil in disguise, and Olivia wasn't about to let him ruin Madison's wonderful play with an uncaring attitude and subpar acting.

"Excuse me." With her smile intact, Madison stood up and extended her hand. "I'm Madison Robinson."

Noah grasped Madison's hand. "It's nice to meet you. Well, as an adult. I remember you as a child. But, listen, I really enjoyed reading *Just One Thing.* I laughed at your insight into the human condition, especially between men and women. You have a lot of knowledge for someone so young."

Madison smiled. "Thank you. My mother always said I was an old soul. I never really understood what she meant until recently. But, as you know, I spent my early childhood in Myra's Diner. From the playpen on, my entertainment was watching people. While my mom and aunt ran the business, I sat with coloring books and toys, but my favorite thing to do was to simply observe. I always found it fascinating." She looked from Noah to Olivia and then chuckled softly. "Still do," she admitted.

Olivia lifted one shoulder in question and wondered what she'd done that was so amusing. She got that a lot.

"Thanks for coming into town to audition. I was very excited when your agent called me. He sent me a head shot and résumé."

"No thanks necessary. I'm glad to have a reason to come home, if only for a while. I know that I have been gone for a long time, but I still think of Cricket Creek as my hometown, and the people here have always been supportive of me."

Olivia barely refrained from rolling her eyes. He sounded so sincere . . . Maybe he was a better actor than she gave him credit for.

Madison tilted her head to the side. "Well, I'm flattered that someone of your caliber would want to audition for a small production like ours."

"Thanks, Madison. I'm looking forward to the opportunity."

What? Olivia raised her eyebrows at Madison, but the young playwright's focus was on Noah. So he had a few commercials, a couple of bit parts, and two years on a soap opera. Big deal! Okay, so she taped *Love in the Afternoon* and watched it every evening while eating her dinner. It wasn't like she cared about the silly story line or watching Noah play Dr. Jesse Drake. It was just something to do while she ate dinner. Although she had to admit that she hadn't seen Dr. Jesse Drake getting blown to pieces coming and, okay, maybe she shed a tear or two. But while Noah Falcon possessed a certain amount of charisma, his acting left a lot to be desired. Madison might be flattered that a television actor was auditioning, but she was about to be disappointed. Olivia couldn't wait to see the look on Noah Falcon's smug face when he failed to land the part. Filling the auditorium was only half the battle.

"Hey, if I can give back to Cricket Creek by generating some excitement and attention to your play, then I'm happy to do it." He smiled. "Well, I just wanted to pop in and introduce myself. I'll be back for the open casting call."

Madison shook her head. "There's no need. You've got the part."

"What?" Olivia squeaked. "But, Madison, don't you want him to audition?"

"I have a monologue memorized," Noah offered.

Madison waved a dismissive hand. "That's not necessary."

"Madison," Olivia insisted, "don't you at least want him to read with me? You have some sides picked out. Let's do a couple of them."

Noah frowned. "Sides?" He looked at Olivia for help, but she remained stubbornly silent.

Madison gave Olivia a "What's up with you?" look and then said to Noah, "Scenes I handpicked from the script to read." She grinned. "Were you thinking green beans or mashed potatoes?"

Noah laughed. "Well, I am getting hungry. I can't wait to eat at your aunt's diner. I've eaten all over the country and there aren't any onion rings or bacon cheeseburgers that compare to Myra's." He glanced at Olivia. "Or cookies from Grammar's. Right, Olivia?"

"I haven't eaten all over the country, but if I had to guess I'd say you're right," Olivia answered honestly and then stood up. "That's another important reason we need for this play to be a success. Myra's and Grammar's are holding on for now, but we've got to bring in some tourists this summer. A lot is riding on the play's success."

Noah folded his arms across his broad chest. "And you don't think I will take this seriously." It was more of a statement than a question.

"I didn't say that."

"Sure you did, between the lines. You think I haven't changed."

Noah took a step toward her, crowding her personal space. But instead of backing down, Olivia put her index finger in the middle of his chest. "If the shoe fits . . ." she said—and then she didn't know where she got the nerve, but she angled her head and gave him a little poke— "wear it."

"Hmm . . . that was a bit trite for an English *tutor*."

"Am I supposed to be impressed?" Her heart beat faster when she realized that he did remember her from high school, when she'd tutored him—no, make that *attempted* to tutor him—in English so he could play baseball. What he'd really wanted was for her to do the work for him, but she had refused and made him actually study. "Because I'm not."

"Surely you can be more creative than that, Miss Lawson," he taunted softly and inched even closer. To her credit, she stood her ground, but she hated that Noah Falcon still had the ability to make her weak in the knees.

Though she'd rather eat chalk than let him know it.

"I wanted to stay on your playing field," she countered, with much more moxie than she felt. She heard Madison gasp and knew she needed to back it down, but her mouth was taking on a life of its own.

"My playing field? Did you forget I was in the major leagues?"

"You're on my turf now." Oh, wow, did she really say that?

He arched one eyebrow. "Maybe I was paying more attention to *you* than you thought." Noah looked down at her finger and then slowly back at her face. His eyes settled on her lips, making Olivia have the insane urge to fist her hands in his shirt and pull him in for a long, hot kiss. Crazy! Some of what she was thinking must have shown in her expression because his gaze lingered, as if daring her to do it. "Ever think of that?"

"No, and just maybe I wasn't paying as much attention to *you* as *you* thought," she replied, but her breathless voice lacked any real bite and gave her away. *Fudge!* "Ever think of that?" She tried to add an edge to her tone while tapping her cheek as if in thought. "Mmm, I'm thinking . . . *no*."

"Really, now? Somebody's got a chip on her shoulder."

"And somebody has a big head." Oh, she really needed to shut her mouth!

"Ah . . . Miss Lawson, trite again."

She ground her teeth. "But oh so true."

"If you say so." He gave her a lazy grin that somehow infuriated her. She'd never poked or shoved anyone in her life, but suddenly she wanted to give Noah Falcon a hard push, stomp away, and slam the door, leaving him standing there staring after her. She shot him a glare that always quelled her rowdy students, but he had the nerve to chuckle. Okay, now she really wanted to kiss him . . . No, wait—*shove* him. Hard. Kiss him and then shove him . . . Yeah, that would be the ticket.

And so she did. Well, shove him, anyway.

To her delight his eyes widened a fraction, but it was like shoving a brick wall—he barely budged, making her want to try again, and she was considering it when Madison suddenly applauded, capturing the attention of both of them.

"See, now, *that's* what I'm talking about," Madison announced with a smile.

"What?" Noah and Olivia asked simultaneously, turning to face the happy little playwright.

Madison stood there beaming and then raised her hands into the air. "You two have explosive chemistry. You *are* Ben and Amy in *Just One Thing*. Amazing! I don't have to look any further." She wiggled her shoulders and did a little jig. "Olivia, I've never seen you lose your cool!"

"You've never seen me pushed over the limit." Olivia narrowed her eyes at Noah.

"It was fairly easy," he replied in a bored tone, but his eyes were full of humor.

"I know! And it's awesome!" Madison gushed. "Olivia, I was wondering if you would be able to bring the emotion needed to Amy's character."

"You were?" Olivia asked with a little frown and tried not to feel offended. But then again, like her mother and aunt Myra, Madison wasn't one to pull any punches. "Seriously? I studied theater at Cooper College and I was a barnie for years."

"A Barney?" Noah asked. "You look more like a Fred."

"Very funny. I was referring to performing in regional summer stock while school was out," she explained and was proud that she kept from rolling her eyes. "The plays were originally performed in barns, so the actors were called barnies," she continued in her best school-teacher tone.

"Is there going to be a quiz at the end of this conversation?" Noah asked. "Because I haven't been taking notes."

"Wow, that's a shocker," Olivia shot back, but when he laughed she had a difficult time not laughing with him. She pressed her lips together and arched an eyebrow for good measure. "Lucky for you, no."

"Phew." When Noah swiped his hand across his forehead, Olivia could barely suppress her grin. Like all great athletes, he had a touch of arrogance, but she somehow got the impression that despite his success Noah Falcon didn't take himself too seriously. She had to admire him for going after what he wanted in life instead of running scared like she always seemed to do.

Olivia suddenly thought of the box beneath her bed full of playbills, rave reviews, and acting offers left unaccepted for reasons she had recently begun not to regret exactly but at least to question. Chasing her dream would have meant leaving her father all alone, and she couldn't stand the thought. But sometimes she wondered what it would have been like to give it a shot. She sighed and looked down at her feet.

"Hey, Olivia," Madison said, "Cooper College has a well-respected fine arts curriculum. I've seen you in several local productions, so I know you're a great actress, but still ... you're always so put together that I wondered if you had the fight in you to play Amy." She fisted her upturned hands and shook them. "You do! Oh, this is fantastic! Thanks, Noah!"

"I guess all I needed was someone who could bring out the worst in me," Olivia commented when Noah stood there looking so darned smug. She was glad neither of them knew what she was really thinking.

He tossed his head and laughed. "I'm more than happy to do my part."

Olivia leaned one hip against the edge of the table and gave him a stern look. "I certainly hope so, because like we said, there's a lot riding on this production. Its success means so much to this community, not to mention that Madison has written a gem of a play. You really do need to take this seriously, Noah."

Olivia was expecting a flippant response but was surprised when his grin slipped and a shadow crossed his features. He looked at her for a long, silent moment, and she caught a glimpse of vulnerability that he was quick to mask. "I will," he answered simply. "You have my word."

Olivia felt a guilty pang wash over her. Had she really hurt his feelings? The thought disturbed her. "Noah ..." she began, "I didn't mean—"

"Don't worry about it," he interrupted. The cocky grin returned, but this time she wasn't really buying his attitude. "Madison, it was a pleasure and an honor. I need to go and get settled in at the place I'm renting and then head to Myra's for a cheeseburger. Call me when rehearsals begin."

"I will," Madison replied with a smile.

"Olivia." Noah gave her a polite but somewhat distant nod that bothered her as well, but before she could think of anything more to say, he turned and walked out of the room.

"You can quit staring at the door. He's gone," Madison said.

Olivia abruptly turned to face her. "Okay, what just happened there? Do you have a clue?"

Madison nodded slowly. "Maybe ..."

Olivia's heart was pounding hard, but she inhaled a deep breath and attempted to appear calm. "So, are you going to enlighten me?"

Madison pressed her lips together and said, "No. This is something between you and Noah Falcon."

"There isn't anything between me and Noah Falcon but friction," Olivia insisted. "Explosive chemistry?" She rolled her eyes. "Give me a break."

"Explosive chemistry. Sexual tension," Madison said with a slow shake of her curly head. "Call it what you want." Her eyes danced with delight. "But you two have it in spades."

"We do not! We are like ... like oil and water, for goodness' sakes."

"Right ... Wow, for someone who has always been a notorious matchmaker you sure are clueless when it comes to yourself, Olivia. Oh, and are you going to tell me about your past with Noah?"

"We don't have a past," Olivia sputtered but felt her cheeks grow warm.

"Really?" Madison untied the ribbon on the white box and opened the lid. "Coulda fooled me." Unable not to, Olivia peeked over Madison's shoulder. "Oh, cinnamon cake. One of your favorites, if I'm not mistaken?" She plucked a hunk of cinnamon crumble off the cake and popped it into her mouth. "So there's no past? That's not the vibe I was getting."

Olivia plopped down on a folding chair and tossed

back a swig of her chocolate milk as if it was something stronger. "Well, unless you consider nerdy-tutor-
hot-athlete unrequited love a past." She shook her
head. "Classic."

Madison sat up straighter. "So you were in love with
Noah Falcon?"

She snorted. "Every girl at Cricket Creek High
School was in love with Noah Falcon. It was a silly high
school crush and . . ."

"And what?"

"Nothing! Can we change the subject?"

Madison laughed.

"What?"

"Girl, you need to loosen up and let your hair down."

Olivia looked at her young friend for a long, thoughtful moment.

"I know . . . trite. Must be in the water tonight."

Olivia narrowed her eyes and then tilted her head at
Madison. Her heart pounded when she had a sudden
lightbulb moment. "Yes, but you know what?"

"No, but judging by the look of wonder on your face,
I'm about to find out. I don't know if you could surprise
me more than you already did today, but give it a go."

"Madison, I'm sorry. I was rude."

"A little. But you know me. I think it's better to speak
your mind, and you did get a lot of things out in the
open."

"You're right."

"I know. Look, I'm thrilled that Noah Falcon is here,
but the last thing we need is a prima donna who thinks
he simply needs to show up. You were right to call him
out."

"No, I mean about me." Olivia reached back and
started tugging the band from her bun. "Ouch," she
mumbled and pulled harder.

"Olivia, what in the world are you doing?"

"You are absolutely right," she repeated firmly. "In fact, I couldn't agree with you more and it's about dog-gone time." She tossed the band over her shoulder. "There!"

"Um, I meant letting your hair down figuratively?"

"I realize that." Olivia raked her fingers through her hair and shook the long tresses free. "But this is a sym-bolic start to a new . . . me." She smiled bravely, but her lips trembled slightly, ruining the effect.

"Oh, Olivia . . ." Madison stood up when Olivia's eyes filled with unshed tears. "What's going on with you?"

"I'm not sure," Olivia answered more to herself than to Madison. "Hormones?" She gazed down at the floor for a moment, then back up at Madison.

Madison put her hands on Olivia's shoulders. "Hey, I was only teasing about letting your hair down. I should learn to keep my big mouth shut. We could all learn from the exemplary manner in which you conduct yourself."

"Yes, but pretty stuffy and boring." Olivia sniffed, but then arched an eyebrow. "Except perhaps tonight," she added in a small voice.

Madison grinned. "Well, yeah, no argument there," she admitted and squeezed Olivia's shoulders.

Olivia put her cool palms to her warm cheeks. "I poked the man in the chest! What was I thinking?"

"You weren't thinking, Olivia. You were feeling."

Olivia groaned. Was she ever!

"But, hey, for the record, I love this new spunk you're suddenly showing!" Madison rose up on tiptoe and gave Olivia a hard hug. "And you know how much I value your friendship."

"Thank you, Madison. I am so glad that you and your mother have moved back from Chicago," she told her as she returned the hug.

Madison grinned. "I am too . . . but don't tell my

mother. It would take the fun out of complaining about missing the city all the time."

Olivia laughed, but when she pulled back she glanced at the wall clock and suddenly remembered who was due to arrive any minute.

"Oh, no . . ." Madison commented. "I know that look. What's going on, Olivia?"

"Promise me you're not going to be angry about this thing I might have done." Olivia held her thumb and index finger an inch apart and then mouthed, "Little thing."

"Might have?" Madison took a step back and looked up at Olivia.

"Well, okay, *did*. But before you say anything just hear me out, okay?"

"You know me—but I'll try." Madison took a deep breath and blew it out. "Okay, lay it on me."

3

Who's the Boss?

"Well," Olivia began, and when she paused Madison suddenly had an inkling of what she was going to tell her and she didn't like it one bit.

"Oh, Olivia, please tell me that you didn't hire Jason Craig to build the sets!"

"You said you'd listen," Olivia accused in her patient teacher voice. She fisted her hands on her hips, but with her hair down, she looked younger, softer, and more appealing. Normally an observation such as this would make Madison smile, but she was pretty sure what was coming and so she narrowed her eyes instead.

"Well, did you?" Madison persisted.

"Now hear me out," Olivia requested and tilted her head, causing her long brown hair to tumble forward, obscuring her eyes. For a second she seemed startled, as if she didn't know what it was, and then she flipped it over her shoulder.

"You did!" Madison smacked her hands on her jeans so hard that it hurt. "How could you?"

"He was the low bidder, by far."

"I don't care! Jason Craig is *im-poss-i-ble*. I can't

work with that man and you know it. All we ever do at Aunt Myra's diner is argue with one another."

"The remodeling job he's doing at the diner is top-notch, Madison."

"There are other contractors."

Olivia leaned forward. "He was low bidder and he does wonderful work. What was I supposed to do?"

"What I told you to do—and that was not to hire him." Madison put her palms in the air and took a moment to wrestle with her emotions. "No, wait. Okay . . . you're right. I'm being unprofessional. But you will have to deal with him, not me."

"Agreed," Olivia responded quickly.

"And this better not be one of your matchmaking schemes."

Olivia pressed her lips together and tried to look totally innocent. "Why would you think that?"

"Because," Madison replied, moving closer to the table, "you have that gleam in your eye."

"I do not have a gleam in my eye. That's absurd."

"I have been observing people all my life and I know a gleam when I see one, Olivia. But you can simply forget it. Jason Craig and I are total opposites and can't even be in the same room with each other without going toe to toe. You already tried this once. Whatever matchmaking radar you possess was and still is out of kilter with us."

"My track record happens to be excellent, I'll have you know."

"Olivia! Give it up, okay?"

"Oh, all right," she glumly conceded.

"Thank God for small favors!" Madison said, borrowing one of her aunt's favorite lines. She took a deep breath and blew it out. "That being said, you are right. Jason does do excellent work. So if you just handle him,

it will all be good." She started picking up the paperwork and putting it in her shoulder bag. "I'll just check
in now and then and give my approval." She zipped the
bag shut and arched an eyebrow. "Or disapproval. Something he doesn't like very much. The man had the nerve
to call me bossy. Um, hello, I *am* his boss." She lifted one
shoulder. "Well, granted, the diner isn't mine, but I am
his boss in a roundabout way," Madison admitted and
then tried not to remember how the rough-around-the-
edges Jason Craig could make her fume and yet melt at
the same time. "Okay, I guess we're out of here for now."

"Um . . ." Olivia gave her a sheepish look.

"Oh, no . . ." Madison stomped her Jimmy Choo bal-
lerina flats that she got for a steal on eBay. "There's
more, isn't there?"

"Jason is due here soon for a short meeting."

Madison felt a bit of warm anticipation slide down
her spine at the thought of seeing him but hoped she
hid it well. "No problem. I'll just scoot before he arrives.
You can answer any questions he might have."

"Well . . ." Olivia wrung her hands together . . . Not a
good sign.

Madison groaned. "Oh, please, just spit it out."

"I have a, um, parent-student conference, so you will
have to meet with Jason," she said, apologizing in a rush.

"No!"

"Just this one time."

"Olivia!"

"Sorry! I have to run." Olivia turned so quickly that
she nearly bumped into Jason Craig as he was coming
through the doorway. "Hi, Jason. Madison is waiting. I'm
very, *very* late for a meeting."

"Okay," Jason answered with a slightly perplexed
expression and moved aside. "Catch ya later, Teach."
He watched her walk away and then shook his shaggy
blond head before turning his attention to Madison.

"Hey, whaddup, Maddie?" he asked in his slow Southern drawl that always reminded Madison of honey dripping off of a hot biscuit.

"I won't even waste my breath telling you not to call me Maddie," she grumbled.

"Smart move," Jason answered and flashed Madison a grin that never failed to make her heart race and tick her off at the same time. "It just seems to fit you better, since you always find a way to make me mad as hell."

"Through no fault of my own."

"Right . . ." He drew the word out with the arch of one blond eyebrow. He had the nerve to look ruggedly sexy in dusty work boots, beat-up jeans, and a cobalt blue T-shirt, which stretched across his wide shoulders and bulging biceps, testing the limits of the short sleeves. After sitting down on a folding chair, he lifted his shoulders and rolled his head as if he was worn out. Madison knew from watching him work at her aunt's diner that he pushed himself to exhaustion, and she suddenly longed to walk over and massage his neck and shoulders. "So tell me about these sets I'm going to build."

"Do you have time for this project, Jason?" She tried to keep concern out of her voice but failed.

"Don't worry about your play. I'll make time and do it right."

Madison was more worried about him overextending himself, but she left it at that. "Could I get you something to drink? Water? Coke?"

"A beer?" he asked hopefully.

"Sorry."

Jason sighed. "Then can we take this meeting down to Sully's? I really need a cold one and some hot food. It's been a long day."

Madison hesitated. Sully's was a cozy little corner tavern with dim lighting, tiny booths, and close barstools. The crowd at Sully's tended to be an eclectic mix of patrons, and Madison loved to people-watch and listen to the animated conversations. In reality the comfort-food chalkboard specials were tasty, but what she didn't want was to bump knees with Jason Craig.

"Is it that tough of a question?" Jason leaned back in his chair so far that Madison was afraid he might tip over but refrained from telling him to sit up straight because that was precisely what he wanted her to do. "Let me guess—Sully's isn't good enough for you, Maddie?"

She ground her teeth together. "Of course it is. I'm just not hungry," she replied, but then her stomach had the audacity to growl loudly.

"Really?" Jason looked at her for a long, sulky moment, and then his boots hit the floor with a thump. "Look, just forget it. Just give me whatever paperwork I need and call me when it's time to start."

When he stood up Madison shook her head in apology. "Jason . . ."

He held up one hand. "It's fine. I get it."

"Get what?"

He gave a short laugh. "Nothin'," he grumbled, but when he pushed to his feet and reached over to grab his jacket, Madison's eyes widened in alarm.

"Jason, what in the world did you do?"

"Since it's you asking, I have no clue."

Madison took a step closer and pointed to his arm. "You're bleeding."

"What?" He bent his shaggy head but shrugged.

"On the back of your biceps," Madison told him. She reached for a napkin left over from the elephant ear and dabbed at his arm.

"I must have scratched it on a nail. Ouch! Just leave it alone."

"Oh, stop it, you big baby. Hold still. I have a first-aid kit here somewhere."

"I'm fine, Maddie. It's just a damned scratch. Believe me, I've done much worse." He tugged his arm away.

She scrunched up her nose while examining the wound. "It's nasty and needs to be disinfected."

"I said I'm fine."

"Don't be stupid."

"Oh, don't worry. I've learned my lesson," he answered, making Madison wonder just what he meant. He looked up from the scratch and met her eyes. He was a good head taller than her, adding to his gruff masculine appeal. He smelled like the outdoors and spicy aftershave, and damned if he didn't make frat boys and metrosexual men pale in comparison.

"Don't move, okay?"

"Still bossy as ever." He sighed. "Go get a bandage if it makes you happy."

"I'll be right back." Madison hurried into the bathroom and located the first-aid kit. One look at her flushed cheeks in the mirror told her that Jason Craig still had the power to make her pulse race. Madison had been taught to be strong and independent by her mother and aunt Myra, and perhaps it was because Jason had a way of making her feel the desire to be wrapped in his arms that she shied away. Weakness was something that she detested and probably one of the reasons she felt the need to be tough around him ... when what she really wanted was to fall into his arms. She took a deep breath and closed her eyes. No one, not even her mother, knew how afraid she was of this play bombing! Olivia was right: The financial future of Cricket Creek Community Theater was hanging by a thread. Not only that, but her aunt Myra and her mother had just sunk a huge chunk of their savings into remodeling the diner, and the success of the production really could make a huge difference. Bringing back tourism for the summer could not only save the community center but potentially rejuvenate the entire town.

Madison took another deep breath and pushed the bathroom door open. She lifted her chin and put her tough-girl expression back on before entering the room. Jason sat on the edge of the table with the napkin against his arm. Since he was hunched down, she was nearly face-to-face with him, and out of nowhere came the memory of how amazing it felt to kiss him. She swallowed hard and tried to concentrate on his arm instead of his mouth.

"I can do it," Jason said after she fumbled with the small packet and unfolded the antiseptic wipe. But when he held out his hand Madison waved him off.

"It's on the back of your arm, Jason. You can barely see it. Just sit still and let me fix you up." When she touched his arm he flinched. "Did I hurt you?" she asked with more gentleness than she wanted, but a muscle was jumping in his jaw.

"No, it was just cold," he said gruffly, making her wonder if it was more than that.

"Sorry," Madison said and then grimaced. "This really is a nasty scrape." She lifted her head just as he tilted his backward to look, and his mouth brushed against her cheek. Madison felt a hot tingle all the way to her toes but pretended she didn't notice his warm mouth against her skin. "You should be more careful," she grumbled as she reached for another packet.

"I didn't mean to kiss you."

She feigned ignorance and then looked up with raised eyebrows. "Kiss me?"

"As you wish, Princess." He slid his hand behind her head and lowered his mouth to hers.

When Madison opened her mouth to protest, Jason took it as an invitation and deepened the kiss. Her *no* sounded like a moan—okay, it *was* a moan—and when

his tongue touched hers a jolt of pure heat had the
packet slipping from her fingers. Her hands slid over the
contours of his hard chest and into his long hair that she
pretended not to like when in fact she thought it was
wild and sexy. She stood between his legs and kissed him
back, savoring the feel of his soft lips and hot mouth. His
tongue tangled and teased, and he kissed her with bold
male thoroughness before pulling back to lightly lick her
bottom lip. But when Madison thought he was finished,
he moved his mouth to her neck, sending a hot shiver
down her spine. She tilted her head and sighed, wanting
to back away, but she simply could not bring herself to
do so. His big, capable hands spanned her waist, pulling
her closer, and when he kissed her again, she clung to his
shoulders and kissed him back like it was her job. She
could feel the heat of his skin, the ripple of muscle, and
she simply melted into his arms.

When the kiss finally ended, Madison rested her forehead against his while trying to gather her scattered wits.
They were both breathing hard but remained silent.

"You shouldn't have done that," she said and when
she would have pushed away his hands tightened on her
waist.

"You asked me to."

"I most certainly did not." She meant to sound huffy,
but it came out breathless. *Damn!*

"You said . . . *kiss me.*"

"I didn't . . . Well, not like that!" she sputtered and
pushed against his chest. "It was a question!"

"And I answered."

"Let me go!" she demanded and pushed harder, even
though she wanted to fist her hands in his shirt and kiss
him all over again. Oh, she was going to get Olivia back
for this!

"Do you really want me to?" he countered in his slow
Southern drawl, but there was something serious in his

eyes that made Madison's heart thump. When she swallowed but didn't answer, his gaze fell away and he released her.

Madison stood there for a confused moment and then took a step back, but when he made a move to get up she put a hand on his thigh. "Let me cover the scrape." She felt the muscle beneath the denim tense, but he gave her a choppy nod.

"Whatever. Make it quick. I'm thirsty and hungry."

She gave him a choppy nod back and then bent her head to her task. After smoothing some ointment onto the scrape, she wrapped it in gauze and then taped the edges together. "Keep this on to protect it and make sure to put more ointment on later, okay?" Madison expected a comment about her being bossy, but when he merely nodded she felt a stab of disappointment and moved away for him to stand up.

Jason shrugged into his coat in silence, but when her stomach rumbled in empty protest once again he gave her a deadpan look. "Too bad you're not hungry or we could grab a bite to eat."

Madison felt heat creep into her cheeks but lifted her chin and said, "Yeah, too bad. Maybe some other time?"

"Right," he mumbled and headed out the door without looking back.

Madison stood there for a long, confused moment and then sank into a chair. She closed her eyes and relived the amazing kiss and wondered why in the world she continued to fight her obvious attraction to Jason Craig. She hated that he thought she viewed his country-boy status as not being good enough for her big-city upbringing. That wasn't the case at all. Sure, she missed Chicago, but Cricket Creek was her first home and she loved seeing her mother leave behind the stress of a four-star establishment to rescue her aunt Myra's restaurant by turning it into the upscale yet homey Wine and Diner.

And while Jason might not wear a suit and tie, Madison admired his work ethic and his small-town values. With a groan she folded her arms on the table and rested her weary head. Right now she could be hanging out with a supersexy man who made it clear that he was into her. She could be sitting next to him in a booth noshing on wings, drinking a cold beer, and laughing like a twenty-three-year-old should be doing. She could be pressing her leg against his in an "accidentally on purpose" flirty way and maybe even stealing a kiss or two . . .

And so why wasn't she?

Madison pressed her forehead against her arms and sighed. She knew the answer . . . well, at least partially. Her mother had been crushed by her parents and rejected by the boy she had given her virginity to as a trusting teenager. And Madison had watched her mother struggle but survive with no one but her aunt Myra for help and guidance. Both women had taught her to be fiercely independent and to rely on no one but herself. She had been encouraged to be driven and focused, and being with Jason made her feel vulnerable and exposed . . . in a word, scared.

Madison sighed. She knew that her writing was her emotional outlet because she could control fiction but not reality. Her work was tightly plotted and made perfect sense in the end . . . Oh, why couldn't life be the same way?

She inhaled a deep breath and then blew it out while pushing herself to her feet. A frozen dinner and iced tea didn't sound nearly as good as fried pickles, hot wings, and a tall beer. And while she loved her condo with the river view, a crowded little bar suddenly had more appeal. But how could she show up at Sully's now? Impossible without swallowing her pride, but when she spotted the paperwork that Jason had left behind she smiled slowly and said, "There's my ticket." She slipped her arms into her pink corduroy jacket and tied the sash, turned off the lights, and locked the door behind her.

Madison's knees felt a little shaky as she walked the short distance to Sully's, but she squared her shoulders, pushed open the door, and searched the crowded room for Jason. He was seated at the bar but as if having Spidey sense, he turned on his stool as she walked toward him. When their eyes met, her heart lurched, but she gave him a cool smile and slapped the folder down on the bar. "Forgot this," she said rather sharply, but when she turned on her heel to go, Jason put a warm, firm hand on her shoulder.

"No, I didn't," he admitted with a slow grin and then handed her a longneck, making her realize that he had been awaiting her arrival. "Bought this for ya."

"What are you, twelve?" Madison gave him her best glare and pretended to accept the beer reluctantly, but inside her heart was beating wildly. He had wanted her to follow him . . .

Oh, my.

4
Top-shelf

"Shhh!" Jason leaned over and said in her ear, "Yeah, I'm only twelve, but don't let on to the bartender. I wanna get served." Damn, she smelled good, and when a whisper-soft lock of her hair brushed against his lips and trailed across his cheek, it was all he could do not to kiss her sweet little neck.

"Drinking at twelve?" Madison whispered back. "Oh, yeah, I forgot that I'm back in Kentucky."

"Right." Jason nodded toward her Bud Light. "Guess you'd rather be drinking an import." He arched an eyebrow. "Or better yet, a perfect martini."

After shrugging out of her pink jacket she took a little sip and then wrinkled her nose but failed to comment.

"And hanging out with men in Italian loafers instead of work boots," he leaned in and said partially to get her goat but mostly to make it look as if they were flirting. It didn't go unnoticed on his part that every guy in the place was giving Maddie the once-over, and he wanted to give the distinct impression that she was with him. "Pop a squat, Maddie." He stood up and offered her his seat and then draped his arm across her back and gave her shoulder a squeeze. "So, am I right?"

"Yes, a dirty martini would hit the spot right about now."

"Really? No problem."

"Right." She rolled her eyes as she drew out the word and gave him an incredulous look. "Like that's going to happen."

Jason shrugged and pretended to buy Maddie's uppity attitude, but in reality he was more onto her than she knew. She couldn't even pull off a believable glare. That didn't mean she didn't get under his skin ... *Oh, no.* The snooty little spitfire could make him mad as a hornet in nothing flat, but damned if she didn't turn him on at the very same time. And Jason knew that she felt a hot spark too, but what ticked him off was that she fought the attraction so hard, making him wonder how she would treat him if he was in a fancy-ass suit in an upscale lounge spittin' some game at her instead of at Sully's in work pants. That mere thought made him angry as hell, and yet all he wanted to do was kiss her like crazy.

"Damn," he unintentionally growled out loud.

"What?" She shot him a curious frown.

He ran a hand down his face. "Damn ... um, I'm hungry. You? Oh, yeah, I forgot. You're not."

She lifted one delicate shoulder, dislodging his arm, but he got her back by letting his hand slowly slide over her skin. "I could eat."

"Are you up for some wings?"

"Sure." She tipped her longneck up, put her tongue on the bottle, and then took a real swig.

Jason watched, remembering how her warm, soft lips felt next to his, and he had to swallow a groan. Who would have thought he could be jealous of a beer bottle? "Do you ..." he began, but when she licked the moisture from her mouth he lost his train of thought and focused on her tongue. "Hot ..." he said out loud as well but managed to keep the *damn* in his head. What in the world was this girl doing to him?

"Oh, hot. Definitely hot."

"Excuse me?"

"The wings, Jason. I like mine hot, too." She tilted her head and gave him a curious stare. "That's what you meant, right?"

"Right. Yeah, the wings." Jason turned and motioned for the bartender. "Hey, Pete, we need twenty hot wings, celery with blue cheese—oh, yeah, and a dirty martini. Chill the glass first," he requested and ignored Maddie's startled expression.

Pete, who was a dead ringer for Charlie Daniels, ambled over to Jason. "Like I wouldn't do that. Whadaya take me for?" He held up a delicate martini glass, added one ice cube and some water. "In the freezer for exactly three minutes." He looked at Madison and arched a bushy eyebrow. "Beefeater, Tanqueray, or Bombay Sapphire? I don't make a martini with nothin' but top-shelf, so don't ask for nothin' else."

Jason turned to Madison, who simply blinked at Pete. "What? You *did* want a dirty martini, didn't you?"

"He— I—" She glanced at Jason and then nodded. "Y-yes." After taking a breath, she turned back to Pete and raised her chin. "Bombay Sapphire, please."

"Excellent choice, if I do say so my damned self," Pete commented in his gruff voice and nodded so vigorously that his beard swayed back and forth.

"Shaken gently, three times, *with* the olive." Madison smiled and held up three fingers.

Pete winked at her. "A girl after my own heart." He placed a hand on his chest and then nodded at Jason. "Whadaya doin' with this here fella, anyways?"

"Good question," Madison answered and then laughed. Jason loved seeing this side of her and wished she could let her guard down and be this way more often.

Pete jammed his thumb toward his chest. "You could do better, if ya know what I'm sayin'?"

Madison gave him a flirty grin. "I know just what you're saying."

"You're about to get an ass whuppin', Pete Sully," Jason warned him.

"Yeah? You and what army?" Pete scoffed and then flexed a muscle for Madison. "I can take that pipsqueak with one hand tied behind my back," he said with a wink. "Your drink will be coming right up, sugar. Can't rush perfection," he added over his wide shoulders and then turned to begin mixing her martini.

"You can pick your jaw up off the floor," Jason said in her ear.

Madison tilted her head and smiled. "I have to admit that I never expected to be served a martini here." She looked around at the crowded bar but saw mostly long-necks and shot glasses. "Care to enlighten me?"

"Absolutely." Jason spotted a free booth in the far corner, tugged Madison to her feet, and grabbed her jacket. "Hey, Pete, we're going to snag a booth. Bring me another beer with the wings and Maddie's martini." He ignored her elbow to his side for calling her Maddie.

"Sure thing," Pete replied as he poured the gin into the shaker.

"Follow me." Jason liked the feel of her small hand in his grasp as he led her over to a rather secluded booth. He nodded to people he knew, but didn't stop to shoot the bull. All he was interested in was getting Maddie to open up and laugh with him. If she would only do that, hopefully more would come later.

They slid into a booth with deep red vinyl-covered cushions and a high wooden back, giving them a bit of privacy. A checkered tablecloth and a fat flickering candle gave the atmosphere a romantic feel ... or perhaps it wasn't Sully's bar but being with Maddie that made the air crackle with pent-up passion. Jason stretched out his long legs and bumped knees with Maddie. When her eyes widened slightly, he said, "Sorry," even though he wasn't.

"No problem," she answered, but she suddenly seemed flustered, making Jason wonder if she would ever let her guard down enough to give him a fighting chance.

A moment later Pete wove his way through the crowd toward them, carrying a longneck in one hand and a martini in the other. "Here you go, sugar." He presented the glass to her with a flourish and then unceremoniously set Jason's beer down with a thump.

"I see how I rate," Jason mumbled. "Trying to steal my girl . . . gonna whup my ass." He sighed and took a long pull on his beer.

"Thank you, Pete," Madison said and gave the big bartender a warm smile. She took a sip and then nodded slowly before taking another taste.

Jason almost laughed at the expectant expression on Pete's face. He took a swig of his beer and watched Maddie tip her head to the side and frown. He thought it was sweet of her to make such a big deal of judging the martini but would never let her know it or she would likely bite his head off.

"Well?" Pete finally prompted.

Madison raised her eyebrows. "Did you know that my mother, Jessica Robinson, was a chef at a four-star restaurant in Chicago known for excellent martinis?"

"Is that right?" Pete shook his head and looked a bit nervous. In all the times Jason had come in Sully's he couldn't remember Pete ever appearing unsure of himself. Jason wanted to ask him for his man card. "Guess you've had a few, then."

"Now and then." Madison admitted, but then she gave him a big smile that did crazy things to Jason's gut.

She held up her glass. "But I have to tell you that *this* dirty martini is perfection, Pete. Supercold and mixed with just the right amount of olive juice. And I can tell that you shook the ingredients with a tender hand. Excellent!" She kissed her fingertips to her mouth.

"Really?" Pete asked.

Madison took another sip and nodded. "Absolutely, no doubt in my mind. And I'm a straight shooter."

"Just like your aunt Myra. Gotta love that." Pete beamed with pride. "Well, then, I'll have to bring you another one on the house. Just let me know when you're ready."

Madison grinned and held up her index finger. "One martini is all right. Two is too many—"

"And three is not enough," Pete finished for her. "James Thurber."

Madison gently set her glass down, stood up on tiptoe, and gave Pete a hug, making the big bartender actually blush. "Now you're talking." She was still chuckling when Pete walked away. "I love it when somebody is totally different from how they appear." She took another sip of her drink and asked, "Don't you?"

"Not always," Jason replied with a grin.

"Well . . . true," she admitted. "Or it can be a good thing."

"What I do appreciate is when someone is simply themselves. No bull, no pretense," he commented. "How about you?"

"Of course," she agreed, but her smile faded and she looked down at the table and toyed with the stem of the glass.

Jason wanted to reach across the table, cover her hand with his, and say, "You can let your guard down and be yourself with me." But instead he cleared his throat and said, "You want to know the story behind martinis here at Sully's?"

"Yes." Her smile returned and she nodded. "I love these sorts of stories."

Jason waited while a busboy placed a basket of wings in front of them. As he put a few of them on a small plate, he said, "During the boating season Cricket Creek Marina gets a wide range of boats, from runabouts to cabin cruisers."

Madison nodded as she gingerly bit into a hot wing.

"Well—and I was here when it happened—this dude wearing khakis and a boating hat, no less, comes waltzing in here and asks for a martini. After Pete made one for him, this dude turned up his nose and told Pete it was the worst damned martini he had ever had in his entire life and stomped out."

"That jerk!"

Jason took a swig of his beer and laughed. "Pete was so pissed. It was like watching an angry grizzly bear."

"Let me guess—after that, Pete Sully was on a martini mission?" Madison dipped a celery stick in the blue cheese and looked at Jason.

"Oh, yeah. Pete has his pride. The food here is good. The beer is always ice cold and the drinks stiff. And although the place isn't fancy, it's clean as a whistle and the staff is pleasant and efficient."

"Like Aunt Myra's diner," Madison said with a nod. "And I actually think there's a lot of atmosphere here too. That's why I want this town to come back, Jason. I have nothing against national chains, but small pubs and local diners have so much heart, you know?" She looked at him with honesty in her big blue eyes. "I joke about wanting to return to Chicago, and I do miss the city, but I never forget that Aunt Myra and Cricket Creek took us in." She laughed and said, "I was told that I was quite a handful."

"Really?" Jason leaned back and put a look of mock surprise on his face. "Hard to believe."

"Mom said that the saying *It takes a village* was coined with me in mind." Madison smiled, but then pressed her lips together as if suppressing emotion.

This time Jason couldn't stop himself. He reached over and covered her small hand with his. "Let me guess—that's why you want this play to be a huge success. Bring in tourists this summer and save the community center." He watched her swallow hard and she finally nodded.

"God, yes. Olivia and I are so excited, but anxious too," she replied in a husky tone that hit him hard in his gut. "Keeps me up at night," she admitted, but then she inhaled a quick breath. "And if you breathe a word to anyone I'll hunt you down."

"I won't," Jason promised and gave her hand a squeeze. When she tried to pull away, he held on firmly. "Maddie, you can call me ... bend my ear any time of the day or night, and I won't tell a soul. Got that?"

Madison nodded. Jason's big hand felt so warm and reassuring, and when he rubbed his thumb over her skin a shot of pure longing hit her with more punch than the martini. She looked into those hazel eyes that seemed to change color with his mood and saw understanding and caring. "Yes, I get that loud and clear. Thank you," she said softly.

"You're welcome, Maddie." Jason's concern chipped away at the cold, hard wall of solid independence that she hid behind, and even though it was a scary feeling Madison let a few pieces fall away and scatter like leaves on an autumn day. "Now, I want you to do one more thing for me." He held up his index finger and gave her a hopeful smile.

"You mean there's more?" She rolled her eyes and drained the last sip of her martini. "Just like Olivia, there's always more. Okay, what?" she asked in her kick-ass Madison voice, but inside she felt warm and wonderful and by the look on Jason's face she wasn't really pulling it off anyway.

"I want you to just relax and let your hair down tonight."

"Unreal." Madison leaned back in the booth and chuckled.

"What?"

"I just gave Olivia the very same advice earlier today. Am I really that uptight?" She hated to think so.

"No." Jason shook his head slowly. "Not uptight exactly, but guarded. And I think you know it." He looked at her for a long moment and then lifted her hand to his mouth and kissed it tenderly. That simple gesture made her breath catch, and she felt more pieces of her protective wall crumble away. But instead of feeling exposed, she looked into his eyes and felt a sense of freedom overtake her.

"You want to get out of here and maybe watch a movie or a game?"

"Sure," Madison answered much more calmly than she felt. Her hand still tingled from his touch.

A moment later Pete walked over and looked at Madison's empty glass. "You ready for another one, little lady?"

"May I take a rain check, Pete?"

"Sure thing. You want the rest of those wings boxed up?"

Madison nodded. "If you don't mind?"

"Not at all. I'll throw in some extra celery and dip too."

"Thanks," Madison replied and looked at Jason when he groaned.

"Am I invisible?" Jason complained.

Pete's laughter was a deep rumble that shook his entire body. "When somebody as sweet and pretty as her is sittin' there? You betcha."

Jason arched an eyebrow. "Pretty, I'll give ya. Sweet . . . mmm, that might be a stretch."

"I don't think so," Pete insisted and then handed the bill to Jason.

"Why, thank you, Pete," Madison said and realized that she meant it. People in Cricket Creek seemed to speak their mind in an honest way that Madison appreciated.

Pete gave her a wink. "Be right back."

"Wow." Jason watched Pete walk away and then turned back to Madison. "I don't think I've ever seen him wink at anyone, but he's been winking at you all damned night."

"I seem to have that effect on men," Madison joked with a flip of her hair but then rolled her eyes.

"You sure have that effect on me," he admitted in a voice that suggested to her that he was serious.

"Well, you didn't bother to wink at me," she replied in a teasing tone, but she was fishing for a real answer.

"No, but I sure kissed your hand like some big-ass lovesick puppy."

"Right . . . like you've never done that before?"

Jason raised his palms in the air. "Seriously, do I look like that kind of mushy dude?"

"No," she admitted, with a soft smile. "And I guess that's what made the gesture so cute," she told him, but then lowered her gaze as if regretting her own honesty.

"Yeah, cute, that's me all right. I get that all the time. Sweet too."

Madison laughed. "Don't worry. Your secret is safe with me."

A moment later Pete brought the to-go box over to the table and handed it to Madison. "Here, sugar. Hope to see your pretty face in here again sometime soon."

"Oh, I'll be back," she assured him with a sound nod.

Pete slapped a dish towel over his shoulder. "And if

this yahoo gives you an ounce of trouble, you just let me know."

Jason shook his head and they both stood up. "Pete, you've got this all backwards. She's the troublemaker," he said, but then he leaned over and kissed her on top of her head—yet another gesture that made Madison's heart skip a beat. She tried to glance up and give him a scowl, but when she looked into those hazel eyes of his she was lost. She knew that she was falling for Jason Craig. She had been for a while. The trick was not to let him know. She couldn't let anything interfere with the production of the play. But when he tucked her hand in his she felt a warm rush of happiness that was going to be difficult to resist.

5

Just Do It

Olivia ducked behind a big oak tree when she spotted Jason and Madison coming out of Sully's Tavern but then had to peek around the trunk to observe them. "Oh!" She put her palm over her heart and smiled. They were holding hands! "Yes!" she whispered and squeezed her eyes shut. "I knew it!" Now all she had to do was to continue throwing them together to keep the spark alive. She just loved it when a plan came together.

"On the lam?" a deep voice asked, startling Olivia so much that she tripped on the brick pavers circling the tree. She fell forward and grabbed the trunk for support, drawing an equally deep chuckle. "Now, I know you drive a hybrid, but that's taking tree hugging to a new level."

Olivia spun around and put her hands on her hips, but since she wobbled off-balance her glare lost some of its punch. "Must you always sneak up on a person?"

"I'm six foot four," Noah replied. "I can't exactly sneak. From my vantage point you were the one sneaking, anyway."

"I was not sneaking," she insisted hotly.

"Hiding, then? Whom are you hiding from? Or is it 'who'?" He scratched his dark stubble as if in thought.

"Whom . . . I mean *nobody*," she replied, but then felt heat creep into her cheeks. "Nobody at all."

"You really suck at lying. And your Southern drawl comes to life when you try. You need to work on that," he teased. "Or maybe not. I kinda like it."

"Oh, really now? Well, you . . ." Olivia took a step toward him, which was a mistake, since the cool breeze carried the scent of his cologne her way, muddling her train of thought. "You . . . suck at—" she began but couldn't think of anything that he sucked at and felt foolish attempting to come back with something.

"Let me fill in the blank for you. I suck at acting." He threaded his fingers through his windblown hair and then sighed. "I went through the motions on the soap, but I really need acting lessons, especially for a live performance. Will you work with me, Livie?"

Olivia felt a hot little thrill at him calling her Livie, even though she pretended to hate it. It sounded like an endearment, but then she became annoyed that he could get to her so easily, just like back in high school. Noah was a natural-born charmer and she wasn't going to fall into his trap again. "We tried this once before, remember?" she asked tightly.

"I know." He put one hand against the tree bark and leaned forward. She could feel the heat of his body, and when the wind blew a lock of her hair across her face, he reached over and tucked it behind her ear. "But I told you that I'm serious, and I meant it," he added, with what appeared to be a sincere smile.

"I—" Olivia wanted to answer, but she was reeling from the feel of his fingertips brushing across her cheeks, and words failed her. She had to fight the urge to tilt her cheek into the palm of his hand and so she stepped away from him.

"Okay." His smile faded when she failed to respond, and he jammed his hands in his jeans pockets. "Look, I know you think I'm an arrogant ass, but do you think you could set your personal feelings aside and do this? You said yourself how much this means to the town. I would compensate you for your time."

"I don't want your money," she stated vehemently.

Noah raised his hands up to the sky. "Now, how in the world did I manage to offend you this time?"

"I don't know. It just felt . . . wrong."

"Are you always this unreasonable?"

"Never."

"Then why with me?" he asked and then smiled slowly. "Ah . . ."

"Ah, what?" She was getting that urge to smack him and kiss him at the same time again. It sent her off-balance and yet felt oddly exhilarating. "I'm not certain that I like your tone."

"You're attracted to me."

"Pffft . . . right! That explosive chemistry stuff that Madison tossed around was pure nonsense."

He rocked back on the heels of his boots. "You think so, huh?"

She poked a finger in his chest again. "I know so."

"Really, now?"

"Absolutely." She pulled her finger back and looked at it as if it were a smoking gun. She really needed to stop poking him.

"Oh, Livie, I'm right and you know it. You're attracted to me but you don't want to be, and it ticks you off."

"I'm not!" she insisted hotly and backed away but came up against the tree trunk. "That's just pure . . . poppycock."

"Poppycock?" He grinned. "Really?"

Oh, why did that silly word come out of her mouth? The man could fluster her no end.

"Nonsense!"

"You don't think so?"

"Yes! Wait! I mean no!" Dear God, she was so confused.

"Really?" Noah took a step closer to her and tilted her chin up. "Then kiss me."

"What? You've got to be joking," she sputtered, but her heart was beating out of her chest. "Why in the world would I kiss you? I can't believe you just asked me to do that."

He shrugged. "Me neither, really, but I did. So go ahead. Prove that I'm right."

"You mean *wrong*."

"Fine," he replied with a bit of a challenge and a taunting shrug. "Even more reason to do it."

"We're in a public place!" She put the emphasis on the *p*'s, sounding a little like Daffy Duck.

Noah looked left and then right and then braced his hand against the tree. "No one is around or watching, Livie. And it's getting dark out."

"This is just plain crazy. I won't do it. I'm a schoolteacher. I have a reputation to protect," she argued, but the breeze blew her hair across her face and reminded her that this was the night to let go and to take a chance, to jump without a net. And hadn't she always dreamed about what it would feel like to kiss Noah Falcon? Maybe it would be a big disappointment. If it was, she could put her imagination to rest. She blinked up at him. Should she really do this?

"Wow, do you have to think about everything this hard? That has to be exhausting. Just do it."

"Just do it?" His comment made her think of sweating, determined athletes in a Nike commercial. Maybe he was right. Maybe she should just do it. Wasn't that sort of supposed to be her new motto? Well, her first motto? Olivia tilted her head to the side. She kind of liked having a motto. It certainly made decisions easier. "Oh, all right." She tried to grumble, but it came out breathless. "Let's put your silly theory to rest once and for all."

Before she could chicken out, she pulled Noah's head down for a quick get-it-over-with kiss, but the moment her lips touched his she was lost in sweet, sultry sensation that tingled at her mouth and oh, so slowly sank to her toes. When he threaded his fingers through her hair and lightly licked her bottom lip, she sighed and opened her mouth for more . . .

Noah knew he was a good kisser, but with Livie he forgot all about the mechanics and simply dived into the experience. There was such a sweet honesty about her reaction to his touch that it made having her in his arms all the more satisfying. He didn't think about what to do next but simply felt his way through. She didn't have a motive or an agenda . . . didn't care that he was Noah Falcon baseball player or television star, and that made the kiss feel real, organic, and amazingly right even given the crazy circumstances. Oh, and her full mouth was so sweet, so supple—he suddenly wished they weren't standing on a street corner but were somewhere private where he could explore every single inch of her body.

Noah pulled her closer against his frame, letting her know just what she was doing to him. Her hair felt soft and he wondered what it would be like to have the silky tresses trail down his bare skin. She gasped but didn't push away. Instead, she slipped her hands up his biceps and to his shoulders as if needing to hold on. Noah felt a hot rush of excitement and would have moved his mouth to her neck, but a car passing by reminded them both that they were standing behind a tree but still basically out in the open on Main Street.

When Olivia stepped back and put a hand to her

mouth, Noah thought she was mortified, but she chuckled softly and said, "I'm not a science teacher, but I'm thinking your hypothesis has some merit after all."

Noah tipped his head back and laughed at her unexpected reaction. "So there *is* some explosive chemistry between us?"

Olivia tilted her head to the side and said, "Mmmm, a tiny bit, perhaps. Then again, we might need more research before coming to a decisive conclusion."

Noah laughed again at her unexpected candor. "I'm a willing participant." He took a step closer and tipped her chin up. "Are you, Livie?"

She blushed, but then looked at him with serious eyes. "Flirting is fun, Noah, but I am completely committed to the success of this play. I hope you will remain committed as well."

He was disappointed that she thought he was merely flirting and wondered if she and everyone else would ever think of him as anything more than baseball and beefcake. Of course, he hadn't helped matters with his recent weeks of excessive partying and spending money like crazy. He needed to get his life back on solid ground—another reason he had taken on this role. "You already have my word. No matter what your opinion is of me, I can assure you that I will do my best," he replied a bit tightly.

Olivia frowned. "It wasn't my intention to insult you, Noah."

He shook it off just like he always did and put a grin back in place. "I know. So you're going to tutor me, I hope?"

"Yes," Olivia replied. "We need to rehearse together anyway. It will be tough for me while school is still in session, but my evenings and weekends are free, and by the time we're ready for full rehearsals school will be out for the summer."

"So when do you want to start?"

"Tomorrow? Construction will begin on the sets or I would suggest the community center, so I suppose my place is the best choice. My house is just a few blocks away." She pointed down the street.

"Sounds good."

Olivia smiled. "Super. See you tomorrow around seven," she replied.

"Okay," Noah replied, but when she turned to walk away he felt a sense of loss. He wanted to be in her company for a while longer and so he scrambled for something to say. "Let me drive you home."

Olivia hesitated. "That's not necessary."

"It's getting dark.

"I'll be perfectly safe."

"I need to know where you live, and I would feel better driving you home." He jerked his thumb over his shoulder. "My car is over there."

Olivia fell in step beside him. "Like I could miss your flashy red Corvette."

"I've never been one to be subtle," he admitted and had an urge to reach over and grab her hand. Odd— although they had a past, he barely knew her and yet already he felt possessive. He refrained, since he didn't want to appear too forward, but after that knock-your-socks-off kiss, holding hands seemed pretty tame. The thought made him chuckle.

"What's so funny?" Olivia asked after they stopped at his car.

"You are." Noah pushed the keyless entry and opened the door for her.

"That's not how I'm usually described, but I'm so very glad you're being entertained," she commented as she slid into the low-slung leather seat.

Noah leaned over. "Okay, you refuse my cookies, but then I end up with a bone-melting kiss." He shook his head. "Just when I'm expecting a curve, you throw me a fastball. You're keeping me on my toes and I like it," he added before closing the door.

Noah was still smiling as he walked around the car to the driver's side. This play was an opportunity to be taken seriously, and although he was nervous, he hadn't felt so alive and lighthearted in a long time. And he wasn't lying. Her knock-you-naked kiss had taken him by surprise. Just thinking about it was getting him aroused. *Damn* . . .

"I live on the corner of Eighth and Oak Street," she told him.

"Not far from the high school."

Olivia nodded. "I walk most days."

"I'm not surprised," Noah commented. "After all, you are a tree hugger."

She laughed. "Yes, I demonstrated that pretty well, didn't I?"

"Yes, you did." Noah liked the fact that she could laugh at herself. He was accustomed to high maintenance, not sweet honesty, and he was more relaxed with her than he had felt with a woman in recent memory. Within a couple of minutes he pulled up to the curb in front of her house, wishing the drive had been longer. "Nice," he said, looking at her cute Cape Cod with a stone front porch. An inviting grapevine wreath decorated the dark green front door, which matched the shutters. Warmth, character . . . the house suited her.

Olivia peered out the window and sighed. "It's a work in progress, but I love it. I'm not very handy, but I'm learning." She slid him a grin. "Mostly by mistake."

Noah grinned back. "Then we do have something in common. That's how I've always learned too, or as my father would tell you, the hard way."

"Where are your parents?"

"I bought them a house in Florida. My dad coaches

baseball at a junior college and my mother gardens and paints."

"How nice of you to do that for them, Noah."

He shrugged. "My dad devoted a lot of his time coaching me on traveling teams and my mother put up with us being gone. I'm glad I could give something back."

She looked at him for a thoughtful moment. "And you gave up something of your childhood too, I expect."

"It's what I wanted," Noah answered, even though it wasn't entirely true. But Olivia was the first person who had had enough insight to realize that his success had not come without cost, and he liked that about her as well. His desire for her to see him as something more than beefcake became even stronger. "Well, here you are." He killed the rumbling engine and hoped for an invitation inside, but she turned and laid a hand lightly on his arm.

"No need to walk me in. I'm sure you want to get settled. Where are you staying?"

"I'm renting a condo down by the river."

She nodded. "Nice. That's where Madison is living. It's another project that got off to a good start but then stalled when the economy went sour."

Noah nodded. "It's a shame. That property overlooking the river is some prime real estate. Seems like something else could be done there to bring in tourists."

Olivia sighed. "I agree. But what? Well, I'll see you tomorrow."

"What time?" Noah asked while wondering how in the world merely having her hand on his arm could be sexy as hell. Her fingers felt cool and soft and he wanted her to slide her hand up his arm and into his hair.

"Since it's Sunday, could we get started fairly early in the evening?"

"How about six o'clock and I'll bring pizza?"

"That works for me. We have the regular chains on

the outskirts of town, or Papa Vito's—he's still trying to compete."

"Oh, boy." Noah rubbed his hands together. "I consumed many a slice of Papa Vito's pizza in my day." He smiled at the memory. "We used to hang out there after ball games, stuffing ourselves and playing pinball until Papa V would finally kick us out. Good pizza and amazing big, fat breadsticks swimming in garlic butter. Does he still run the place?"

"Yes, and he's as cranky as ever. But you're right. Papa Vito's pizza beats the chains hands down. He learned making pizza from his father, who had a pizza parlor in Chicago. I just wish the kids around here were aware of what a gem they have. Everything there is made fresh, not brought in on some big truck." Olivia shook her head and swallowed hard. "I'm sorry," she apologized and then cleared her throat. "I hate to see shops that have been here forever closing right and left and the rest hanging on by the skin of their teeth. These hardworking families are suffering. The community center is a source of art and theater and could end up closing its doors as well. Federal funding has been cut, making revenue from ticket sales even more important. We can't raise prices . . ." She shook her head. "And slips at the marina are empty, Noah. Boats are for sale. You remember how vibrant and fun summers here used to be?"

"Yes, I do."

"Okay." She inhaled deeply. "I'll stop my rant now. But it's just all so very sad."

Noah put his hand on her shoulder and squeezed. "Listen, I know I need some work, but I'm a blue chip player, Livie. You can count on me to give one hundred percent."

"I believe you." She gave him a trembling smile that shot straight to his heart and, unable not to, he put a gentle hand on her chin. "It's just that—"

"Shhh . . ." He rubbed his thumb over her chin and inadvertently touched her bottom lip. "Worrying won't help." Despite the fact that he didn't mean it as anything sexual, the touch of her mouth sent a surge of pure longing through his body. But he didn't want her to get the wrong impression. She needed to know he was serious and not some player trying to score, so he pulled back and nodded toward her house. "Now go on in there and unwind. You need some rest. As you already know, teaching me will take some serious energy."

She put her hand on his arm again. "You don't have to get out. Thanks for the lift." She squeezed his forearm. "You'd better rest up too, Noah Falcon. I'm going to be a lot tougher this time around."

"I will." He reached over and opened her door and he thought it was cute when after getting out she leaned over and gave him a shy wave before turning to walk up her sidewalk. He smiled at her pressed khaki pants and sensible sweater, but her long hair blowing in the breeze suggested a sense of untamed freedom that he wished he could explore with her.

Olivia paused at the top of the steps, and for a moment he thought perhaps she would turn and wave once more. When she didn't, he experienced a bit of disappointment but watched until she was safely inside before turning the key in the ignition.

After he rumbled away Noah took comfort in familiar sights, and faded memories sprang back to life as he passed the Dairy Hut and Papa Vito's Pizza. He slowed down past the high school and felt a stab of emotion upon seeing the baseball fields. Darkness had fallen, but when he stopped he could make out the backstop and rows of stands. After a moment he cut the engine and stepped out of his car, needing to get just a little bit closer to a place and time that had been carefree and simple. He curled his fingers into the chain-link backstop and inhaled the scent of freshly turned dirt and green grass that would soon be ready to play on.

He could almost hear the cheering fans, the crack of a ball hitting a bat, and the sharp shout of an umpire calling strike three. While making it to the major leagues had been an absolute dream fulfilled, Little League and especially Cricket Creek High School were where his love of the game had come to life. Noah looked out at the pitcher's mound and smiled. Major-league baseball had been an amazing ride, but this field would forever hold a special place in his heart.

While Noah stood there leaning against the fence, it dawned on him how very quiet it was. Except for the rustle of the breeze through the trees, the only sound he heard was the occasional hum of a car engine, a bark of a dog, and in the distance . . . music and laughter. A sense of peace washed over him, and he thought to himself that this was the heartland, small-town living at its best. Lately he had been waking up at loose ends, with no real reason to get out of bed. He'd always been someone who was driven and focused, and this new status left him feeling oddly disjointed. He told himself he was crazy. Who cared if he was let go from *Love in the Afternoon*? At thirty-eight years old, he had more money than he would ever need even if he didn't work another day in his life. And so began his mindless spending spree and endless nights of partying, each day blending into the next with no real beginning or end. But instead of feeling carefree and happy, all he felt was depressed.

Seeing this little town struggling had been his wake-up call. Hardworking families were trying to put food on the table while he had been blowing money on crap he didn't need or really even want. How damned ridiculous was that? He needed to have a work boot shoved right up his butt. He wanted to help! For the first time in a long while Noah felt a sense of real purpose, and it made his throat clog with emotion.

As he pushed away from the backstop, thoughts of Olivia Lawson popped into his head and he had to smile. She was nothing like any of the flashy women he had been gravitating toward recently. As he drove to his rented condo all he did was think about her and what it would be like to have her in his arms once again. But he knew that this play was important not only to his career but also to Madison Robinson and Cricket Creek, so he made a promise not to do anything that might jeopardize its success—and getting involved with his leading lady was at the top of the list of things to avoid. But then he remembered Olivia's soft, full mouth and subtle sensuality and sighed. Keeping his hands off sweet Livie Lawson wasn't going to be easy.

6

Caught Up in the Moment

Jason pounded the nail into the two-by-four with more force than necessary and then rocked back on the heels of his steel-toed boots. Working on Sunday wasn't his favorite thing to do, but normally he just sucked it up and dealt with it, especially in lean times like these.

Not today, though.

Today, what he really wanted to be doing was spending some time with Madison, maybe a long drive through the countryside or four-wheeling so he could have her arms wrapped around him all day long . . . Well, and all night long too. He had to grin slightly when he pictured her city slicker tush on the back of a quad, but then again he knew she would do it. His little Maddie had been working hard to find her inner redneck. Well, okay, without a great deal of success, but it sure was fun watching her try. Jason chuckled. Someday she would go mudding without screaming or ducking her head the entire time. He kept reminding her that she was born here and needed to reclaim her Kentucky roots.

But he looked down at his hammer and his smile faded. Working wasn't the only thing that had him in a pissed-off mood. The nails he was pounding into the set frame were bought at Home Depot instead of Tucker's Hardware, where he had been doing business for years. Why? Because Tucker's was yet another local store that had just fallen victim to big chains. It simply could not compete. So after fifty years, the family-owned store had finally closed its doors.

Jason scrubbed a hand down his face. His own remodeling business had remained fairly steady, but he had cut his profit margins to get jobs and also to help locals who were hurting even more than he was. "Damn." He blew out a long sigh. For the first time, he had to face the possibility of bidding out-of-town jobs, or even relocating if things got worse. Oh, he could do it. He had connections and a reputation for excellent work. He just didn't want to leave friends and family or sell his five sweet acres high up on a ridge overlooking the creek, where he planned to build a kick-ass home.

Jason squeezed the weathered handle of the hammer that his grandfather had given him. He had newer, fancier tools, but something about knowing that his grandfather had pounded nails with this old tool gave him a feeling of comfort and satisfaction while he worked. Oh, he had earned a business degree to please his mother, but there was never any question in his mind that he would be wearing boots and a tool belt rather than a suit and tie. He sat there quietly and looked out over the auditorium, hoping that Noah Falcon would bring in a packed house. Although the small businesses and the outlying farming community were no strangers to lean times, the summer tourism had always given them the extra boost they needed to stay afloat. But with the entire country struggling to climb out of this recession, tourism had dropped off sharply. With another sigh, Jason thought about the pressure on Madison to produce a hit play and then shook his head. Of course his thoughts never strayed far from her.

Jason closed his eyes and inhaled a deep breath. Oh, boy . . . He could almost smell her perfume, he thought, and then smiled when he realized that she was sneaking up behind him. He sat still and let her think she was surprising him even though he wanted to turn around and grab her.

She knelt down next to him and put cool hands over his eyes. "Guess who."

"Give me a clue. Are you blond or brunette?"

"Blond . . ." She drew out the word in a low, sexy tone.

Jason rubbed his chin. "Hmmm, I know lots of blondes. Straight or curly?"

"Natural blond, natural curls."

"Natural blond?" Jason questioned in an amused, skeptical voice. "Don't think I know any of those."

She groaned. "Okay, I highlight a tiny bit."

"Narrows it down just a little," he teased to get her going. Getting Madison riled up was one of life's pleasures. "Give me something more to go on."

She gave him a sharp nudge with her knee. "Like what?"

"Ouch!" Jason chuckled. "Well, that was a pretty good clue. But give me something tangible. Swing around and let me touch something. How about your . . . mouth?"

"All right, but keep your eyes closed."

"Not a problem." Jason swung his feet up and swiveled around on the stage floor but parted his legs so she could kneel between them. "Okay, help me out."

"Let's see." She braced one hand on his knee and then took his hand in hers and brought his index finger to her mouth and slowly traced her top lip and then her bottom one. "Anything?" she asked in a breathless voice that made him want to pull her against his chest and kiss her senseless.

"Hmmm." Jason shrugged slowly and then tilted his head to the side as if in contemplation. She touched the tip of his finger with her tongue and he almost groaned. "I need more."

"Okay, now keep those eyes shut." She leaned in so close that her silky curls brushed against his cheek. God, she smelled good. "See if this helps," she whispered hotly in his ear and then eased away from him.

What was she doing? Jason waited with anticipation, barely resisting the urge to open his eyes.

"Keep them closed!" she warned, making him grin.

Jason expected a kiss, but instead she took his hand and—Oh, God—curved his palm around her smooth warm breast. "You took your shirt off?" His eyelids fluttered, wanting to open, but she blocked his vision with her hands.

"Yes. The doors are locked and we are all alone," she softly assured him. "Who am I, Jason? Do you know yet?"

"Ummm . . ." He cupped his hand around her firmly and then circled his thumb over her nipple until she sighed and arched into his touch. "Let me think. . . . You do feel familiar." He inhaled a deep breath. "And you smell amazing." He frowned and then leaned forward and found her other breast. "Now, let me see how you taste," he said and took one breast into his mouth. He swirled his tongue over the perky nipple, and when she groaned he sucked until she gripped his shoulders for support and then straddled his legs. He reached up and threaded his fingers through her thick curls while feasting on one breast and then moving to the other.

"Do you give up?" Madison asked and then gasped when he nipped her lightly.

"I have a pretty good guess. Just let me try one more thing. . . ." He pulled her head down for a long, sweet kiss. When she sank into his embrace, Jason wrapped his arms around her and splayed his hands over her bare back. He loved the silky texture of her skin and the delicate, sensual feel of her nestled against his chest. The thought went through his head that no other woman had ever felt so right in his arms and damned if he couldn't just stay like this forever. When he finally pulled his mouth from hers, he kept his eyes closed and leaned his forehead against hers. "I'm going to go out on a limb, but I think perhaps you could be Madison Robinson?"

"The one and only."

"No truer words were ever spoken." Jason chuckled softly. "Maddie, just for the record, I'd know your touch, your taste, your scent anywhere." He opened his eyes and gently brushed her hair from her face. "But I sure do love lookin' at you."

"Really?" Her shy smile tugged at his heart. She put up this big, confident front, but he saw right though her. Jason wanted her to lean on him.

"Absolutely."

"I can't believe I took my shirt off." She covered her breasts with her hands and then pressed her lips together. "I tend to get caught up in the moment."

"I'm caught up in every moment I'm with you," Jason admitted and was confused when she turned her head away. "Hey," he said and gently turned her back toward him. "I'm not some fancy dude spittin' some game at you. I'm just a country boy puttin' myself out there. The only thing I know how to be is real. You know that, right?"

She nodded.

"Maddie, you might call it getting caught up in the moment, but I think you're just being yourself. You can do that with me." When he saw the uncertainty in her eyes, he rubbed his thumb over her bottom lip. "Always."

"Thank you," she said and her smile trembled at the corners. "My mother taught me to be strong, and I love her for it. But sometimes," she began, but paused when her voice cracked, then finished, "it's hard."

"God . . . come here, baby." When Jason wrapped his arms around her, she laid her head on his shoulder and gave him a shaky sigh. "My parents have had their differences over the years, but they have a strong marriage. I can't begin to imagine how tough bein' a single parent must have been for your mom, especially at such a young age. I guess she had to be tough or crack."

Madison nodded into his shoulder and sniffed. "Mom's parents are wealthy. I refuse to call them my grandparents because I've never even met them. But my mother gave up a life of privilege for me."

Jason thought of his own loving grandparents and his heart ached for her. "Maddie, that's all just . . . stuff. Your mother didn't give up nothin' that was important." He tilted her head up to look into her eyes. "But just the same, remind me to thank her."

"I will." She smiled and then laughed softly.

"What's so funny?"

"I came here to bring you lunch from the diner, but I got sidetracked by our little game." She angled her head toward a shopping bag. "We have ham and Swiss on wheat, potato salad, and fresh fruit. I made it myself."

"Really?"

"Well, not the potato salad. Aunt Myra's red skin potato salad is the best on the planet."

"But you made the sandwiches with your own two hands?"

"Only for you, baby."

"I am impressed."

She wrinkled her nose and gave him a shove. "Hey, it's a start. My mother keeps bugging me to learn how to cook. So, do you want to dig in?"

"I'm just teasin'." Jason nodded. "Sure I do," he replied, but then peeled her hands away from her breasts, replacing them with his own. "But I'd like my dessert first, if it's all the same to you."

Her face fell. "Oh, I didn't bring dessert, unless you count the fruit. There was apple pie. Oh, I should have brought—"

He silenced her with a fingertip to her lips. "You are my dessert, sweet cheeks."

"I like the way you think, Jason Craig," Madison said and began unbuttoning his shirt. "As a matter of fact, I truly am in the mood for something hot and"—she leaned forward and licked the exposed skin—"decadent. Mmm, just what I had in mind."

Jason leaned back on his elbows and let her go to town. Her hands felt cool, but her mouth was warm, and when she nibbled on his neck a silky shiver slid down his spine. "How do I taste?"

"Sinfully de-licious." She licked his earlobe, making him groan. "And calorie-free. I just love win-win situations. Don't you?"

"Yeah, baby."

When she reached for his belt buckle Jason sucked in a breath and then chuckled.

"What?"

"I was just thinking that working on Sunday isn't so bad after all," he replied and then watched her tuck her bottom lip between her teeth while she slid the leather from the loop. She did this whenever she concentrated and he thought it was incredibly cute. When she was nervous she nibbled on her left thumbnail. God, and when she was about to climax, she raised her hands above her head. It seemed as if he learned something new about her every day, and he hoped it would always be that way.

"Just what are you looking at?"

"The prettiest girl in the whole damned world."

"Oh, stop," she chided, but he tucked a finger beneath her chin and tilted her head up. "I'm a geek."

"Okay, the prettiest geek in the whole damned world."

Their eyes met and she licked her lips . . . a sure sign that she was getting emotional. Jason swallowed, tried to keep from saying it but he just couldn't. "I love you."

"Oh, Jason . . ." She blinked rapidly and then pressed her forehead to his, but he tilted her head up again.

"You don't have to say it back or worry about stayin' in Cricket Creek or anything at all. I just had to let you know." Of course, that was all a big, fat lie. He wanted her to throw her arms around him and say it back. And he wanted her to live here permanently. At least the worry part was true. But now he was adding to her worry. "I'm sorry, Maddie. I shouldn't have laid that one on you."

"Telling someone that you love them isn't something you apologize for," she replied with a smile, but it wobbled at the corners. "Jason, I—" she began, but he silenced her with a kiss. He wanted her to say it when she was ready, and he could tell that she wasn't. He also knew that when she said it she would mean it. And yet she threaded her fingers through his hair and kissed him with a deep desperation that told him she wanted him. She needed him. He wrapped his arms around her and held her close. It would have to do for now . . .

Maddie's mouth felt so warm, so pliable and so very soft. Her tongue felt dainty and feminine against his, and yet she kissed with such passion that it seemed to be an extension of her personality—sweet as honey but hotter than an August night. She moved against him with sensual grace, her breasts against his chest while the kiss went on and on. Then, unable to stand it, his hands found her zipper. He tugged her jeans over her hips and groaned when he located a delicate little wisp of silk and lace. "You wear the sexiest damn underthings."

"For you," she whispered in his ear.

"All I can say is thank you, baby."

"My pleasure," she replied with a throaty laugh.

"Your pleasure? Oh, you ain't seen nothin' yet," he

warned her, then slipped his finger beneath the lace, toying and teasing until she gasped.

"Well, then, let's see it!" Maddie laughed and seconds later she was tossing articles of clothing into the air while urging him to do the same thing and so he joined her. "That's what I'm talking about!" Madison shouted when his boxers went sailing off the stage. Making love to Madison was always an adventure. Just like she did with her kisses, she poured her whole self into the experience, never just going through the motions. She had gone on birth control a while ago just for him so they could be spontaneous and not worry.

Jason lifted her onto his lap to straddle him and then pulled her head down for a long, sweet kiss that quickly heated up. He splayed his hands across her back, loving the feel of her smooth, warm skin. "I don't think there is anything on this earth softer than your body."

"And nothing harder than yours."

"Ah, babe, you got that right," he answered with a strained chuckle.

"Oh, Jason, I've thought about you all morning long," Madison confessed, and he was so relieved to hear her admission. So it wasn't just him . . .

"Me too," Jason said and gave her a smile. Madison moved intimately against him, slow and easy, driving him crazy with wanting her, but he prolonged the moment. He cupped her breasts and then took one into his mouth, licking and sucking until she moaned. Finally, unable to wait any longer, he spanned her waist and lifted her upward.

"Oh, Jason . . ." Madison gripped his shoulders and sank back down onto his erection. "You feel so amazing," she breathed into his ear, and then moved slowly back up to her knees. She started a leisurely rhythm, as if savoring each stroke, but then allowed him to guide her harder, faster. Her breasts rubbed against his chest and her hair swung forward, lightly brushing against his skin. "God!" She closed her eyes, but Jason watched the play of emotion on her face, thinking that he had never seen anything so erotic or beautiful. Unable to hold back, he thrust upward and climaxed in a hot rush that lasted longer than he thought possible. With a throaty cry, she raised her hands above her head and arched her back. "Oh!"

Jason moaned while her sweet, sexy body squeezed every drop of pleasure from him. When she fell forward with a long sigh, he wrapped his arms around her and held her tight. For a few moments neither of them spoke but simply lay there breathing shakily. Serious thoughts simmered beneath the surface. He could almost hear what she was thinking, and he knew that this was not the time for her to worry about anything. He could kick his own ass for dropping the L word, but he decided that bringing it up again would only complicate matters, so he decided to keep things light. Finally, he kissed the top of her head and said, "I've worked up an appetite. How about you?"

She nodded against his chest. "You ready for your sandwich?"

Jason threaded his fingers through her thick curls and tilted her head up. "Mmm, I was thinking along the lines of dessert."

"You already had dessert."

"But I can never get enough," he said and captured her mouth in a lingering kiss. She wrapped her sweet little body around him and he made love to her slow and easy, thinking that there was nothing in the world better than this.

7

Thinking Outside the Bun

Olivia glared at the clothes in her closet as if they had somehow sneaked onto the hangers while she was sleeping and kidnapped her other, more stylish wardrobe. Pressing her lips together, she pushed through the khaki pants and cotton blouses with a little extra force and then groaned. "Someone needs to send me on *What Not to Wear* for a major makeover," she grumbled. She could imagine Stacy clucking her tongue and Clinton shaking his head and both of them making snarky remarks while they tossed her drab clothes into the trash. Then they would fly her off to New York City and hand her the five grand and she would follow all the rules and return to Cricket Creek for her big reveal! Myra, Madison, and even Jessica would get teary-eyed when they witnessed her amazing transformation, and best of all, Noah would be blown away by her beauty.

"Oh, stop dreaming and start doing," Olivia scolded herself in a stern voice. She often talked to herself. It was a habit formed during her childhood. Being an only child without a mother meant talking to yourself or to your stuffed animals. "There has to be something in here worth wearing!" She thought of a recent segment on

Good Morning America where a fashion expert insisted that you could shop in your own closet and combine clothing in inventive ways to create a whole new wardrobe. "Yeah, right," she groused. "Match boring with boring and you get . . ." She paused and raised her arms upward. "Boring!" In college she had always wanted to look like other theater and art students who wore flowing bohemian skirts and chunky jewelry. She even bought a beret at a flea market but never had the nerve to wear it. Back then she wore jeans and sweater sets, and now all she owned was practical, comfortable clothing. She had a plain black sheath for funerals, several suits for conferences, and dress slacks and silk blouses for special occasions. And yes, she had a themed sweater for each and every holiday. Loungewear consisted of baggy sweats and hoodies.

Nothing cute. Nothing sexy.

"Damn," she muttered and then slapped her palm over her mouth. She never cursed! She fisted her hands on her hips and shook her head. "Noah Falcon, this is your fault." The man had her turned all topsy-turvy. Kissing on the street in broad daylight! Poking him! And now cursing? What was wrong with her? And yet she hadn't felt this alive in, well . . . She tapped her index finger against her cheek. "Ever." Olivia looked down at her watch and then smacked her palms against her cheeks. Noah would be here in just a little while with pizza. She couldn't answer the door in her underwear! She simply had to put something on and just go with it. After all, she was tutoring him, not seducing him. And yet . . . "Oh, stop!"

Olivia pushed past her Dockers and found a pair of faded jeans that she gardened in. They were tattered and torn from real work and not ripped in some factory, but they looked pretty cool, like something her students might wear. Could she rock the tattered jeans?

Olivia tossed them onto the bed and looked at them for a long moment. "I don't think so." With a groan she turned back to her closet, but then a flash of pink jammed between her gray sweatpants caught her eye. "Oh . . . yeah." She reached for the pink sweat suit that Madison had bought her for her birthday. It was a medium, though she would have bought a large, but when she modeled it Madison had insisted it was a perfect fit and made her promise not to take it back for a bigger size. Madison was forever telling her to stop hiding her banging body behind baggy clothes.

While nibbling on her inner cheek, Olivia tugged on the stretchy white shirt that went with the outfit and then slipped on the light pink velour pants. She tried to pull them up, but they were the style that settled on your hips and had a white drawstring that was merely for show. She tucked in the shirt and then looked in the mirror. "Damn," she said for the second time and then shook her head. The pants molded to her butt and the white piping down the side made her legs appear even longer. The clingy top hugged her breasts, so she put on the matching pink hoodie in hopes of hiding her curves, but it was short and snug, making matters worse if anything. "Grrr . . ." Olivia shook her head and her perky ponytail slid over her shoulder. She flipped it back with a small smile. This morning she had automatically started to put her hair up and the ponytail was the result of her continued effort to break the bun habit. She hadn't worn her hair in a ponytail in forever, and she had to admit that it was fun.

Olivia stared at her reflection for a moment, thinking that she looked ten years younger. She had always worn conservative clothing, even in high school. She had simply never wanted to cause her father any trouble and had tried to be the perfect daughter in every way possible. No cursing, no drinking, no trampy clothing. "Oh, boy, this just isn't me," she muttered and was about to peel the pants all off when the doorbell chimed. "What?" Noah had always arrived late for tutoring in high school, but today he was fifteen minutes early! She stood there uncertainly while her heart thudded. She glanced at the ripped jeans and then at her closet and then back in the mirror. What was she going to do? The doorbell chimed again in the slow way that said he was holding his finger on the button thinking she hadn't heard it the first time.

"Well, damn it all to hell and back!" Olivia didn't even mutter it this time, and then felt a sense of freedom from saying her father's favorite expletive. Who knew it could be so empowering? She stomped her bare foot, but when the doorbell rang for a third time she hurried down the hallway and across the living room. "I'm coming!" she shouted, something else she rarely did even while teaching. But when her hand found the doorknob she paused and tried to regain her composure, which had taken an extended holiday since the arrival of Noah Falcon. With shaking fingers she turned the gold knob and pulled the heavy wood door open. "Hello, Noah," she said brightly, hoping her cheeks weren't as pink as her too snug pants.

Noah's gaze swept over her and he silently stood there holding a big pizza box.

"Are you okay?" she finally asked. He was staring at her as if he was at the wrong house.

He frowned slightly and then seemed to snap out of it. "Yeah, I, uh . . . was waiting for you to invite me in."

"What, are you a vampire?"

He angled his head at her and gave her a slow grin that made her stomach do flippy-floppy things. "I don't think so. Why?"

"They have to be invited in," Olivia explained and thought to herself that he must think she was a complete nut.

"Good to know," he said with another grin.

"That you're not a vampire? You betcha." She stood back for him to enter. "Please, come on in." She swept her arm in an arc of welcome.

He laughed as he walked past her. "No, that they have to be invited in."

"I'm a teacher. I know all kinds of weird stuff. Ask me anything."

"Where do you want the pizza?"

Olivia rolled her eyes and put her hands on her hips. "Well, that wasn't very challenging. In the kitchen. Follow me," she added and then wondered if her butt looked huge in the tight pants. She considered squeezing her cheeks together and then wondered if she had a visible panty line. She made a mental note to do something about her underwear situation the next time she went shopping for cute and sexy clothes. Well, the first time she went shopping for cute and sexy clothes, since it was glaringly obvious that she had never gone that route before. "Right here is fine." She gestured toward the table and then turned to face him. He was still grinning, making her wonder if she did have a panty line. She decided to ask . . . well, in a roundabout way. "What are you smiling about?"

Noah shrugged his shoulders, making her admire the way his yellow V-neck sweater molded to his muscles. She just bet that he hadn't obsessed over what to wear. Of course, when everything looked good on you what did it matter? "I don't really know. You just make me smile."

Olivia found his unexpected yet simple admission touching and was rendered speechless.

"It was a compliment," Noah explained when she gave him a perplexed look.

"Thank you," she replied shyly, and damn if he didn't want to pull her into his arms and kiss her. When she'd opened the door dressed in that pink jogging thing, he about swallowed his tongue. He had already guessed her baggy clothes had been hiding a great body, but actually seeing her sweet curves had blown him away. And her long brown hair pulled back into a ponytail gave her a fresh girl-next-door look that he found to be flat-out sexy. "Can I get you something to drink?"

"Sure."

"Sweet tea okay? I made it fresh today."

"Sounds great," Noah replied and watched her bend over to retrieve the pitcher from the fridge. She had a kick-ass butt and endless legs that were meant for wrapping around a man. "Hot damn . . ." Oh, crap, he hadn't meant to mutter that out loud.

She straightened up and turned around. "Excuse me?"

"Uh, hot damn, that pizza smells good. I'm hungry."

"Well, hot damn, me too," she said as she brought two tall glasses of tea to the table.

"Why, Miss Lawson, I'm shocked," he said in a teasing tone, but in fact he was shocked in more ways than one.

Olivia shrugged as she placed plates and forks in front of them and sat down. "I'm trying to learn to loosen up," she casually admitted, but the color in her cheeks gave her away. "Is it working?"

Noah found her quirky personality endearingly amusing, and he chuckled.

"I guess I need a little more work in that particular direction."

"Well, you're in luck."

"I am?" She took a sip of her tea and waited. The look she gave him suggested that she was never in luck, and he found that a little sad. Pretty little Miss Lawson needed some pampering and he was just the man to do it.

"Yep, I happen to be an expert in being laid-back. In return for acting lessons I'll teach you how to chill. Deal?"

"Deal." When Olivia nodded, he placed his hand over hers and squeezed. The gesture was merely meant to be reassuring and friendly, but simply touching her sent a jolt of awareness tingling up his arm. When her warm brown eyes widened slightly, he wondered if she had felt the same reaction. He sure as hell hoped so, but then he reminded himself that he wasn't supposed to go there and reluctantly removed his hand from hers.

Olivia opened the pizza box, closed her eyes, and inhaled deeply. "Oh, that smells heavenly."

Noah grinned. "Surely there's gotta be pizza in heaven."

She opened her eyes and nodded, making her ponytail swing back and forth. "Papa Vito's pizza," she agreed and slid a pie-shaped spatula beneath a slice. When the cheese clung in long strings, she pulled it free with her fingers and then laughed. "Let's hope there are napkins too," she added, but when she licked some sauce from her thumb, the simple gesture somehow seemed incredibly sensual.

"Of course, first I have to make it there," he said in a teasing tone, but he wasn't entirely joking. Too much money, too much time, and no real direction had been a bad combination. He had been on a fast track toward his own reality show.

Olivia put a slice of pizza on her plate and then gave him a wry smile. "You were reading my mind." Of course, she was joking, and he wasn't about to let her know how close to the mark she really hit.

"One of my many talents." *Good thing you aren't reading my mind*, he thought as he watched her take a bite. When the cheese stretched, she circled the gooey goodness with her tongue and then licked a dollop of sauce from the corner of her bottom lip.

"Wow, this is so good," she said and took another healthy bite. "I haven't had it for a while."

I could help you in that direction skittered across his mind, but he wasn't thinking about pizza. "I wasn't sure what toppings you liked, so I went with basic pepperoni. I figured it was easy to peel off if you didn't like it."

"Classic pepperoni is fine, but I like anything except for anchovies, so you couldn't go wrong."

"Pineapple and ham?" he challenged.

"Sure." She lifted one shoulder. "I'll go Hawaiian when I'm in the mood."

In the mood? He had another sexy visual. The girl was killing him.

"How about you?"

Noah nodded. "Definitely an in-the-mood kind of combo." He tilted his head and said, "Let me know when you are."

"Are what?"

"In the mood."

"Okay," she answered innocently. "I try to be good and stick to mostly veggies, but when I visit my dad, he has to have a meat lover's." She groaned and put a hand to her midsection.

Noah laughed and beat on his chest. "It's a guy thing." He was used to women who picked at their food, and it was refreshing to be with someone who enjoyed eating. Olivia Lawson wasn't his type at all, and yet he couldn't take his eyes off her and he was attracted to her in ways he couldn't even explain. They munched in silence for a few moments.

"So you were impressed with Madison's play, *Just One Thing*?"

"I really was." Noah nodded and then dabbed at his mouth with his napkin. "I found it laugh-out-loud funny but also a compelling and insightful look into the relationship between a man and a woman. Too often we go after what we really don't even want and then wonder why we're not satisfied," he said and then wondered if he had just found the reason why he was so drawn to Olivia. Was she the type of woman he really wanted? "And I think Madison's message was spot on," he continued slowly. "We're looking for happiness in every which way, sometimes overlooking the one that matters most. I know I was," he revealed and then had to clear his throat. There was something about Olivia that made him open up and say things he hadn't disclosed to anyone else. Perhaps it was the warmth in her eyes or the compassion in her voice?

"Wow," Olivia said and blinked across the table at him.

"What?" It disappointed him to no end that she looked as if she couldn't believe he actually had a brain. It hurt like a kick to the gut. "So you're surprised that I have an opinion?" he asked a little stiffly.

"Of course not," Olivia replied easily.

Noah tilted his head to the side. She kept surprising him and he liked that. "Sorry. I have a chip on my shoulder when it comes to the whole dumb-jock thing."

Olivia arched an eyebrow. "I'm a high school teacher, remember? I don't let athletes get away with sliding by. Because you can hit a ball doesn't mean you don't have a brain. I can't stand stereotypes."

"Ah, smart *and* sexy . . ."

She leaned forward. "You can be both."

"I wasn't talking about me," he replied and watched her cheeks turn as pink as her cute little hoodie.

"Oh." Olivia opened her mouth and closed it, clearly flustered, making him wonder if anyone had ever told her how lovely she was. Noah wanted to drive his point home, but he was afraid she would take it as mindless flirting and so he refrained. But then she lifted one shoulder. "Really? Well, I was talking about you."

Noah was floored by her admission. "So you think I'm smart?"

"It's easy to hide behind a stereotype."

"And you think I did that?"

"I always knew you were smarter than you'd let on."

Noah arched one eyebrow. "So you think I'm sexy?"

"You know you're sexy."

"That's not what I asked."

"Let's move on. Shall we?" Olivia folded her hands on the table and raised her chin a notch as if trying to channel her prim and proper persona, but her perky ponytail and tight pink outfit totally blew that out of the water. For some reason that made him want to kiss her. Then again, everything made him want to kiss her. "Well, I'm glad that you were so moved by the play and have such a strong opinion. Being passionate about it will certainly help you in your role as Ben."

"That makes sense."

Olivia nodded. "Closeness to the part is called perception of yourself in the part and the part in you. This will be an important aspect of your acting process. It isn't just about executing the lines or the physical action, Noah. It's about your own inner feelings and taking over the role of Ben as if it was your own life. We'll go over the methods and tools you'll need to use to fulfill the obligations of the material."

"I really do want to bring Ben's character to life on the stage."

"The fact that you understand the theme of Madison's play is key," she told him and then paused.

"But?"

"Always remember that you are bringing your vision of the play to the audience. You can understand your part and sympathize with the character, but you also need to put yourself in Ben's place so that you will act as he would." Olivia leaned over and tapped his chest.

"Use your own feelings, and when you speak the lines they will be coming from your heart alone, not even from Madison's." She settled back in her chair. "Does that make sense?"

Noah nodded. "On the soap I memorized the lines but never really put myself into the role of Jesse Drake. I pretended, but I didn't really feel as if I was him. But I get it. I just hope I can do it."

Olivia took a sip of her tea. "The big difference between the art of an actor and all other arts is that in all other arts the artist creates when he is inspired or in the mood. Actors in the theater must call forth inspiration during the actual hours of the performance. Not always an easy task."

"The-show-must-go-on kind of thing?"

"Exactly. And I'm sure you experienced some of that during your baseball career. You had to go out there and play ball and give it your all whether you felt like it or not."

Noah nodded. "As a relief pitcher I had to be ready at a moment's notice and of course come into the game during a stressful situation."

"So you understand."

"Absolutely. I didn't realize there were so many parallels."

"To tell you the truth, me neither!" She seemed excited about the revelation and waved her slice of pizza in the air. "And, Noah, to be a truly great actor you have to draw from your life experiences."

"Oh, I have plenty of that . . ."

"Then you use affective memory recall."

"Um, explain, please?"

"This is an emotional preparation technique used to reactivate an emotional or psychological experience from a past event and then trick your psyche into thinking it is the present."

"How in the world do you do that?"

"You answer the questions that you ask yourself with your senses, not with words."

Noah leaned back in his chair. "Oh, boy . . ."

"Hey, we'll do some exercises, and after a while it will come as second nature. As an athlete you have a couple of key things going for you that will help you. First, you have to believe in yourself and be confident onstage. If not, you will never convince the audience. As a professional pitcher you have to have this same kind of belief in your ability or you would never get the ball over the plate."

"True again." Noah nodded in agreement.

"As a pro athlete you have had amazing life experiences. And to be a great actor you have to live life a little over-the-top. Know what's going on around you. Understand human nature. What did you feel when you were on the mound pitching?"

"I had to get into the head of the batter. Outsmart him." He tapped his head. "Yeah, and understand human nature."

"The sign of a great actor. I bet that every move you made on that mound had a motive. A reason for the particular action."

Noah nodded slowly. "You're right."

"That's how it is in a play. Every movement across the stage has a reason. Your actions should be based on inner feelings. For homework I want you to go through the entire play, find the right physical actions, and imagine yourself executing them from start to finish. This will help you grasp the role concretely and you will sense a real kinship with Ben."

"Okay. It sounds like an interesting exercise and I get why it will help."

"Great! I'm going to do the same thing with the role of Amy. It's the first step in merging with and living with your part. Make a list of physical actions you would do if you found yourself in the same situation as Ben. It really brings the character to life."

Noah put another slice of pizza on his plate and then offered Olivia one. She seemed to feel more at ease with him, and he found her knowledge fascinating. "I'll be honest. I'm intimidated by live theater."

Olivia leaned forward. "Noah, you've been performing before a crowd almost all of your life."

"Oh, this is way different."

She shrugged. "Yes, but then again, in baseball you wanted to engage the crowd. You were still entertaining. In theater you have to engage the audience as well. You want them to pull for you much like cheering fans. When you engage the audience you'll feel it. You wouldn't pitch as well to an empty stadium, right? You know how it feels to have the crowd on your side. The spectators are a creative participant in the performance. There's nothing like it!" Her face flushed with excitement, and she reached over and put her hand on his forearm. While there wasn't anything sexual or even flirty about the gesture, Noah was acutely aware of her small hand resting on his skin, and when she pulled away he wanted to reach over and put her hand right back.

"I sure know the rush of playing before an excited crowd."

She nodded briskly. "You want them not to just sit there and watch but to have an emotional experience. Talk about it all the way home." Her smile had him smiling, and the sparkle in her eyes made her pretty face glow. "Noah, *Just One Thing* is excellent work! We have to do it justice."

Feeling compelled to touch her, Noah reached over and put his big hand over her smaller one and left it there. Her eyes widened just slightly, and her quick intake of breath told him that Madison was right. There was chemistry between them that couldn't be denied. But Noah knew he had to be careful. Olivia was a sweet, trusting soul and could easily be hurt. He needed to put his emotion into the play and try to keep his distance otherwise.

Lofty plan . . . he just didn't know if he could do it.

8
Rock Soup

Olivia crumbled crackers into her bowl of vegetable soup and then dipped her spoon into the savory broth. Between school and rehearsals with Noah she hadn't been to Myra's Diner very often lately, and she had been missing her favorite country classics. After taking a generous bite, she looked up from her perch on a swivel stool at the front counter and motioned for Jessica Robinson to come over.

"Something wrong, Olivia?" Jessica tucked a lock of dark gold hair behind her ear and leaned one hip against the counter.

"On the contrary." Olivia pointed her spoon at the steaming bowl. "This soup is divine."

"Why, thank you," Jessica replied with a grin. "And by the way, I've been meaning to tell you that you look so cute without the bun. I never knew you had such a pretty natural wave."

"It was your daughter's doing." Olivia angled her head at Madison, who was sitting next to her.

"Oh, if I had a dime for every time I've heard that particular phrase." Jessica shook her head at Madison, who gave her mother a look. "She still manages to stir up trouble."

"I learned from the master," Madison shot back. "'Say what you mean and mean what you say,'" she mimicked, but then grinned at her mother. "You taught me to speak my mind and to stand up for myself. Gets me into hot water sometimes."

"It's better than getting taken advantage of, and it seems to have served you well," Jessica responded and blew her daughter a kiss. "Like mother, like daughter?"

Madison nodded. "With a big dose of Aunt Myra tossed into the mix. Speaking my mind and a little bit wacky." She put the heel of her hand to her forehead. "Heaven help me."

Olivia watched the exchange with envy. When Olivia was just a little girl, her own mother had gone off to study art in Savannah while her father supported her and funded her dream, only to learn that she was having an affair with a professor. She never returned to what she referred to as a stifling small-town existence. Although Olivia's father didn't know it, a few years ago her mother had tried to contact her, but Olivia couldn't push past the pain and had refused her call. She wondered if her mother's rejection of her life and home had made her, Olivia, even more protective of Cricket Creek, but she shook off the hurt like she always did and took another bite of her soup.

"Hey, Mom. Olivia is right. The soup rocks. Did you do something different?"

Jessica shrugged her slim shoulders. "Maybe. You know me—a little of this, a pinch of that, and then taste as I go. Sometimes I add leftover vegetables of the day so as not to waste them."

Olivia arched her eyebrows. "Instead of 'the soup rocks' . . . it's really rock soup."

Madison nodded. "I get it. Like the fable?"

After swallowing another bite, Olivia nodded in agreement. "Yes, it started with the fable about the soldier using a rock to get villagers to add ingredients to his rock soup, but it's now used to describe soup made from anything you find in your pantry."

"You two are too much." Jessica laughed, but then she said thoughtfully, "Y'know . . . I think I'm going to call the vegetable soup 'Rock Soup' on the new menu for Wine and Diner. I've been trying to come up with fun things to add and I like that! Maybe we can think of some other similar stories or fables. But to answer your question, daughter-who-thinks-microwaving-is-cooking, the basic ingredients are the same, but every batch has its own personality."

Madison raised her palms upward in question. "Why would I learn to cook when my mom and aunt own a diner?"

Jessica rolled her eyes. "Why indeed?"

"Mom, you are the only one I know who gives human qualities to food."

"There's a name for that." Olivia tapped her spoon against her bowl and then brightened. "'Anthropomorphism.'"

"Not 'personification'?" Madison asked.

"I suppose one could argue either one," Olivia replied. "But I think 'anthropomorphism' is more correct."

"And *that's* why I went to culinary school instead of college," Jessica said, pressing her fingertips to her temples. "English makes my head hurt."

"Oh, Mom, you're so full of it," Madison told her. "You're as smart as they come and you know it. Head chef at a four-star restaurant? Um, you're no slouch, Mother dear. I'm sure the Chicago Blue Bistro misses you."

Jessica patted her daughter's hand. "Ah, but it's much more fun making Rock Soup."

"And less stress, I imagine," Olivia commented while she crunched more crackers into her bowl.

"The remodeling hasn't been without stress, but Jason and his crew are doing a bang-up job," Jessica admitted. "The addition is going to be fabulous. Jason even came up with a see-through fireplace to connect the two rooms. I love it!"

"That does sound fabulous." Olivia slid a glance at Madison, who pretended to be concentrating on her soup, but the color in her cheeks told a different story. "Jason is a good guy and a hard worker."

"Not to mention easy on the eyes," Myra added as she came out from the kitchen with a heavy tray of food hoisted on her shoulder. "Makes me want to add another room just to have him around in tight shirts and a tool belt."

"The scary part is that she's serious." Jessica rolled her eyes and then turned her attention to Olivia. "I hope that by expanding and having a bit of a coffee shop and bistro vibe but keeping the comfort food favorites we'll bring in some folks from the burbs, along with more tourists. I'm even thinking of having music on Friday and Saturday nights, and if things go well we might extend the patio so patrons can dine alfresco. Jason said he can do brick pavers, and Aunt Myra said that your father can add some landscaping."

"Dad would love that," Olivia said. "All we need is a reason for both locals and tourists to come back into town. Success will breed success. It will liven up the marina too. I sure miss seeing boats on the river." Olivia folded her hands on the table. "I know I've said it before, but we are so lucky to have you and Madison back here."

"You got that right!" Myra Robinson announced as she pushed through the kitchen double doors again, this time with two fat slices of apple pie. "It's good to have my girls back." She set the plates down in front of Madison and Olivia. "Thought you two could use something sweet."

Olivia eyed the pie. "Mmmm, I shouldn't."

"Oh, go for it," Madison said. "That's been my motto lately." Olivia noticed that Madison's comment drew a look of interest from Jessica.

Olivia thought of her own "Just do it" motto and grinned. "Mottoes are fun. We should all have one."

"Wanna hear mine?" Myra asked.

"No!" Jessica answered and then everybody laughed.

"Do you want the pie?" Madison asked again. "Baked fresh this morning."

"Oh, stop tempting me. I really shouldn't . . ."

"Well, well." Myra gave Olivia a wide, sassy grin and flipped her long braid over her shoulder. "Maybe you're gettin' some sugar someplace else? Like from a certain hunky baseball player?" She wiggled her hips, making her big hoop earrings dance back and forth. Olivia had always admired Myra's style, a funky mix of hippie with a Southern flair that only she could pull off.

"Aunt Myra!" Jessica scolded and turned to Olivia. "Don't mind her. She is such a busybody."

Myra slapped the thighs of her vintage Levi's. "Oh, like Olivia isn't? She's always trying to hook people up."

"Tell me about it," Madison chimed in.

"I don't know what y'all are talkin' about." Olivia tried to appear innocent, without much success.

Myra rolled her eyes. "Your Southern drawl is getting heavy, which could mean only one thing."

"That she's lying?" asked a deep voice that made Olivia feel warmer than the rock soup.

"Well, now, speak of the devil," Myra said and gave Noah Falcon a wink.

"Me, the devil?" he asked with a dramatic sigh and then pointed at Olivia. "I think that putting up with Miss

Lawson's acting lessons makes me more of a saint. Do you know that I have homework?"

"Something that was foreign to you in high school," Olivia muttered. "Oh, right, unless someone else did it for you."

"Well, I'm making up for it now. By the time Miss Lawson is through with me I'll be able to win an Oscar."

"A Tony is for theater," Olivia corrected.

Noah sighed again. "Are you going to make me write that two hundred times as punishment, Miss Lawson?"

"Maybe I'll just stand you in the corner," she countered, amazed that he could still make her heart beat faster just by entering the room. After the past few weeks, though, her comfort level with him was becoming easier, and she looked forward to the evening acting lessons much more than she let on. And she had to admit that his progress had been nothing short of amazing.

Myra raised an eyebrow. "How about a spanking?"

"Aunt Myra!" Jessica scolded, but Madison laughed at her aunt.

"Just a suggestion," Myra answered without batting an eye and then turned her attention to Noah. "I bet your ears were surely burnin'," Myra told him. "You're still the talk of the town around here, sweet cheeks."

"Please, don't mind her," Jessica said and gave her aunt Myra a stern look. "I don't think I've taken the opportunity to personally thank you for coming here to Cricket Creek to be in Madison's play. We're thrilled."

"It's been my pleasure," he said, and Olivia was sure that every female eye in the diner was on him, but she tried to act as if his presence was no big deal and slowly swiveled around in time to see him fold his long frame onto a stool next to hers. "How's it goin', Teach?"

"Just fine, thank you, Pupil." When his leg brushed hers she felt a tingle but lifted her chin and said, "Were you attempting to sneak up on me again?" She tried to remain calm, but with his leg pressed against hers it was difficult.

"Not sneaking . . . stalking," Noah corrected with a lazy grin that made her drop her spoon. She left it there, hoping he would think she'd tossed it down in exasperation. The weather had turned spring-fever warm, and he was wearing a short-sleeved midnight blue golf shirt that was the perfect accent for his jet-black hair and steel blue eyes. "What smells so good?" Dark stubble covered his jaw, making Olivia want to rub both hands over his cheeks to feel the soft abrasion. When he reached for the glass of water that Jessica placed in front of him, Olivia couldn't help but notice his tanned, muscled forearms.

"Rock soup," Madison leaned over and answered with a chuckle. "My mother's specialty."

"Rock soup, huh?" Noah angled his head. "Interesting. I'll have a big bowl of rock soup and some sweet tea," he said, as if rock soup was a normal menu item.

"Coming right up," Myra told him. Just minutes later she served him a tall glass of sweet tea and a steaming bowl of soup. "Here you go, hot stuff. And I'm not talkin' about the soup."

"Oh, Myra, please don't inflate his ego," Olivia complained in her stern teacher voice. "It's already bigger than a Macy's parade balloon."

Myra, however, had a mind of her own and smiled at Noah. "Seriously, how'd you get so tan?"

Noah swallowed a spoonful of soup and said, "I've been working out with the Cricket Creek baseball team in the afternoons."

Myra fisted her hands on her hips. "Wow, I bet they love that, Noah. It's very cool of you to donate your time."

"I enjoy it," he said, dismissing her compliment with a slight shrug. "We have some talent this year. I'm looking forward to the games."

"It's still nice of you," Olivia added firmly. She'd noticed that it was a habit of his to do good deeds and not want credit. "Don't play it down."

"Do you have to argue with me about everything?" He frowned at her, but his eyes were dancing with amusement.

"It was a compliment," she insisted.

"Oh, and that is coming from someone who can never accept a compliment."

"Yes, I can!"

"Okay—you look really pretty today."

"You just said that to prove a point."

"Um, yeah, and I just did because I meant it!" Noah looked at Jessica and Myra and said, "See what I mean? I can't win for losing."

"That doesn't even make sense," Olivia said.

"Yes, it does."

Madison laughed with delight. "I swear, you two really are Amy and Ben. Mom, isn't it just uncanny?"

"Sure is," Jessica agreed with a grin, but there was something wistful in her eyes that made Olivia wonder if she'd ever had a special man in her life. Olivia got the impression that Jessica had devoted her time to Madison and her career. But she was so pretty, smart, and talented that the matchmaker wheels in Olivia's head started turning as she thought about who in Cricket Creek might be right for a savvy Chicago transplant. Jessica needed someone strong who'd be able to hold his own with her. Nobody readily came to mind, but Olivia filed the idea in the back of her mind for future consideration. "But I am sure that the baseball team soaks up every minute of your instruction," Jessica continued.

"Kinda like me with Livie," he said before squeezing the lemon wedge into his tea.

"Oh, would you stop callin' me that?" Olivia pleaded and felt her face grow warm. "My name is O-liv-i-a."

"What would be the fun in that?" Noah asked and then looked at Jessica and Myra. "If *O-liv-i-a* hadn't tutored me in English back in high school, I would have missed the regional play-offs where there were baseball scouts on hand. So I guess you could say that she was instrumental in getting me to the major leagues."

"Oh, come on," Olivia said and felt another blush creep into her cheeks. "You're giving me way too much credit."

Noah took a long pull of his tea but then tilted his head. "Not so far-fetched. You played a hand in my future back then, and you still are if you think about it." He put his hand over hers and squeezed.

"Nonsense."

"You mean 'poppycock,' right?"

"You ruined that expression for me," she answered glumly.

Madison snorted. "Well, thank goodness for small favors. I actually said 'fudge' the other day and I thought Jason was going to die laughing." She shook her head. "But if I said 'poppycock' I'd have to slap myself."

"Yep, Livie, you're rubbing off on me," Noah said.

"Lucky you," she responded as a joke, but he didn't laugh.

"Yeah, lucky me," he answered thoughtfully and then added, "Hey, it's a nice night out. When we're finished eating will you walk over to the Dairy Hut for an ice cream?"

"I have apple pie," she answered, but Myra reached over and snatched it away. "I'm going to wrap this up for your breakfast. Go have an ice cream with the man, Olivia. Day-um, are you plumb crazy, girl?" She flipped her braid over her shoulder and shooed her with her hands.

"It is a lovely evening," Olivia answered slowly, but she hesitated. The more time she spent with Noah, the more she was starting to like him. But not wanting to interfere with the play, she had been careful to keep her emotional distance. It was darned difficult, since when she wasn't with him he was constantly on her mind. She even found herself daydreaming at school. And she had relived the kiss a million times. Walking to the Dairy Hut with him was something she had fantasized about as a teenager. And lately she had fantasized about something way better than ice cream. Oh, boy . . . nice night or not, she should refuse.

"Don't get too excited," Noah complained after polishing off his soup.

Therein lies the rub, she thought with wry humor. His tone was teasing, but she sensed just enough disappointment to be tempted.

Madison gave her a hard nudge and a bug-eyed you've-got-to-be-kidding-me stare.

Olivia swallowed hard. Being attracted to him was a given. The man was drop-dead gorgeous and a natural-born charmer. But really liking him was traveling into dangerous territory. Add it all together and she could very easily fall for Noah Falcon yet again. And if she'd thought he was out of her league in high school—well, *now* Noah Falcon wasn't just big man on campus. He was a celebrity. He could very easily sweep her off her feet and then be gone in an instant.

"It's just ice cream." Noah leaned in and said close to her ear, "But I'll even spring for a sundae if you say yes."

"Do you ever take no for an answer, Noah?" Olivia had to ask. She wondered if eyes were on them and tried to act casual.

"I never go down without a fight when it's something I want," he answered without the teasing tone she was expecting.

"I believe it." Olivia had to admit that he had been working hard to improve his acting skills, and although he was rough around the edges he had the talent and the drive to do an excellent job. She had been involved in live theater long enough to know that his stage presence was going to be compelling. And he had joked about homework, but the character biographies they had just worked on during the past week had helped both of them connect with Ben and Amy. Noah Falcon was nothing if not determined, and she liked that about him. But when he reached for her check, she pushed his hand away. "No, you don't."

"Yes, I do," he insisted and with lightning speed he slid his hand across the counter and grabbed the slip of paper.

"Give me that!" Olivia reached toward him, but he stood up and held the ticket just out of her grasp. "No-ah Fal-con!" Without considering that they were in a public place, Olivia jumped up and lunged toward him. She lost her balance and suddenly found herself flattened against Noah's chest and clinging to his wide shoulders.

9

Check, Please!

"Would you let go? I bet everybody's looking at us," Olivia frantically whispered in his ear.

Olivia's back was to the dining room, but she assumed correctly. Everybody was looking at them with curiosity. Silverware stopped clinking and glasses paused in midair. "You're the one clinging to me," Noah replied, and damned if he didn't wish they were all alone and away from prying eyes.

"Oh," she said with a little nervous titter and then stepped back. "Right. Well, you were the cause!" She pointed at him, and for a second he thought she was going to poke him in the chest again.

"You know, you keep doing that," he said and gave a quick wink to Myra, who was doing her best not to laugh.

"Doing what?"

"Blaming me for what you're already doing." It was the first time he'd had Livie in his arms since he'd rumbled back into town, but not a day had gone by that he hadn't wanted to grab her and kiss her once again. It didn't help that the script itself was chock-full of sexual tension.

"I don't do that," she protested.

"I beg to differ. She does, doesn't she?" Noah looked over Olivia's shoulder at Madison for help.

Madison put her hands in the air. "I've already learned not to get between you two when you argue. I'm staying out of this." But then she grinned and looked over the counter at Myra and her mother. "Besides, it's way too entertaining. These two are going to flat-out light up the stage, aren't they?"

"I'll say," Myra said. "Y'all need to get a room."

"Aunt Myra!" Jessica warned and shook her head upward.

"I'm just sayin'," Myra answered with a shrug.

"Well, keep your thoughts to yourself," Jessica pleaded, but Myra just laughed.

"Oh, Mom, it's pointless. Let her go."

"Thank you, Madison," Myra said but then frowned. "Wait—I think I thank you."

"See what you're causing?" Olivia accused Noah with a shake of her head. Her hair slipped over one shoulder, and while the simple white blouse and her usual khaki pants shouldn't have been provocative, Noah couldn't stop staring at her. Although her hair was rarely secured in a tight little bun anymore, she still had that prim-and-proper thing with sensual undercurrents going on, and tonight in particular it was driving Noah nuts.

"What?"

"Trouble."

"Who, me?" Noah pretended innocence. Lately it was like getting a double dose of heat every time they rehearsed, and he was holding back but hanging by a thread. Luckily there was a kiss in the next scene, so he had that in his favor. He would just have to mess up so they'd have to do the scene over and over. The thought made him chuckle. He was also amused that Olivia seemed to have forgotten all about the bill. He handed the check and a twenty to Jessica behind his back. "Let's head over to the Dairy Hut." He certainly needed something to cool him off, but watching her lick an ice-cream cone might not do it.

"I just have to pay my bill." She gave him a pointed look and reached for her purse.

Jessica waved her off. "It's been taken care of."

When Olivia opened her mouth to protest, Myra stepped in. "Olivia, for pity's sake let the man buy your doggone dinner. It was only a bowl of soup!"

Madison pointed her fork at Olivia. "Aunt Myra's right, Olivia. You're always staying after school, volunteering your time, and helping others. Allow someone to do something nice for you for a change."

"I'll say." Myra came around the counter and handed Olivia the apple pie. "Now you two lovebirds head over to the Dairy Hut before they close up for the night. Tell Big Joe I said hi."

"See y'all later," Noah said with a wave. "Hey, and the rock soup was delicious."

"We're not lovebirds," Noah overheard Olivia whisper to Myra before she turned to leave.

"I call 'em like I see 'em." Myra whispered back. "It's only a matter of time. And take it from someone who has made some mistakes . . . don't let something special slip through your fingers." She added the last a little bit louder.

When Olivia sent a startled glance his way, Noah pretended not to hear, but Myra was a pretty savvy chick and he wondered if those words were meant more for him than for Olivia. But as he walked toward the front door he had to wonder . . . Was Myra right? Maybe he was way off base by holding back when he should be going after something that felt so special. Noah had always put his career first, and his father had made it abundantly clear that he should stay focused. Those words, however right or wrong, had stayed with him during his life. But as he watched Olivia smile and wave at people she knew, the thought hit him that he was so much more comfortable with her than with the starlets and models he had dated throughout his career.

Noah had never felt the strong connection that he experienced with Olivia Lawson with any other woman, and he had a sudden urge to put a possessive arm around her waist. In truth, they were seen together so often lately that he knew people were starting to link them as a couple. He didn't care, but he hoped the paparazzi didn't come swooping into town and splash her picture all over the tabloids. He wasn't exactly tops on the list of celebrities to stalk, but he did get his share of exposure in the rags and he didn't want Olivia to have to endure that kind of crap.

He was still deep in thought when they reached the sidewalk outside.

"Are you okay?"

"Sure." Noah looked at her upturned face in question. "Why do you ask?"

"You had a troubled expression on your face," she replied with a slight frown.

Noah shrugged, but he couldn't tell her his thoughts. He was touched, however, that she cared. It had been such a long time since anyone gave a damn about anything other than what he could do for them. "Hey, I'm fine."

Olivia nodded, but then her eyes suddenly widened. "Listen, if it's because—" she began, but then she stopped and gave a quick shake of her head. "Never mind."

"Oh, no, you don't." He took her hand and tugged her over to the side of the building away from watchful eyes. "What do you want to know?"

She glanced down at the ground and then pressed her lips together.

"Livie . . ." He tucked a finger beneath her chin and forced her to look at him. "Tell me what's going on inside that head of yours. Would you, please?"

"Okay, are you concerned that people are talking about us . . . ? You know, like we are . . . together?"

Noah leaned back against the brick wall and gazed at her in surprise. "That sure came out of left field. Why on earth would you think that?"

She tilted her head to the side. "Well, people were whispering and staring at us in the diner, and we have been seen together almost every night for the past two weeks. This is a small town and people talk. Walking over to the Dairy Hut will get tongues wagging even more."

"Ah, so the good old Dairy Hut is still the hot spot in town?"

Olivia nodded. "Some things are slow to change around here. I just wanted you to know."

"Olivia . . ." Noah shook his head slowly and then sighed. "That's not what I meant. I realize that people are speculating about us. But why would you think it would upset me?"

She toyed with the wrapper on the apple pie. "Oh, come on, Noah. I'm not exactly the caliber of woman you're usually seen with."

"Yes, you're certainly right about that."

"I get it." She swallowed hard. "You have an image to uphold. If you want me to set the record strai—" Noah dipped his head and cut her off with a gentle kiss and then cupped her cheeks between his palms.

"We're in public!" she reminded him breathlessly.

"Exactly. Have I made my point?"

She smiled slowly. "Yes."

"Damn!" He slapped his thigh.

"Now just why are you saying that?"

"I wanted you to say no so I'd have to make my point again." When Olivia laughed and gave him a playful shove, he grabbed her hand. Although her eyes widened a fraction, Noah was relieved when she didn't pull away. Holding her hand in public would indeed start tongues wagging, but he suddenly heard Myra's words in his head: *Don't let something special slip through your fingers.* All day long Noah looked forward to their lessons. He thought about Olivia constantly. Just seeing her raised his spirits, even though he hadn't really known they needed raising and filled a void that he hadn't known was there. "Wow." Noah shook his head with a sense of wonder.

"What?" she asked in a breathless voice that suggested she was feeling the same emotions. At least he hoped so.

"Are you ready?" Noah asked, and he wasn't really talking about ice cream.

"I most certainly am," Olivia answered.

Olivia's sweet, genuine smile took aim at Noah's heart and he smiled back. "So am I." He tugged on her hand and led her over to his Corvette. "Let's put your pie in the car," he suggested. He took the plate from her and placed it on the passenger seat. He wanted a reason to come back to the car and perhaps entice her to go for an evening ride before taking her home for his acting lesson. Or then again, perhaps he could convince her to take a night off.

"It sure is a nice night out," Noah commented while they waited for the traffic light to change.

"Oh, I agree." She smiled up at him. The unseasonably warm evening carried the sweet scent of blooming flowers and freshly cut grass. "Spring has always been my favorite season."

"Yeah, me too. It means baseball," he said and then was surprised at his own response. Baseball was his past, not his future. Until coming back here he'd tried not to think much about spring training.

"I imagine that you must really miss it," she said as they crossed Main Street.

"That part of my life is over." Noah shrugged, feeling a little confused. "I don't really know where that came from."

"What do you mean? Baseball is in your blood." She patted her chest. "A part of who you are, Noah." She looked at him as if surprised at his admission and tugged on his hand for them to stop in front of the city park. They sat down on the brick wall overlooking the playground. Little children played on the swing sets with their parents watching. A group of teenagers laughed and shoved each other, and an elderly couple walked their dog.

"You're right." Noah inhaled a deep breath and then grinned when after three misses a little boy wearing a baseball glove finally caught a pop-up.

"Great catch, son!"

"Thanks, Daddy! Hit me another one! Higher this time."

"Okay, be ready!"

Noah recalled doing the very same thing with his father and was swamped with an odd sense of longing that he didn't quite understand. After a moment he turned his attention back to Olivia. "For most of my life baseball defined who I was. I lived it and breathed it. When it ended I felt lost. Without any real purpose. In some ways I still do. And after I was booted off of *Love in the Afternoon*, I started leading a lifestyle that left me feeling empty." He squeezed her hand and said, "You are the only person I've admitted that to."

Olivia looked at him with sincere eyes. "You're back in your hometown, with so many memories. And you've been working out with the Cricket Creek baseball team. It's only natural to have some melancholy feelings." She extended her arm in an arc, taking in the park. "This is where it all began for you. Your roots."

"And it's a good thing I came back here. This little town helped me get my sorry ass back on track." Noah tilted his head. "Did you ever think of moving away from Cricket Creek, Livie? Pursuing that acting career that you wanted so much?"

Something of a shadow passed over her features, but she gave him a firm negative shake of her head. "Never, except for college, and Cooper isn't very far away. I could have commuted, but my father wanted me to experience campus life. Like I mentioned, I was a barnie and did summer stock but never very far away. This is my home. I choose to bloom where I was planted. I don't need to run off searching for something better," she answered with a touch of bitterness that was at odds with her usual gentle nature. He had a feeling there was more to her answer than what she was giving him. Acting was in her blood like baseball was in his. There had to be a reason that she decided not to go after what she was so passionate about. "There is such a sense of community here. Strong family values. We're not just a dot on a map, Noah. This town is worth saving. If not, all of these little storefronts will soon be swallowed up by big business. Cricket Creek will become pretty much a ghost town."

"No more butter cookies," he said and then squeezed her hand.

"Nope," Olivia answered with a small smile. "And that would just blow," she continued hotly.

Noah tipped his head back and laughed.

"How is no more butter cookies funny?"

"Oh, believe me, it's not. But prim and proper Miss Lawson saying 'That would just blow' is hilarious."

"Why does everybody laugh at the things I say?" she grumbled.

"Because you're funny. Nothing wrong with that, is there?"

"Yes! People are laughing *at* me!" She grumbled louder, but then her eyes widened. "Omigod, watch out!"

"What?" Noah watched in amazement as Olivia suddenly raised her hand in the air and then dived forward from the wall and snagged a fly ball in an ESPN-worthy catch marred only by the girlie yelp she gave when the ball smacked her bare hands. She landed facedown in the grass and rolled to her back, but to her credit she had the ball still clutched in her right hand.

"Olivia!" Noah quickly knelt down beside her and felt a stab of alarm. "Wow, are you okay?"

She nodded, but when she tried to verbalize her well-being all that came out of her mouth was a wheeze and two blades of grass.

He put his hand against her cheek. "You got the wind knocked out of you."

She nodded and tried to gulp in some air.

"Great catch!" Noah said and got a wheezing laugh in return. A moment later the young father and son came rushing over. When Olivia tried to sit up, Noah put a gentle hand on her shoulder. "Sweetie, slow down and breathe," he advised her. "You'll be fine in a minute or two." He knew she would be okay, but seeing her in pain had his stomach in knots.

"I am so sorry," the dad said and gazed at Olivia with concern. "I hit that one a little too hard." He looked back at Noah. "Is your wife okay?" he asked and then recognized Noah. "Oh, wow, you're Noah Falcon!" He turned to his little boy. "Adam, this is a major-league baseball player and he's from Cricket Creek. We just moved here this spring and thought it was so cool."

"Wow!" Adam's eyes widened. "Are you really, *really* Noah Falcon?"

Noah nodded. "Last time I checked." He always found that question amusing.

"Did you know that your name is on the sign down the road?" Adam asked in a high-pitched, excited voice, pointing over his shoulder with his glove. "Hey, will you sign my baseball and my glove too?" he asked and then peered down at Olivia. "Can I have my ball back, please?"

When Olivia wheezed a weak "Yes," Adam reached down and plucked the ball from her clutches. Noah was happy to see that color was returning to her pale face. "Want to sit up?" he asked, but she shook her head. "You'll be okay in a minute. You hit the ground hard." He was willing to bet she had never had the wind knocked out of her before, and he put a reassuring hand on her shoulder.

The young dad looked at her with sympathy. "I'm so sorry, but, hey, that was quite a catch. It saved Noah from getting smacked in the head. Do you guys have kids?"

"Not yet," Noah said with a grin down at Olivia. "Honey, we need to work on that."

Sputter. Wheeze.

"Well, when you do you'll have one heck of a base-ball player on your hands."

"Who speaks correct English," Noah added and had to laugh, but his smile faded when Olivia tried to sit up but then flopped back down with a breathless groan. Her shoulders rose with the effort of trying to get air back into her lungs. Noah quickly signed the baseball and glove and handed it to Adam.

"Thanks!" Adam gushed with a wide grin. "Dad, isn't this awesome! Look, it has my name and everything!" He then looked up at Noah with adoring eyes. "This is the bestest day ever. Hey, will you come to one of my games?"

"Adam," his father said with an apologetic shake of his head at Noah, "I'm sure Mr. Falcon is busy."

"I can't promise for sure I can be there," Noah answered, but then he tilted his head at Adam and said, "but when and where, Tiger?"

Adam's eyes got round. "Cricket Creek grade school fields on Tuesday nights. Um, what time, Daddy?"

"Six thirty."

"I'll try my best." Noah gave Adam a high five and shook the dad's hand.

"I'm Dan Forman, and I have been a fan forever. Thanks for coming back here to Cricket Creek to be in the summer play. I hope it's a big success. I know I'll be attending."

Noah nodded. "It's good to be back. Spread the news about the play," he said and then turned to Adam. "Keep your eye on the ball and practice hard, okay?"

Little Adam shook his head so hard that his too big baseball cap slipped sideways. "I will!" he answered so seriously that Noah hid his smile and put on his game face.

"That's what I'm talking about." He watched Adam tuck his hand into his father's as they walked across the playground. He could hear the excited chatter from Adam and made a mental note to do his best to at least show up for an inning or so.

"That was amazing." Olivia pushed up to her elbows and gave Noah a warm smile.

"You mean your catch? Yeah, baby . . . a diving catch, no less, and you held on to the ball." He squeezed her shoulder. "It should be the ESPN play of the day."

"Oh, stop," she scoffed but then gave him a slow grin. "Really?"

Noah nodded. "Major league, baby."

"Sweet!" she said and raised one fist in the air. "Maybe I'm not such a nerd after all," she added with a little head bop that made Noah laugh. "Okay, maybe not."

"I happen to like nerd balls."

"But I was referring to your conversation with little Adam. You certainly made his day."

Noah shrugged. "Yeah, well, he made mine. It's been a while since I've signed a baseball."

"Are you really going to his game?"

"I'll do my best. Hey, do you want to go to his game with me, *Mrs. Falcon*?" he joked, but he was a bit startled when he realized that the thought of her being his wife held a certain appeal. Where in the world did that come from?

"Oh!" Olivia's eyes widened. "We should have set them straight! Rumors are really going to fly!" She put a hand over her mouth and then chided, "No-ah!" But instead of appearing mortified, she suddenly giggled. "I don't think I've ever been on the receiving end of juicy gossip."

"Welcome to my world," Noah responded drily and then helped her up to a standing position.

"Oh, it's not always fun when rumors fly, I suppose."

Noah shrugged. "I've always tried not to worry so much what people say unless it hurts someone I care about. That being said, I attempted to be a baseball player that kids looked up to, you know? Sports have lost so much of that—I'd like to see integrity brought back, especially to baseball." He took her hand and started walking. "I talked about that with the players over at Cricket Creek High School. I reminded them that they are representing their team and school when they play."

"Good for you, Noah," Olivia said with a serious nod. "Believe me, kids today need positive role models." She angled her head and then continued. "I've given you a hard time from the moment you roared into town, but I misjudged you. I'm sorry for that."

Noah pulled her to a stop at the street corner before

they reached the Dairy Hut. "Hey, I will be the first to admit that I'm no saint, but I try to live by a certain moral code. Being back here really has helped me remember to keep those beliefs intact." He frowned. "Coming home has been a good thing for me in more ways than one." He felt a measure of emotion clog his throat and had a strong urge to draw her into his arms, but he suddenly felt overwhelmed at the intensity of his feelings for Olivia. His life was in transition, and he needed to remember that while he was only here for the summer run before going on with his life, Olivia Lawson had made it clear that she wanted to live in Cricket Creek. She was the last person on earth he wanted to hurt, and so he smiled and said, "Well, actually, a little bit of gossip about us could be an added draw for the play, as odd as it seems."

"Oh, I get it—create some buzz," Olivia said with a slow nod coupled with a look of disappointment that she quickly masked, confirming his guess that she was developing feelings for him as well. "Smart thinking." She cleared her throat and glanced away for a second. "Sure, I think we can pull it off—you know, like holding hands and things like that."

"Right," Noah replied, and for a heartbeat he considered setting her straight, but then he decided that letting her assume that any advances on his part were all for show was an easy way to be able to enjoy getting close without the risk of hurting her in the end. "What do you think?"

10

Spring Fever

"Excellent idea. We can get a little Hollywood-style buzz going. Noah Falcon and the high school English teacher an item? My tumble in the diner was a good start, and like we said, people are already beginning to gossip. This walk to the Dairy Hut was a better idea than I imagined." Olivia knew she was rambling on, but she couldn't stop herself. She hid her disappointment with a choppy laugh followed by a wave of her hand. "I consider myself a good actress. We can totally fool everyone." Except for herself, she thought sadly. "I'm totally down with this," she added and realized she sounded like she was seventeen. Whenever she tried to tell a lie her Southern accent prevailed, and when she was nervous or upset she tended to play a role instead of being herself. She had learned to act upbeat and happy as a child for the benefit of her father, and she could surely do it for the sake of the play. But right now she sounded like a Southern Valley Girl hybrid, if there could be such a thing.

"Dude, for real?" Noah asked with a slight grin.

"Sorry." She felt heat steal into her cheeks. "I'm around teenagers all day long, and I tend to pick up their lingo even though I preach using correct English. But yes, getting people talking will add some buzz building up to opening night. Let's do it," she said and tugged on his hand. "We'd better hurry or the Dairy Hut will close. Spring hours are earlier than summer," she added and kept walking, even though she got the impression he wanted to hang back and say something to her. An odd lump had formed in her throat and ice cream no longer held any appeal, but she would do her damnedest to fake it. "I'm dying for a dip top. You?"

"Still thinking . . ."

Ahh . . . she was fooling herself to think that he was truly falling for her. Cricket Creek would never be good enough for the likes of Noah Falcon. He would soon be off to bigger and better things and never look back. The thought made her feel unreasonably upset, and she suddenly wanted to go home.

"Are you okay?" Noah asked and stopped on the corner.

"Sure. Why do you ask?" She tilted her head in a questioning gesture and pasted a smile on her face.

"Maybe because you have a death grip on my hand. Is this making you nervous?"

"Of course not." Olivia swallowed hard and let go of his hand. "But it is getting late. Real rehearsals at the center begin on Monday night. We should probably head back and practice unless you're hell-bent on getting a creamy whip."

Noah chuckled. "Hell-bent? Why, I'm surprised at your language, Miss Lawson."

"I don't know where that came from." Olivia found herself smiling in spite of her jumbled emotions. "Well, are you?"

"I've been known to be hell-bent. Yeah, I am really craving a soft-serve ice cream. I can't remember the last time I had one. I'm thinking chocolate dip top too," he admitted with a boyish grin that reminded Olivia of how carefree he was back in high school, and it occurred to her that Noah wasn't as sure of himself as he pretended and that she and Madison were putting a lot of unfair pressure on him to make this play a success and to help save his hometown in the process. "So will you indulge me?"

"Oh, okay." She rolled her eyes but had to give in. Who could resist those dimples and that smile? Apparently not her.

"Thanks," he said with another lopsided grin that tugged at her heartstrings. This unexpected vulnerable side drew her to him even more, making her want to pull him into her arms and give him a reassuring hug. When he took her hand again, she didn't protest. Guarding her heart, she decided, was pretty much pointless, since mistake or not, she was already in love with him and she might as well just face the facts. She was a goner the moment she saw him in the bakery, even though she had put her nose in the air and pretended otherwise. Of course she would never let him know it, but this little farce they were concocting would be her ticket to be with him as his girlfriend, if only for a little while. So from this moment on, she would pretend to be pretending and soak it all up like a sponge until the play concluded at the end of the summer.

"You sure you don't want sprinkles? I've always been a fan of rainbow, although I'm in a chocolate kind of mood tonight." She had to laugh when his eyes widened before he shook his head up at the blue sky.

"Too many choices," Noah complained with a long sigh. "But you know what?"

"Probably not, but I'll bite."

"I haven't had this much fun eating in a long time."

"You mean you don't miss sushi, steak, and sea bass?"

"Are you kidding?" Noah closed his eyes and took a

deep breath when they reached the edge of the parking lot, which was surprisingly full. Apparently they weren't the only ones with spring fever. After a second he raised his index finger in the air. "Cheeseburgers, fries, waffle cones, and chocolate. Oh, wait a minute . . . and hot dogs. I've been missing out on a lot. I just didn't know it." He opened his eyes and looked at her, and for a heart-stopping moment she thought he meant something entirely different, but then he swallowed and said, "Surely there's a Dairy Hut in heaven too. Not just Papa Vito's pizza?"

"Oh, without a doubt and open all year long, not just summertime. And Grammar's butter cookies."

"Myra's onion rings and chili cheese fries?"

Olivia nodded. "And I think I have to add Jessica's rock soup to the list," she said. "Oh, and her apple pie," she said and was startled when she was given a nudge from behind.

"Don't leave out a dirty martini from Sully's!"

Olivia glanced at Noah and then laughed. "What? Madison? Jason? How long have you been standing there?"

"We just walked up behind you," Madison explained, but then she grinned. "But you two *lovebirds* were so into each other that you didn't notice."

"We're not lovebirds," Olivia corrected, but this time without much conviction.

"Hey, you were walking hand in hand to the Dairy Hut. That's what all the lovebirds do in Cricket Creek."

Olivia angled her head at Madison and Jason. "Oh, really, now?"

Madison raised her palms in the air. "We weren't holding hands," she informed everyone, but the color in her cheeks suggested to Olivia that the two of them were getting very close. Yes!

"I offered a piggyback ride," Jason said, "but she declined."

"You offer a lot of things that I decline."

Jason put his arms behind his back and stretched. "It's only a matter of time."

"In your dreams," Madison shot back, but Olivia could feel the sexual tension humming between them. They weren't fooling anyone. Madison turned her attention to Olivia. "What were you two talking about so intently?"

"The fine cuisine in Cricket Creek," Noah replied and rubbed his abdomen. "Wait. What's this I hear about a dirty martini at Sully's? Are you kidding me?"

"It's a long story, but trust me and try one," Madison replied. "You won't be sorry," she said and grinned up at Jason.

Jason extended his hand to Noah. "Hey, man, heard you're working out with the Cricket Creek baseball team."

"Yeah. They've got a talented roster this year. How've you been, Jason? Haven't seen you in Myra's in a while."

"Been busy, but doin' all right."

"Working too hard," Madison said with a shake of her head. "He barely takes the time to eat. The promise of a hot fudge sundae was the only way to get him to take off his tool belt for the night."

"I could think of a better reason," Jason answered and got an elbow jab from Madison.

"Jason!" Madison looked at Noah in apology. "I think he's been hanging around my aunt Myra a little too much."

"Man's got a point," Noah said and got the same exact treatment from Olivia, but he only grinned, gave Jason a knuckle bump, and blew it up. "What can I say? We're guys."

When Jason lifted his hands in innocent agreement, Madison groaned. "Olivia, I feel like we're trapped in a beer commercial."

"Hey, I resemble that," Noah said and got a round of laughter.

"Ya think?" Madison asked with a grin and rolled her eyes at Olivia.

"I know," Olivia agreed, but she was amazed that a major-league baseball player turned soap star could make the people around him feel so at ease, and it occurred to her that she truly had misjudged him.

"Oh, hey, Noah, I'll be drawing up the plans for the dugouts over at the baseball field right after I'm finished framing the sets," Jason informed him.

Olivia looked at Noah with surprise. "You're funding building new dugouts at the high school?"

Noah lifted one shoulder, shrugging it off. "The ones there now are falling apart. Those kids work hard and they deserve better." Noah gave Jason a nudge. "And Jason's bid was way under what it should have been."

"I'm not surprised," Olivia commented and gave Madison a look that said that Jason was a good guy. "He did the same thing for the sets, which happen to be beautiful, by the way. The art students at Cricket Creek have been painting them."

"It's all coming together," Jason said and gave Madison's arm a squeeze. "I think it's safe to say that we all want the best for Cricket Creek."

Olivia was glad that Jason seemed to be a shoulder for Madison to lean on, since her young friend was fiercely independent to a fault. "Opening night will be here before we know it. Which reminds me, we should get our ice cream and head back to read through the script. Come on, guys," Olivia said and started walking toward the Dairy Hut.

They quickly became the center of attention and made the Dairy Hut patrons stop in mid-lick. "If you love ice cream, raise those cones in the air and give me a yee-haw!" Noah said.

"Yee-haw!" was the collective response from families and couples standing in groups or sitting at picnic tables.

When Noah looked Olivia's way with another boyish grin, she shook her head. "You are something else, Noah Falcon."

"You mean that in a good way, right?" he asked.

"Sure," she assured him but then rolled her eyes.

Madison gave Noah's shoulder a shove. "Don't worry. I get that all the time too."

"But in a good way as well?" Jason asked and got a much harder shove from Madison.

"Why, of course."

Olivia had to laugh and then shook her head at Madison and Noah. "Along with your mother, Madison, you are the shot in the arm that this town needed. There hasn't been this much excitement about summer arriving in a long time."

"I can't argue with that." Jason grinned at Olivia and then draped his arm over Madison's shoulders. "Can you, baby?" he asked Madison.

"Nope," Madison answered, drawing a chuckle from Jason.

"You agree with me? Now that's a first."

"No, it's not." Madison laughed and when she eased up and gave Jason a light kiss on the lips, his eyes widened as if surprised at her public show of affection. He seemed so pleased that Olivia's heart did an internal tap dance. When Madison glanced her way, Olivia gave her a slight I-was-right nod.

Madison rolled her eyes skyward, but it occurred to Olivia that Madison was starting to believe the theme threaded throughout her beautifully written play. Rich or poor, young or old, city bred or country born, there was still just one thing that really mattered at the end of each day.

Love.

As if reading Olivia's thoughts, the young playwright smiled, but then in true Madison form, she said, "Are we going to stand here all day or get some ice cream?"

"I was thinking about standing here all day." Jason casually glanced down at his fingernails and was rewarded with a jab to his side from Madison. "Do you have to keep doin' that? I've got bruises every damned where." He made a show of wincing while rubbing his ribs.

"I was simply thinking of Noah, who is dying for his dip top. Am I right, Noah?"

"You are correct," Noah agreed and put his hands up in surrender.

"See, I'm good that way." Madison angled her head at Jason, who in turn tweaked her wrinkled-up nose.

Noah reached over and took Olivia's hand, causing a warm thrill to snake down her spine. All it took was one look, one touch, and he simply made her melt. She smiled at him and gave his hand a good squeeze. Madison's play truly was spot on. Unable to be bought, sold, or bartered, love remained the most highly sought-after and valuable possession. Olivia recalled Myra's advice about not letting love slip through her fingers and stole a glance beneath her eyelashes at Noah. Perhaps it wasn't just pure chance that had brought Noah Falcon back to Cricket Creek but something that was meant to be? Her heart hammered at the thought.

Chances, Olivia realized, were nothing if not taken. And that meant that she was going to have to put her heart on the line if she wanted a future with Noah. But did she have the courage to do it?

Knowing that her emotions tended to be written all over her face, Olivia turned and walked up to the window at the Dairy Hut. After clearing her throat, she jammed her thumb over her shoulder, "Hey there, Big Joe. Ice cream for these guys is on me."

"In that case make mine a large," Noah said from behind Olivia.

"Noah Falcon!" Big Joe, who was actually small in stature, shoved his hand through the open window and grinned. "Last time I saw you standing at this here window you were in a Cricket Creek uniform." He shook his head. "Man alive, those were some glory days. Three state championships in a row. Golly!"

"Sure were some fun times." Noah shook Big Joe's hand. "The roster looks strong this year. The team has some depth."

"Yeah, well, the boys sure are pumped about you helpin' out. Heard you're building dugouts too. Mighty nice of you, Noah."

"No big deal. This town's always been behind me. I'm glad to give a little back," he said modestly.

"All the same, it's great to have you back here." He turned away for a second and then handed Noah a blue Slush Puppie.

"A Cricket Creek blue Slush Puppie after every win. You remembered." Noah grinned as he accepted the cold cup.

"Noah, you gave this town lots of memories." Big Joe winked at Olivia. "Most of them good."

"Some of them legend," Jason said and then backed away from Madison's elbow.

"Oh, come on, I had to raise a little hell," Noah protested and then took a long slurp of his Slush Puppie. He backed away so the rest of them could order.

"I'll have a small vanilla-chocolate swirl with chocolate sprinkles," Olivia said. It occurred to her once again that Noah wasn't quite the cocky superstar that she had thought him to be, and without thinking she reached up and patted his back. He seemed surprised at her spontaneous gesture, but then smiled with what appeared to be a bit of emotion. While Madison and Jason ordered, he offered her a swig of his drink and she accepted, thinking that it felt like a very couplelike thing to do. She was getting used to him being around and determinedly pushed the fear of him leaving out of her mind. For now the spring sliding into summer seemed endless, and she refused to ruin what felt like a rare perfect night.

"Your tongue is blue," Olivia observed with a giggle.

"Correction—Cricket Creek blue. Let me see yours."

"Oh, like I'm falling for that old trick," Olivia replied and clamped her mouth shut.

"Fall for what?" Jason asked after swallowing a bite of hot fudge sundae. "You need me to kick some Noah Falcon butt, Teach?"

"Like you can," Noah countered in a tough-guy voice that was hard to take seriously while he licked a dip top. "Damn, lost a piece of chocolate. My dip-top skills need some polishing."

"What did he want to see?" Madison asked.

"My tongue."

"Oh, baby." She gave Noah an arched eyebrow. "You've still got some game."

"Right, I know . . . for an old dude. I keep getting that."

Madison laughed. "Well, you've got an ice-cream cone in one hand and a Slush Puppie in the other. I think you're an overgrown kid."

Noah stuck his tongue out at her.

"Eew, with a blue tongue," Madison observed.

"Cricket Creek blue," Olivia corrected.

Madison shook her head. "You people are just weird."

"Isn't she just the sweetest thing?" Jason asked drily.

"Thank you, Jason," Madison said in a singsong voice and blew him a kiss.

Olivia laughed, then licked a creamy drip from her cone. When she looked up, Noah's eyes were on her and her heart skipped a beat.

11

The Only Game in Town

Noah was right. Watching Olivia consume an ice-cream cone sent his pulse racing. It wasn't just the sensual act of licking the vanilla swirl but rather the pleasure she took in something so simple. "Let's find a place to sit." He located a vacant spot beneath a huge oak tree and sat down on top of a picnic table with his boots on the bench seat, just like he did as a teenager. A month ago, going out on the town meant an upscale hot spot where one drink cost more than an entire meal at Myra's Diner. Noah had thought that was the lifestyle he had always aspired to and that it spelled success, but sitting here with warm and friendly people felt so relaxing . . . so damned good that he was beginning to rethink his goals.

Since returning to Cricket Creek he had felt a sense of peace, of belonging. He woke up in the morning looking forward to the day ahead, and he realized that had something to do with the gentle woman sitting beside him.

"A penny for your thoughts," Olivia said.

"My thoughts are worth more than a penny," Noah teased and then bumped his knee against hers. "Actually

I was thinking about how I love New York but always felt swallowed up by the city. It's different here."

Madison nodded. "I get what you're saying. Chicago felt the same way. Everybody knows everybody here. There is a sense of caring." She rescued a piece of chocolate from her cherry dip top and said, "Mom and I were talking about that recently."

"Really?" Jason rested the heel of his work boot on the bench of the picnic table next to where Madison was sitting. "So you think you're going to stay beyond the end of the play?" Although he asked casually, Noah could sense the seriousness in his question.

"Now that I know I can get a fabulous martini at Sully's, I'll give it some consideration." She concentrated on her cone but then looked up at Jason. "Unless you can think of a better reason?"

"I could come up with a thing or two," Jason answered.

"Promises, promises . . ." Madison replied, but the blush in her cheeks made Noah think that Jason had already shown her a thing or two. The vibe between them was hot enough to make his ice cream melt. He could relate.

"You going to the game tomorrow, Noah?" Jason asked with a sideways tilt of his head.

Noah swallowed a crunchy bite of cone coated with chocolate. "You mean Cricket Creek baseball?"

Jason grinned. "It's the only game in town—the season opener against Morgan County. No beer allowed, but the hot dogs are good."

"I had planned on it. You going too?"

"I might be late, but I try to make most of the home games." He stood up and brushed crumbs from his jeans before extending his hand to Madison and playfully tugging her to her feet. "Hope to see y'all there." He looked at Olivia as well, and Noah realized that people really were starting to connect them as a couple.

" 'Bye, guys," Madison said. Noah thought that she seemed more happy and relaxed than he had seen her since his arrival. "They seem to be hitting it off," he observed after they walked away. "Maybe you were right in hooking them up."

"I usually am."

Noah took a bite of chocolate and angled his head at her. "Why do you do it?"

"Do what?"

"Play matchmaker?"

She looked a bit uncomfortable for a second, but then shrugged. "Part of it is to keep people here in Cricket Creek. I hate it when people leave when all they really need is right here in their own backyard."

Noah sensed there was more to it than that, but he chose not to put a damper in the otherwise excellent evening. "Is it okay if we go to the game and rehearse late tomorrow?" he asked and was glad when she nodded and seemed to brighten.

"Sure, I'd love to go. Try to make as many games as I can," she answered before crunching the last bite of her cone.

"I . . ." Noah had a comment on the tip of his tongue but when Olivia licked a chocolate sprinkle from her bottom lip all coherent thought fled his brain. "Uh . . ."

"What?"

"You, uh, missed some."

"Here?" When she licked the wrong side of her mouth Noah shook his head and leaned closer.

"Other side," Noah informed her but chuckled when she missed the sprinkles.

"Oh, can't you help a girl out? For heaven's sake, I don't want to walk around town with chocolate-sprinkled lips. People laugh at me enough already. Where is my napkin, anyway?" She looked around, but he reached over and cupped her chin in his hand.

"Allow me." With the pad of his thumb Noah brushed a sprinkle or two from the center of her bottom lip. He didn't mean it as anything overtly sexual, but he felt the impact of her moist mouth slide like hot fudge down his spine.

"Thank you." Her voice was husky, and the evening breeze blew strands of hair across her cheek. She looked at him with soulful eyes that held a hint of expectation. Noah desperately wanted to lean in and kiss her.

And so he did.

Softly. Gently. But the feel of her mouth beneath his packed a punch that had him threading his fingers through her hair in search of more. She tasted like ice cream, smelled like flowers, and he simply couldn't get enough.

"Noah, we're in public." She pulled back and whispered it in his ear.

"I don't give a—"

"Fig?"

"Yeah, a flying fig," he responded gruffly. He was beyond caring about anything other than kissing her, touching her, and they were secluded enough not to be a spectacle.

"Me neither," she admitted with a trembling smile that hit Noah hard. Olivia Lawson was falling for him. He could see it in the depths of her warm brown eyes. She was so sweet, honest, and good ... and she didn't deserve to have her heart broken. She shook her head and put a hand on his cheek. "Don't do that to me."

"What?"

"Look at me as if I'm made of spun glass. Noah, I might not be the kind of woman you're used to, but I'm not going to shatter right before your very eyes. Small-town girls are made of sturdy stuff."

"Olivia?" Noah's heart pounded like it was the ninth inning and he'd been brought in to close a one-run game with three men on base and no outs. "What are you saying?"

Olivia cleared her throat and then said, "I'm saying that we need to go back to my house and ... and rehearse." She gazed down at the grass and then back up at him. "Are you ready?"

"I've been ready." Noah nodded and stood up so quickly that he almost fell over and had to steady himself on the edge of the picnic table. If he wasn't mistaken, Olivia Lawson wanted him as much as he wanted her—and not just to rehearse lines that they already knew by heart. He leaned in and said next to her ear, "Are you planning on having your small-town-sturdy-self way with me?"

She caught her bottom lip between her teeth and lifted one slender shoulder. "Maybe."

"Well, then, let's blow this Popsicle stand."

Olivia laughed when he tugged her to her feet. "Don't go feeling so sure of yourself, Noah Falcon."

He arched one eyebrow and gave her what he hoped was his best winning smile. "So I have a chance?"

She held her thumb and index finger an inch apart.

"Baby, that's all I need."

"We'll see." Olivia's light, playful laughter washed over him like warm summer rain. Noah was used to bold, confident women. Olivia was pure and natural in comparison, and yet there was an earthy sexiness about her that simply blew him away.

When Noah took her hand, he wasn't surprised to feel a slight tremble. A light rose blush stained her cheeks, and he could tell that she was nervous. He couldn't wait to kiss away her inhibitions.

Oh, boy ... but when he started walking, he found that his own legs felt a little shaky. He had dated models and starlets, but he couldn't remember when he had felt such a sense of sweet anticipation.

They started strolling at a normal pace toward his car, but the closer they got to Main Street the faster they walked. The sexual tension that had been building since day one suddenly heightened to a fever pitch.

"Oh, my goodness!" Olivia yelped when she nearly sat on the apple pie.

Noah hopped into the car and threw it into gear. "Hold on tight." He had to force himself to go at a safe pace while driving to her house, but as soon as he pulled into her driveway he rushed over to the passenger side of the Corvette, yanked open the door, and tugged her to her feet. Not caring about who saw them, he scooped her into his arms and carried her up the steps.

"What are you doing?" Olivia clung to his shoulders and laughed with pure delight.

"I don't know. I felt the need to have you in my arms right away." When she fumbled with the doorknob, Noah said, "It's not locked?"

"This is like Mayberry, Noah. I never bother to lock my doors."

Noah shook his head. "I know, but all the same, promise me you'll keep your doors locked from now on, okay?" The thought of anything happening to her clenched his gut, and he hugged her closer.

"I promise," she replied in that husky voice edged with Southern comfort. "And thank you."

"For what?"

"For caring, Noah."

"This whole town cares about you, Livie."

"Yes, but in an abstract way. Your concern for my safety means a lot to me. And I care about you too. This isn't about who you are—you know that, right?"

"Yes, I do know that." But she had no idea what that statement meant to him. As a baseball player Noah had been taught to keep his game face on. So when emotion suddenly clogged his throat, he was taken aback, but then he gave her a slow smile. "You know, it was always my dream to make it to the majors, and don't get me wrong, I enjoyed everything about it, including the female attention." He cleared his throat and continued. "But, Livie, what you just told me is the sexiest thing a woman has ever said to me."

She looked at him and nodded. "I get it."

Noah looked up at the ceiling and shook his head. "You know everyone in this town makes it clear that they are proud of me. But at the same time Mabel rides my ass when I go to the bakery. Madison keeps me in line and, well, Myra gives it to me real. Even Jason treats me like a friend and not a celebrity. It's pretty cool to feel needed, wanted, and liked as a person instead of a franchise that's losing value."

"Losing value?" Olivia put a hand on his cheek. "You don't give yourself nearly enough credit."

He sat down on the sofa with her on his lap. "Ahhh, Livie, thank you for making me feel good about myself again." He chuckled. "Even as a kid I felt worthless when I wasn't hitting."

"And yet you love the game."

"Absolutely. I miss playing, but I didn't know how much I missed the game until I started spending so much time with the high school team. Being behind the scenes has been great—I didn't know I'd still be able to enjoy baseball from a coaching angle.

"You know, I was lucky I got noticed when I was playing here. Small-town teams like Cricket Creek don't get scouted as much as the big schools."

Olivia shrugged. "Maybe you can find a way to change that. Even small-town kids need a chance."

Noah smiled at her and then tucked a lock of hair behind her ear. "Or even a second chance." He met her gaze and then dipped his head and captured her mouth with his. The kiss began tenderly, but the moment his tongue tangled with hers Noah was lost in sensation that went beyond just physical. He didn't simply want Olivia—he needed her . . .

And yet he hesitated.

Olivia reached up and cupped his cheeks between her palms. "I want this, Noah. Let's go to my bedroom."

"So do I." With her still in his arms Noah stood up. "Down the hallway?"

"Yes, the room on the left," she answered in a voice full of heat. "And hurry!"

"Not a problem," he said and laughed as he picked up the pace.

They entered the bedroom and he eased her to her feet and kissed her hotly before pulling back to begin unbuttoning her blouse.

"Your fingers are trembling," Olivia said with a sense of wonder.

"Kinda ruins my player reputation," he said with a slight grin.

"No, it's incredibly, adorably sexy."

"Just like you," he said as he continued to undress her. "I've fantasized about your underwear from the moment I saw you in Grammar's Bakery."

Her eyes widened. "Truly?"

He nodded. "You were so prim and proper but with a mouth made for kissing. I imagined silk and lace."

"You would have been oh, so wrong."

After pushing the soft cotton blouse down over her shoulders, he sucked in a breath. "But I'm not."

She pressed her lips together and looked down at the floor. "I went shopping."

Noah felt his chest tighten. "For me?"

She nodded slowly and then raised her gaze in a question. "How did I do?"

Noah cupped his hands around pale blue satin edged with just a hint of white lace. The tiny white bow that peeked between her breasts was demure and yet enticingly sexy. With an intake of breath, he rubbed his thumbs over the creamy skin spilling out over the top of the bra and said, "Perfect."

"The bra?"

"No . . . you. The lingerie is just an added treat." He brushed her hair to the side and kissed her neck. "Do the panties match?"

"Why don't you find out?" Her voice was soft, breathless. And when he sucked her earlobe into his mouth, she moaned and held on to his shoulders for support.

"You don't have to ask twice." While nuzzling her neck he unbuttoned and then unzipped her pants. He slowly slid them over her hips and down her thighs. "Ah . . . satin," he said, cupping her ass in his palms. He tucked a finger under the elastic and sighed. "And lace. Bikini." While toying with the panties, he ran his tongue over her bottom lip, teasing, tasting until he felt the moist heat of her desire beneath his hand. When she sucked in a breath, he said, "Olivia, lie down on the bed so I can see you."

12

Cowboy Up

Olivia eased down onto the bed and gazed up at Noah. It had been a long time since she had been with a man, and she should have felt shy, unsure . . . but the passion smoldering in Noah's eyes made her feel bold and confident. The bra and panties had been an impulse buy and had looked so enticing in her drawer next to her Hanes Her Way that she had slipped them on this morning. Just wearing the slinky underwear had given her an attitude, and she thought with a smile that she was going to fill her dresser drawers with silk, satin, and lace.

"You can't smile like that without telling me what you're thinking."

"I'm thinking that you are overdressed for the occasion."

"I like how you think, Livie Lawson."

She eased up to her elbows.

"And I love how you look," he added and then tugged his shirt over his head. A moment later he was gloriously naked. She gazed up at wide shoulders, a sculpted chest, and muscled thighs. A thatch of dark hair covered his chest and tapered to an enticing line pointing to an impressive package.

Oh, my . . .

"You're gorgeous, Noah . . ." she said but then hesitated.

Noah sat down on the bed and tilted her chin up to look at him. "I hear a *but* in there somewhere." He rubbed his thumb across her bottom lip and waited for her to elaborate.

"This sounds corny, but I find you sexy from the inside out."

She leaned in and kissed his chest, loving the feel of his warm skin beneath her lips. Her tongue darted out and licked his nipple, swirling and teasing. His spicy, masculine scent filled her head and curled her toes. She loved touching him, tasting him. When her hand brushed against his penis, he inhaled sharply and threaded his fingers through her hair.

"Livie . . . damn, girl."

She looked up with a smile and asked, "So do you find me sexy from the inside out too?"

"Inside? Outside?" Noah pushed her into the pillows and began a trail of kisses starting at her neck and heading south to the soft swell of skin above her bra. "I just find you flat-out sexy."

"Good answer." Olivia sat up and stroked his cheeks. His dark stubble felt soft yet abrasive as she rubbed it back and forth.

His gaze met hers and locked. "It's not just an answer. It's true."

"Oh, Noah . . ." She threaded her fingers through his thick hair but then fell back against the mound of pillows when his hand slid up her thigh and caressed her intimately. And then he kissed her.

Her heart pounded, her pulse throbbed, and she kissed him back with more passion than she'd known she possessed. But then again, no man had ever made her feel this way. She arched her back in an effort to get closer, to slide her skin next to his. Her hands found his back and savored the ripple of muscle when he moved. With a moan she slid her hands over his butt and squeezed, bringing a deep, sexy chuckle from his throat. "I don't know where I found this inner sexpot." She lightly nipped his shoulder. "But it sure is fun."

"I'd like to think I brought it out in you."

She laughed. "I think you did."

"I just knew there was a sultry side beneath that prim and proper exterior. And damn if that isn't so much sexier than low-cut and in-your-face."

"Really?"

"Absolutely. Ah, you feel so good. I've wanted you in my arms like this for so long," he whispered in her ear and then rolled to the side. He caressed her lightly and said, "Take your bra and panties off for me, Livie. I want to see you, touch you ... taste you."

"Okay ..." With her heart pounding, Olivia reached around and unhooked her bra. When her breasts tumbled free, Noah swallowed hard and gently cupped them in his big hands. "There's not a lot of me."

"Ah, Livie," he said and circled her nipples with his thumbs, causing heat to uncurl and sink downward. "You're sweet perfection." When he leaned in and took one nipple in his mouth, Olivia arched her back and fisted her hands in his hair. He licked and sucked until she thought she would go crazy with wanting him. And when he slipped one finger beneath her panties and found her slick heat, she gasped.

"Noah ..." Her voice was husky, needy. "Dear God ..." She tugged her panties down her thighs and tossed them up in the air in pure abandonment. "Oh, no!" she cried and clapped a hand over her mouth.

"Baby, what is it?" Noah looked at her with concern.

"So much for being cool." Olivia pointed to the ceiling, where her pale blue panties hung from the blade of the ceiling fan. "My inner sexpot is a dork like me," she said with a shrug of her shoulders. "At least I'm consistent."

Noah leaned back against the pillows and laughed.

"Um, should you be laughing right now? Hello, I'm trying to be sexy. Work with me."

"Ah, Livie, laughter is incredibly sexy." He ran a fingertip down her cheek. "You make me feel so good."

"I know a way to make you feel even better," she offered with the arch of one eyebrow.

"Wow, I'm thinking that your dorky inner sexpot kinda rocks." Noah captured her mouth, playfully at first, but Olivia wrapped her arms around him and deepened the kiss. With a moan Noah lifted her up to straddle him.

"Noah, do you have protection?" she asked softly.

His eyes widened slightly as if surprised at himself. "Yes, let me get it," he replied and then shook his head. "I was so caught up in the moment that it didn't occur to me. You do that to me." He gently eased her to the side, and a moment later he was sheathed and boldly ready.

Noah joined her on the bed but took his sweet time, loving her with a slow, gentle hand. He caressed her, kissed her, and explored every inch of her body until she was mindless with wanting him. She savored the taste of his skin, the moist heat of his mouth, and when he entered her she wrapped her legs around him and matched him stroke for exquisite stroke. Warm, delicious pleasure washed over her in waves . . . building, climbing, until she let go . . .

"Ah . . . Livie!" He entwined his fingers with hers and made love to her with achingly sweet intensity, holding her close until she cried out his name. And still she clung to him, skin to skin, heart to pounding heart. He kissed her hotly, deeply, over and over, as if he never wanted the moment to end.

Finally he rested his forehead against her and sighed. "Am I crushing you?" His eyes remained closed.

"Never. I'm a strong, sturdy small-town girl, remember?"

"Strong, sturdy, *sexy* small-town girl." He chuckled weakly. "And you plumb wore me out."

"Wimp," she teased even though her chest was rising and falling just like his. "But I like it that you're starting to sound like you came from here."

Noah chuckled. "I never did give up my cowboy boots and I still eat grits."

"Mmmm . . . cowboy up?"

"Give me a minute. 'I ain't as good as I once was . . .'" He sang the first line of the chorus of the Toby Keith song.

Olivia giggled. "Okay." She relented but then moved suggestively against him.

"Or two," he pleaded. He rolled to his back and then laughed at the blue panties twirling around on the paddle fan. He pointed at them and said, "You should leave them up there."

"I think I will."

"Seriously?"

"No."

"I think you should."

"Might be hard to explain."

"True." Noah shook his head. "I'll be right back. Don't go anywhere."

"I won't," she answered with a slow grin and then watched his cute butt cross the bedroom and disappear into the bathroom. She pulled back the comforter and scooted beneath the covers, hoping that he was going to spend the night that she didn't want to end. She put her head on the feather pillow and sighed while thinking she had never felt so relaxed and so content. "Ahhh . . ." A girl could get used to this . . .

*   *   *

When Noah came back into the bedroom, he turned the light off before crawling under the covers and pulling Olivia against him. His warm, bare skin brushed against hers, and he felt a hot shiver of arousal even though he was bone-tired. Truthfully, he had never been one to snuggle, but having Olivia curled up next to him with her head on his shoulder felt peaceful . . . right. A sense of pure contentment washed over him, and he hugged her closer. With a small sigh she reached up and cupped his cheek before resting her hand back on his chest.

Her sweet, simple gesture moved him beyond all measure, and he kissed the top of her head while caressing her shoulder. No words were spoken, but something shifted in their relationship and it wasn't simply about sex. In that moment Noah knew that they were moving in the direction of something deeper, lasting . . . meaningful. She tucked her leg between his and leisurely trailed her fingertips over his chest as if she couldn't get close enough or touch him enough. He smiled and murmured, "That feels nice. Don't stop."

"I won't," she whispered in his ear and then kissed his neck. She rubbed the pad of her thumb over his bottom lip and then splayed her hand over his chest once more. He felt as if a new level of trust and comfort settled between them, and he covered her hand with his. He could have told her that he loved her right here and now and he would've meant it, but he knew it wasn't the right time just yet.

Before Olivia, the women in his life had equated to fun but he had never shared the kind of conversation or companionship that Olivia provided. She made him laugh, she warmed his heart, and she filled a gap in his life that he hadn't really known was there until recently.

She sighed once more and rubbed her leg against his, and then her breathing became soft and even. Noah smiled as he reached out and pulled the covers up over her bare shoulder. Olivia was asleep in his arms and that was just fine, since he had no intention of leaving her bed until morning.

Although his eyes were heavy and his body drained, sleep evaded him and yet he was content to simply hold her close and listen to her breathe. What, he wondered, would it be like to do this each and every night and then wake up next to a woman that you loved?

Amazing . . . filtered into his mind and set up shop.

And yet in the back of his brain the reminder that he was leaving after the conclusion of the play buzzed around like an annoying fly that needed to be swatted. While he couldn't fathom the thought of Olivia not being in his life, he had to wonder what was here for him or what there was outside of this small town for her.

Unable to come up with an answer, Noah closed his eyes and ground his teeth together.

Funny, in Madison's play Ben and Amy fought their attraction while they concentrated on everything else in their busy lives except each other, but in the end they realized what mattered most, making Noah wonder if he and Olivia were life imitating art.

But could they find a compromise? A solution? Noah also sensed that there was something in her past that she hadn't told him about; he needed to know what it was in order to piece together the reasons for her fierce loyalty to this struggling town.

The thought of hurting her clawed at his heart, but he finally drifted off to sleep hoping that somehow, some way, they would find the path that would eventually lead them to that elusive happy ending.

13

Walking on Sunshine

Olivia found herself daydreaming and humming throughout the day, and when she went into the ladies' room during lunch, she noticed a goofy smile plastered on her face. She frowned and tried to put her no-nonsense teacher attitude in place, but her smile popped back out as soon as she thought of Noah, which was about every other second. "This will never do," she mumbled, and she decided to pin her hair up in a bun in an effort to appear serious for fourth period. "There." She gave her reflection a firm nod and then clicked down the hallway in her sensible pumps.

She sat down at her desk and waited for the students to get settled. "Okay, I'll give you the first half of the class to work on your essays. Feel free to come up to me with questions, and remember that the rough draft is due on Monday, so now is your time to ask away." She folded her hands on her neat-as-a-pin desk and attempted to appear all business, but then she felt the song "Walking on Sunshine" bubbling up in her throat. She wondered what her students would think if she burst into song like in *High School Musical*, and that thought sent her into a sudden fit of giggles, which she had to disguise with a cough.

Apparently, waking up to Noah Falcon kissing her neck was the way to start the day.

Olivia slipped on her glasses and attempted to grade yesterday's quiz, but once again her brain decided to take a side trip to Noah-land. When her phone vibrated, she discreetly picked it up but failed to maintain her poise when she saw that Noah had sent her a text message saying she was the sexiest woman on the planet.

"Miss Lawson?"

Olivia looked up to see Chrissie waving her hand in the air. The rest of the class stared at Olivia expectantly, making her wonder how long she had ignored Chrissie's raised hand. She quickly dumped the phone that she shouldn't have had out anyway into her desk drawer and tilted her chin up to peer over her glasses. "Yes, Chrissie?"

While twirling her ponytail Chrissie asked, "Um, do you think we could have until Monday to turn in our rough draft instead of tomorrow?"

Olivia blew an errant strand of hair that had escaped her bun out of her face and angled her head. "And why should I extend the due date?" she asked crisply, hoping that her face wasn't beet red from the text message.

"Well . . ." Chrissie hesitated but then continued in a rush. "The Cricket Creek baseball team is playing the Morgan County Colonels and they are our archrivals. I really, *really* want to go, but I can't if I have to work on my paper. I mean, after all, it is a big game, Miss Lawson, and the team needs our support, but I want to get a good grade too." She played with her ponytail and shrugged. "I'm just sayin'."

The class looked at Olivia expectantly. Although she encouraged them to support school functions from band contests to baseball games, she always preached that academics came first. "I do believe," she began, and it seemed as if the entire class leaned forward and held a collective breath, "that Chrissie has a valid point."

"I do?" Chrissie asked with surprise but then flipped her ponytail over her shoulder and sat up straighter. "I mean, I know. Makes sense, right?"

Olivia nodded slowly. "I'll extend the deadline," she began and then held up her index finger, "but to get the extension you must attend the game." She grinned and then asked, "Everybody down with that?" Heads bobbed and eyes widened at her use of slang, and so she added, "Sweet," just to mess with them. "I'll see you there." She smiled, then cleared her throat. "Okay, now back to work."

Heads bent to their tasks and Olivia went back to trying to grade papers. It might have been her imagination, but she thought the class seemed to be working diligently, perhaps in appreciation of her extension of the deadline. Her red pen paused in mid-check while she mulled this over. She knew she was a good teacher. She had the test scores to prove it. She worked hard, and whenever possible she was accessible to her students. But she had a reputation for being strict and grading tough, which didn't always make her popular with parents or students. Ever since the day Noah Falcon rumbled into town, though, Olivia's view on life had been changing. He had awakened something soft and warm, melting a cold, hard ball of fear that had been knotted in her stomach since the day her mother left. She was learning to trust, to believe . . . to love.

Olivia thought of her father, who had lived his life in quiet anguish, crushed by the desertion of a woman he had adored. For the first time Olivia understood how he could be so hurt, but she also knew that he deserved another chance at happiness. In her matchmaking attempts she had never once considered someone to bring the joy of love back into her father's life.

"Oh, my gosh!" she said out loud when the absolute perfect person popped into her mind. Ignoring the startled looks from her students, she shook her head with a sense of wonder. "How could I not have known this?"

"Known what?" Chrissie had the nerve to ask.

"Something I should've seen a long time ago." Olivia nibbled on the inside of her cheek and had to brush a tear away.

"You okay?" Chrissie asked, and all eyes were upon her.

"Perfectly fine." Olivia nodded. "Thank you, Chrissie." She realized that she could dig deep for emotions for a scene in a play, but in her real life she had been going through the motions, just like her father. A good cry, a flash of anger, a belly laugh had all been replaced by strict self-control. Olivia had been taught this by her father's example, and she had thought it served her well. After all, letting go meant feeling and feeling meant hurting.

She brushed at another tear. She rarely lost her composure in front of her students, but instead of feeling embarrassed she swallowed the moisture clogging her throat and inhaled a shaky breath. Not knowing how to explain her emotional state, she glanced down at her desk and found the script to *Just One Thing*. Inspired, she held it up. "I've already mentioned it before, but this is the play that is being put on by Cricket Creek Community Theater. I know that you've heard that our very own Noah Falcon has come home to star in the play."

"You mean *your* very own?" Head cheerleader Jackie Swanson asked with an arch of one blond eyebrow. "Way to go, Miss Lawson. That man is mighty fine."

Olivia felt another blush creep up her neck. "Noah and I are working together."

"Closely," Jackie said with a slow nod, but she hushed when Olivia gave her a "That's enough" look. "I'm just sayin' what I've heard."

Olivia felt a little surge of feminine pride that people

really were connecting her with Noah. She also hoped that it really did make people want to attend the play. "Back to my point," Olivia said in her teacher voice. "What you may not realize is that the play was written by Madison Robinson, who also lived here as a child. Her aunt Myra owns the diner in town. Anyway, Madison is only twenty-three years old." Olivia inclined her head. "Just a few years older than each of you," she added. "Can anyone guess where I'm going with this?"

Seventeen-year-olds weren't always eager to contribute thoughts, but shy, rather nerdy Allie Cooper halfway raised a tentative hand. Olivia gave her an encouraging smile, thinking that Allie reminded her of herself at this tender age. "Thoughts, Allie?"

"Well," Allie began softly, "Noah Falcon was a major-league baseball player turned television actor, and Madison Robinson is a budding playwright." She swallowed and continued. "They obviously had high aspirations and achieved them."

"They sure did. Any other observations?" Olivia raised her eyebrows at the class. Jimmy Walters, a star athlete in both football and baseball, casually raised his hand. "Jimmy?"

He sat up straighter. "It's tough to get scouts to come to smaller independent schools unless you do something off-the-wall like the Cricket Creek Tigers did back when Noah was playing. When he was a senior they went undefeated and won the state championship." Jimmy shrugged his wide shoulders. "It's impossible to make it to the next level when you never even get a good look."

"Impossible?" Olivia shook her head. "Jimmy, they did it. If Madison's play gets good reviews, it could end up at a bigger venue, maybe even Broadway. Jessica Robinson started out cooking in a diner and became a chef in a four-star restaurant. You can still dream big in a small town."

"Yeah, you can dream big and then leave if you want to get anywhere," Jimmy replied. "Miss Lawson, let's face it—everything is closing up in Cricket Creek. If that happens this school will shut down and we'll get bussed out to the county."

Olivia stood up, leaned forward, and said, "I remember when this town was thriving. The marina was packed. You had a tough time walking down Main Street on a Saturday afternoon. You had to book a bed-and-breakfast a year in advance."

Jimmy shook his head. "Dude, those days are gone."

Olivia responded, "They don't have to be. Our baseball team is good this year. Let's all go out and support them. And eat at Myra's. Hang out at the Dairy Hut and the marina this summer. Attend the production of *Just One Thing*! Play some sand volleyball at the city park. Let's breathe life back into this town one day at a time." Olivia pounded her fist on the desktop. "This is our town. Let's save it!" Okay, her fist really smarted, but she raised it up without so much as a cringe and said, "Are y'all with me?"

"Yes!" Chrissie, bless her heart, was the first to jump in. She pumped her fist skyward and looked at the rest of the class in challenge. "Come on, you guys. I am third generation and proud of it. Raise your stupid fists!"

Allie raised hers with an unexpected "Woo-hoo!" Jimmy followed and soon the entire class had jumped on the bandwagon.

Olivia's heart beat faster and she smiled broadly. She had never felt so alive, so driven . . . so happy.

"Causing chaos, Miss Lawson?"

Olivia looked over and saw Noah leaning against the doorframe and wearing a Cricket Creek Tigers uniform. "Chaos is my middle name," Olivia answered drily, causing a titter of laughter from the students.

He took off his baseball cap and grinned. "So I've

heard." He looked incredibly sexy in the blue jersey and tight baseball pants, and even though she felt a hot shiver of excitement just seeing him, Olivia arched one eyebrow, pressed her glasses up on her nose, and asked crisply, "So, Mr. Falcon, to what do we owe this pleasure?" She meant her comment to sound businesslike but stumbled over the word "pleasure."

Noah gave her a lopsided grin. "I would say it's simply your lucky day, but I admit that I have an agenda."

"Imagine that," Olivia responded. She nodded toward the uniform. "Aren't you a bit over the hill?"

"I've still got some game," he said, drawing a laugh from the students. "Actually, the team gave me this uniform yesterday. Even has my old number—fifteen." He turned around to display the number, bringing a round of applause and some whistles.

"Should have been retired," Jimmy shouted over the cheers.

"Thanks. Pass that thought on to the powers that be. But that's not why I'm here interrupting class," he said with a cute expression of apology to Olivia, who tried her best not to blush. "I'm going from classroom to classroom to encourage you guys to come to the game today."

"Miss Lawson already encouraged us," Chrissie announced with an I-had-something-to-do-with-it grin. "She even said we could turn in our homework on Monday if we went to the game."

"No kidding?" Noah looked at Olivia with pleased surprise. "Wow, you could knock me over with a feather."

"I fully support extracurricular activities," she said primly and dearly hoped that everything she said sounded suggestive only to her own ears. "And this is a big game."

"Sure is, so I hope to see y'all there. You too, Miss Lawson." He slapped his cap back on his head and gave her a wink as he moved on down the hall.

She was met with openmouthed stares.

"Wow," Jackie cooed with a shake of her head, "Noah Falcon sure is into you, Miss Lawson."

"Well, we are starring in a play together," Olivia reminded them, hoping that her breezy tone hid the flutter in her stomach. "Let's get back to our essays, shall we?"

After her students returned to their assignment Olivia pulled out another quiz, but all she could see when she stared at the paper was Noah Falcon's handsome face floating in front of her.

And there it was again—the smile that would not go away.

14

It's Five O'clock Somewhere

$\mathcal{M}$adison's mind kept wandering to thoughts of Jason while she filled napkin holders at the diner. She smiled, thinking that a few months ago she would never have believed that she would be going on a date to a high school baseball game, much less looking forward to it. But then again, it wasn't so much where she was going as who she was going with. She glanced at the clock and sighed. Time seemed to be crawling at a snail's pace. The lunch rush was well over, and the dinner crowd would be small since the Cricket Creek Tigers were playing a home game.

When the bell on the door jingled, she looked up from her task. "Well, hello, Mr. Lawson."

"Hi, there, Madison."

Madison smiled when Owen Lawson walked to the front counter and sat down. "What brings you here this time of day?"

"I trimmed some trees and bushes over at the library, but I worked through lunch so I could go to the game. Olivia reminded me that the Tigers are playing Morgan County. I try to make as many home games as I can."

"Good for you. Sweet tea?"

"Yes, please. I'm parched. What are you doin' workin' here this afternoon? Don't you have enough to do with the play coming up?"

"I'm filling in for my mother. She has a rare afternoon off for some retail therapy."

"Retail therapy?"

Madison grinned. "Shopping, but Mom will relieve me so I can go to the baseball game too. Apparently it's the popular thing to do."

"In Cricket Creek it's still our favorite pastime," he said with a ghost of a grin. "Nice of you to cover for her. I know how busy you've been. She raised you right."

Madison inclined her head. "Thank you, Mr. Lawson. I got a good start here in Cricket Creek," she acknowledged, but then she leaned in close and said, "Mom sure did have her work cut out for her, but we were lucky to have Aunt Myra help us out. Speaking of, are you here for Aunt Myra's famous meat loaf special?"

Just as she spoke those words, Aunt Myra breezed in through the double doors with a tray laden with salt and pepper shakers. "I think you mean '*famous* Myra's meat loaf.' That's how I told Jessica to put it on the new menu. I think it should have my picture by it too."

Madison came back with, "You're a legend in your own mind."

"Uh, I think you meant 'infamous,' Myra," Owen quipped with dry humor. Like his daughter, he had a quiet, funny way about him without trying. But there was an edge of sadness around his mouth that tugged at Madison's heart.

"Oh, go on with ya," Myra said with a wave of her hand, but Madison noticed that color was high in her aunt's cheeks and she had to hide her smile. This was good stuff.

"Would you start me off with a tossed salad too?" Owen requested. "With Olivia rehearsing every night she hasn't been bringing me her leftovers and my diet has suffered sorely. 'Course, I should learn to cook for myself," he added, but then he shrugged.

"But if you cooked we wouldn't have you in here as often," Madison commented, reaching over to pat his hand. Owen Lawson was one of the nicest men she knew, but it sure was hard to coax a smile out of him.

"True enough. And the food don't get any better."

"Doesn't," Myra corrected from where she was busy setting out the salt and pepper shakers.

"Who are you, the grammar police?" Madison called to her aunt. She rolled her eyes at Owen and tried to squeeze a smile out of him.

"That's Olivia's job," Owen said. "Sometimes I say 'ain't' just to get her goin'." He glanced over at Myra, who was concentrating on her task. "Myra's meat loaf is one of my favorites, but your mama sure does have some really good fancy fixin's. She talked me into trying that chicken something or other . . ."

"Chicken cordon bleu?"

Owen snapped his fingers. "That was it."

"Did you like it?" Madison asked with interest. Her mother was worried that some of the regulars would balk at menu changes.

Owen nodded. "To tell you the truth, I didn't think I would, but it was real tasty. I'm sure this place will be hoppin' after the renovations are complete. Draw in a fancy-pants crowd but keep the regulars as well." He tapped his temple. "Smart thinkin'. And Jason sure does a bang-up job."

"He certainly does," Madison acknowledged with a smile. She thought to herself that Owen Lawson was a ruggedly handsome man with his jet-black hair threaded with silver. His light blue eyes were accentuated by a deep tan, and she admired the way his white shirt stretched across his wide shoulders. Yeah, he was pretty darn ripped for an older dude, but she guessed that his lawn care business kept him fit. Madison knew that her aunt Myra was sweet on him and got all aflutter whenever he came in, but disguised it with a sassy attitude. Maybe it was Olivia rubbing off on her, but Madison wondered if there would ever be a chance of Aunt Myra and Owen Lawson hooking up. She angled her head, thinking it would do both of them a world of good. "The renovations should be done by the opening of the play. Jason is working overtime to make it happen."

"Is he here now?"

Madison shook her head. "He was laying tile earlier. But now he's over at the community center finishing up the sets."

"He's a hard worker, that one," Owen commented in his quiet way, lifting his glass of tea for a sip, but then he paused and frowned. He pulled out a sprig of green and held it up. "What the devil is this?" he asked, catching Myra's attention.

"That would be a sprig of mint," Myra told him in a voice that suggested no argument. "Put it right back in there and take a swig before you go complaining."

"I wasn't complaining, Myra. Just askin'. Never had anything green stickin' out of my tea here before tonight."

"There's a first time for everything."

"And a last," he commented and placed the mint on his napkin.

Uh-oh. Madison stood back and watched her aunt sashay over and pick up the sprig. "We're throwing in classy touches here and there in preparation for Wine and Diner. The mint, I will have you know, is in honor of the upcoming Kentucky Derby. You might just enjoy it, Owen." She shoved the mint in his direction.

"Maybe I would if it was a mint julep instead of sweet tea. Now that's Derby Day." He winked at Madison.

"Now you're talking, Mr. Lawson."

Myra shook her head. "We don't have our liquor license yet, so I can't make you one." She propped one hand on her slim hip and said, "I do fully admit, though, that I can make one kick-ass mint julep with some single-barrel bourbon. But whatever. Quit being as stubborn as a mule and try the mint in your tea."

"Me stubborn?" Owen put his palms on the counter and leaned forward. "That's like the pot callin' the kettle black."

"I'm not at all stubborn," Myra argued stubbornly, causing Madison to hide her snort behind a cough. When her aunt glanced her way, she concentrated on wiping down the already clean counter.

"Really, now?" Owen shook his head slowly. "Have you already been hitting some of that Wild Turkey?"

"I prefer smooth twelve-year-old Weller. Turkey has too much bite for me. But to answer your question, no, I have not," she said with a flip of her braid and a jingle of her hoop earrings. "Not that it isn't a pretty darned good idea, now that you've planted that seed in my brain, thank you very much."

"You're welcome," Owen countered with an edge of humor, and yet he failed to smile.

"Well . . ." Madison began, deciding that she needed to step in, "Aunt Myra, why don't you knock off early? Head over to Sully's and ask Pete to make a couple of mint juleps for you and Mr. Lawson." She suggested in the same innocent voice that Olivia used when she was in matchmaking mode. "I just bet he makes a good one."

Myra put her hand to her chest. "Sugar pie, it's three o'clock in the afternoon."

Madison gave her a wide-eyed look. "Since when do you follow the rules?"

"I . . ." Myra sputtered, at a rare loss for words.

"It's five o'clock somewhere," Owen answered in a deadpan tone that had Madison laughing.

"Just what are you sayin', Owen?" Myra asked with a hint of a challenge. "Surely you're not thinkin' of sippin' on a mint julep in the middle of the afternoon?"

Madison held her breath and waited.

"Well?" Owen picked up the sprig of mint and studied it. "What if I was?" His blue eyes suddenly lifted and zoned in on Myra, who seemed frozen in her tracks.

Ask her to join you, Madison shouted in her head. She wished she could telepathically send the message to Owen but thought she had a better chance of bending the spoon in her hand. Ugh! "We have plenty of mint," Madison offered brightly. She reached beneath the counter and held up a bunch.

Myra glanced at the mint and then back at Owen.

"Well?" he persisted. "What do you think?"

Madison barely refrained from pounding her fist in her palm. *So close, Owen . . . Go for it, dude!*

"I think you've taken leave of your senses," Myra finally sputtered.

"Asking Pete Sully to make me a mint julep? Yep, I do believe you're right." He arched one dark eyebrow. "So, you wouldn't join me?"

"Of course I would. I never claimed to have any sense. Welcome to the dark side, Owen Lawson," Myra replied with a big grin.

"Thank you," he said quietly. "I think." He tossed the silly sprig into his tea and started to lift the glass to his mouth but then set it down with a thump.

And then he laughed.

At first it was simply a small, rusty chuckle, but then it turned into a deep belly laugh that shook Owen's shoulders and had him clinging to the counter for support. Myra's tinkling laughter joined his guffaws. "Oh . . . my." Owen slapped his leg and looked so carefree and happy that Madison put her hand over her mouth and had to turn around so as not to show her tears. No one ever spoke of it, but Madison knew that his wife had left him with a young daughter to raise on his own and she had heard Aunt Myra say that he had never complained. She headed to the kitchen for the meat loaf before they could see her emotions get the better of her. No wonder Olivia liked setting people up. It was so satisfying!

When she reentered the dining room, Myra and Owen were still laughing. She set his food in front of him, but he barely noticed.

When he came up for a breath Myra said, "So you like the dark side? Sweet!"

Her comment had him laughing again. "Apparently."

"So are we on?" Myra asked in a shy tone that Madison had never before heard from her feisty aunt.

"Soon as I get done eating famous Myra's meat loaf," he answered, taking a bite of his salad.

"Well, then, eat up." She shooed him with her fingers.

"You always this bossy?"

"Yes."

"Aunt Myra, why don't you go on upstairs and freshen up? I'll hold the fort. That way Owen can enjoy his food without you hounding him."

"Good idea," Owen teased and he tucked into his mashed potatoes.

"Whatever," Myra answered, but Madison could see the fluttery feminine excitement in her aunt's eyes. She wanted to grab her and hug her hard. It occurred to Madison that her mother and her aunt had worked so hard to make her life special, but not without sacrifice, and she suddenly wanted to burst into noisy tears. She braced herself against the counter and swallowed hard as she watched her aunt exit the room and head up to the modest but comfortable apartment above the diner that had been her home for so many years. And then she felt a warm, callused hand fold over hers.

She turned to Owen with tearful eyes. "You know, my

life wasn't traditional in any sense of the word, but I sure am lucky." When she blinked at him, he squeezed her hand.

"Love comes in all shapes and forms," she said, "and one isn't better than the other. I think we all lose sight of that sometimes."

"Madison, you have quite a bit of insight for one so young."

"So I've been told."

Owen looked at her for a long moment and then closed his eyes and sighed. "Ah, girlie, thank you." He inhaled another deep breath. "This is called something . . ."

Madison gave him a warm smile. "An 'Aha!' moment."

"Yeah, that's it." Owen scratched his chin and said, "I've been wastin' my time mourning what I don't have instead of celebrating the blessings that I've got." He smacked his leg. "I'm such a dumb ass," he lamented in a voice as close to a shout as Madison had ever heard from him.

"I'll second that!" Myra called from the hallway.

"Oh, really now? Well . . ." Owen began, but his jaw dropped when Myra entered the room.

Madison sucked in a breath. Rather than her usual jeans, her aunt wore a lavender broomstick skirt and a cream-colored peasant blouse edged with deep gold piping. And her hair, instead of being woven in a braid, fell in rich chocolate brown waves over her shoulders. And although her makeup remained subtle, a light dusting of rose blush highlighted her high cheekbones, and her full mouth had a touch of gloss. She looked soft . . . sweet.

"Would y'all stop gawking at me?"

Madison grinned.

"What?" Myra demanded.

"I was thinking that you looked soft and sweet," Madison answered.

"Looks are deceiving," Owen commented.

"Oh . . . ha-ha-*ha*," Myra said with a little head and shoulder bop, but Madison noticed that Owen couldn't stop staring at her. "Are we going to get a drink or not?"

Owen dabbed at his mouth with his napkin. "Just hold your horses, now, Myra. I need to settle up my bill."

Myra waved a hand at him. "It's on the house. Now come on."

Owen shook his head firmly. "No, I am going to pay my bill."

"The hell you say."

Madison shooed her hands at Owen when he reached for his wallet. "You won't win this one."

Owen sucked in a deep breath and blew it out before turning to Myra. "Fine, but then you have to agree to go out to dinner with me," he insisted.

"Whatever."

"You say that way too damned often."

"What-evvvv-*er*."

Madison laughed and handed Owen the bunch of mint. "Tell Pete to make yours a double," she called as they argued all the way out the door.

"You got that right," Owen answered over his shoulder and caught a sharp shove.

"Okay, now what?" Madison looked around the empty diner and realized that her chores were all caught up. She smiled, thinking that her mother was going to have an easy time closing up tonight.

She was still chuckling to herself when the bell chimed over the door again. She looked up and felt a flash of heat when Jason walked in. He paused and looked out the window, then turned back to Madison and said, "Wait—was that *Aunt Myra* with *Owen Lawson*?"

"Yep."

"In a skirt?"

"If you mean Aunt Myra, yes," she answered with a grin.

"Where are they goin'?"

"To Sully's for a mint julep."

"What?"

"Long story."

"Oh." His eyes lingered on hers for a heated moment. "Are you here for an early dinner?"

Jason shook his head slowly. "No, had a late lunch."

She took in his damp hair, cargo shorts, and green striped polo shirt. He appeared freshly showered and looked incredibly hot in his casual clothes. "Then what are you here for?"

"I was finished over at the community center." He shoved his fingers through his shaggy hair and then shot her a slow but oh, so sexy grin. "So I thought I'd come over and get some . . . *dessert*," he said, using their code word. "Any suggestions?"

"As a matter of fact, yes." She smiled and said, "Something sweet and covered in whipped cream."

"Sounds delicious."

"Oh, believe me, it is. Wait!" She twirled her index finger in a circle. "Turn around."

He raised his eyebrows but did as requested.

"See the blue sign hanging on the door?"

"Yes."

"Move the handles on the clock to read 'be back in thirty minutes.'"

Jason glanced over his shoulder. "Now we're talking."

"Talking," Madison said as he walked purposefully her way, "isn't what I had in mind." Her eyes held his, and the closer he came, the harder her heart pounded.

"Well, then, baby, we're on the same page." His voice was gruff . . . laced with his sexy Southern edge that made her melt quicker than a Dairy Hut dip top. A moment later he was behind the counter slipping his hand through hers. "I take it we're all alone?"

"Yes."

"Then let's get away from prying eyes through the front window." He tugged her past the double doors into the kitchen. With a low groan he pushed her up against the cool wall and kissed her hotly, deeply. Madison shoved her fingers into his hair and met his passion with a heat of her own. When his mouth found her neck, he said, "I've been thinking about kissing you all damned day. Hit my thumb with my hammer half a dozen times and cracked two pieces of tile."

"Sorry."

He smiled. "Cussed my fool head off, but it was worth the pain to have you on my mind."

"Not exactly Hallmark card material, but I love it . . . the thinking-of-me part, that is," she explained.

Jason tucked a curly lock of hair behind her ear. "Couldn't stop if I wanted to," he told her, but then shook his head. "Damn, I sound like such a girl . . ."

Madison laughed. "I'm thinking we need a little less talk . . ."

"And a lot more action?" He arched a golden eyebrow and then dipped his head, capturing her mouth in a sweet kiss that curled her toes and had her clinging to his shoulders. He tasted like mint and man, and the warm ripple of muscle beneath her palms had her arching her body closer, eager for more contact. With a groan, he reached up and took her hands, weaving his fingers through hers. He extended her arms up against the wall and pressed close, letting her know just how much he wanted her. He kissed her over and over until she was crazy with wanting him. Needing him.

"Ah, Jason . . ."

Clothes fell to the floor until they were skin against skin. "You feel so good." He cupped her bottom and lifted her up. "Wrap your arms and legs around me," he whispered hotly into her ear.

And so she did . . .

"Maddie, you're driving me nuts. You're on my mind with my first cup of coffee and you're the last thing I think about when I hit the sack."

"I know. I've never felt this way before either." Madison clung to him and kissed him wildly while he made love to her with such heat that it took her breath away. Giving yet demanding, he brought her to the brink of passion and then slowed down as if savoring each taste, each touch, and each stroke. He looked into her eyes with raw honesty, and for the first time in her life Madison let go and allowed herself to love without holding back. She watched the play of emotion on his handsome face until he closed his eyes and thrust deep. The throaty sound of his pleasure sent Madison flying over the edge and her climax exploded with achingly sweet intensity.

"Wow!" Madison buried her face in his neck and remained wrapped around him. There weren't any candles, soft music, or wine, and yet she trembled with emotion. "That was unbelievably beautiful," she said and hugged him hard. She had yet to tell him that she loved him, but she knew without a doubt that she did.

Jason lifted his head so he could look at her and gave her an endearingly crooked smile. "I didn't even miss the whipped cream."

Madison laughed. She loved his easy manner and sense of humor. "Another time," she promised, and then her eyes widened. "Oh, boy, we'd better get dressed. My mother will be coming back soon."

Jason nodded but dipped his head and captured her mouth for one last kiss. He pulled back and said, "Just remember to keep Madison à la mode off the main menu."

Madison felt a surge of feminine satisfaction that he wanted her all to himself. "Don't worry. Madison à la mode is reserved just for you."

"Sweet."

"Exactly."

They laughed as they scrambled back into their clothes. Madison felt so lighthearted and happy that doing the Snoopy dance in a circle wasn't out of the question, but her mother would be returning shortly. "Hurry!" she urged as she looked around for her panties and then giggled when she spotted them near the stove.

"I'm trying," he answered and hopped on one foot while trying to yank his cargo shorts on. He toppled sideways and had to brace his hand against the wall.

"When my mom gets here, act all cool and everything, okay?" she said, but she was distracted by the ripple of muscle as he pulled his shirt over his head.

After his head popped through, he said, "Really? I thought I'd tell your mother that we just had incredible sex in the kitchen."

"Oh, stop!" Madison gave him a playful shove but then thought about the fact that although while living in Chicago her mother had dated here and there, she hadn't had a man in her life for as long as Madison could remember. Knowing how great this felt made Madison experience a pang of sadness for her hardworking mom.

"Hey, baby, I was just teasing," Jason assured her with a frown.

Madison put her palm on Jason's chest and looked up at him. "I know. I was thinking of something else."

"You have a lot on your mind," he said softly and drew her into his arms. He kissed the top of her head and said, "Just remember that you can come to me with anything, if just a shoulder to lean on."

Madison felt emotion clog her throat and she nodded against his shirt. When his arms tightened around her, she sighed. It felt so good to be in his arms.

"Hey," he said gruffly and tilted her chin up, "I mean it." His eyes held hers for a long moment, and then he

captured her lips with a sweet and tender kiss that was
at odds for someone so big and so strong.

Madison melted into the kiss, but the thought hit her
that this should not be happening. It was never her intention to remain in Cricket Creek. Even though she loved
the little town, she was still a city girl at heart. After *Just
One Thing* ended its run, she planned on returning to
Chicago. Her mother and aunt had the diner, but what
would she do in Cricket Creek? The irony, of course,
wasn't lost on her. The theme of her play was that in the
end there was just one thing that really mattered.

Love.

And now that she had found it, could she ever let
it go? Madison tried to picture Jason in Chicago and
couldn't, and yet the thought of living without him
struck terror in her heart.

"Hey, don't look so worried. I'll sneak out the back,"
he offered with a grin and a quick kiss on her cheek.

"You don't have to do that," she said, but when she
heard a knock on the front door she put a hand to her
mouth. "Okay, that would be cool," she decided and followed him to the back door so she would remember to
lock it.

"I'll see you at the game," Jason said and gave her
one last quick peck on the cheek before heading out the
door.

When Madison heard another sharp knock, she
hurried toward the front door. Thinking that only her
mother would be so persistent, she began formulating
a valid reason for closing up for thirty minutes in the
middle of the day. She was a writer—surely she could
come up with something reasonable.

15

Islands in the Stream

Olivia put her face up next to the window and peeked into the diner. As long as she could remember Myra's had never closed in the middle of the day, and she wondered if something was wrong. With that disturbing thought in mind, she banged harder on the door. Then, out of the corner of her eye, she spotted Jason Craig sneaking around the corner of the building. He slipped into his red truck and pulled away just as Madison flung the front door open.

Bingo.

"Why, you little devil." Olivia pointed a finger at Madison.

"What?" Madison gave her a wide-eyed, innocent look. "I am an angel. Ask anyone."

"Right, anyone who doesn't know you." Olivia put her hands on her hips. "Just what have you been up to, young lady?"

"Chores."

"Ha! Behind closed doors? It's hardly a chore to have a little afternoon delight with Jason."

"Dear Lord, you're channeling Aunt Myra." Madison flipped the sign from the clock over to OPEN and tried to smooth her hair as she walked over to the counter. "Now just why would you think such a far-fetched thing?"

"Well," Olivia began as she sat down on a stool, "for one, I witnessed Jason sneaking out the back way and hightailing it away from here. For two, your curls are tousled and you have a glow about you that says you were up to somethin' good."

"You should know," Madison pointed out as she slid a glass of sweet tea toward Olivia.

"Why, I never . . ." It was Olivia's turn to put an innocent hand to her chest.

"Oh, stop with the acting. Save it for the play."

Olivia grinned. "Okay. We're not fooling each other anyway."

"I'm just glad that it was you instead of my mom knocking at the door." She wrinkled her nose. "That would have been awkward." But then Madison poured a glass of tea for herself and leaned one hip against the edge of the counter. After taking a long swig she said, "Oh, Olivia, I'm falling for Jason big-time." When her voice trembled, Olivia reached over and patted her hand. "He already told me that he loves me."

"And what's wrong with that, sweetie?"

"Olivia, I never intended to stay here in Cricket Creek." She inhaled a shaky breath. "But that flies all out the window when I'm with him."

Olivia nodded, since she knew exactly where Madison was coming from.

"My play is all about love finding a way and I don't see how this can ever work out." She put the heel of her hand to her forehead and closed her eyes. "I really tried hard to resist him. But I caved." After a long, silent moment she turned tortured eyes to Olivia. "Now what do I do? What in the world was I thinking? Olivia, I can't hurt him!"

Olivia looked at her young friend and said, "We can't

choose when, where, or why, but when it comes our way we need to accept love with open arms. For in this life, if we could choose *just one thing*, love would always win."

"Stop quoting me."

"Madison, it's true."

"To quote *you*, it's . . . bull *feathers*." Madison pounded a fist on the speckled counter so hard that the silverware jumped. "If you don't agree, then just what are you going to do when Noah leaves at the end of the summer? Huh?"

Olivia toyed with her straw and watched the ice twirl in a circle.

"I know you're falling for Noah too. So don't even try to deny it."

"I won't deny that there is an attraction. Noah suggested that we play it up for the sake of the production. Create some Hollywood-style buzz." She lifted one shoulder. "I'm having fun. It's working. End of story." She tilted her head sideways and began folding her napkin like a fan.

Madison took a swallow of her tea and then crunched some ice. "You are so full of it."

"As my father would say, it is what it is and it ain't what it ain't."

"Would you leave Cricket Creek if he asked you to?"

Olivia looked at Madison with surprised eyes. "Well, we're putting the cart way before the horse, but to answer your question, no. This is my home." Olivia stopped fiddling with the napkin and swallowed hard. "My father lives here and he means the world to me," she added and then could have bitten her tongue when Madison's eyes widened. "Oh, Madison, how callous of me!"

"No problem." Madison waved a dismissive hand at her. "Olivia, I know we share a bond where parent abandonment is concerned. It truly sucks and it's shaped our way of viewing the world. But, look, I can't control the fact that my father chose not to be a part of my life or that my grandparents were so narrow-minded. And you can't change what your mother did." She inhaled sharply and looked up at the ceiling. "My mother and aunt Myra taught me to be fiercely independent and to never rely on others." She shook her head. "I know they meant well, but it sure is nice to have a soft place to land . . . a shoulder to lean on. I just hate to feel weak and needy." She inhaled deeply once more. "The past is difficult to shake."

Olivia reached out and finished for her. "But we can't let it rule our lives. Make us afraid to let go and love."

"Oh, boy"—Madison shook her head slowly—"I talk a good talk, but I sure don't know how in the world all of this will play out. And speaking of plays . . . fiction sure makes a hellava lot more sense than reality."

"Yes, too bad we can't write our own ending," Olivia responded.

"So true—but one thing I know for certain. We've got people who love us." She smiled softly and said, "I just told your father that we might not have had traditional upbringings, but love comes in all shapes and forms. One isn't better than the other. Just different. I truly believe that."

"As usual, you're right." Olivia took a sip of tea and then sputtered. "Wait—you were talking about this to my father?"

"Does that upset you?"

"No, I suppose not," Olivia replied evenly, but then leaned forward on her elbows. "Oh, there's more?"

Madison suddenly seemed to be gathering her emotions. After a moment she cleared her throat and said, "That simple statement seemed to somehow set your father free."

"Oh, my goodness." Olivia looked down at the speck-led countertop and expelled a shaky sigh. "I know that he always blamed himself for my mother leaving. He thought that in his own way he wasn't good enough to keep her here, and he always assured me that I wasn't the reason she left either, although I sometimes think that I was."

"Olivia!" Madison reached out and grasped her hand.

"And I do believe now that he hated my loss of a mother more than his loss of a wife and so he devoted himself to me instead of ever looking for the love that he so deserves." She felt tears well up in her eyes and looked up. "Oh, you are so right! His love and devotion more than made up for my mother's absence. Why didn't I ever tell him this?"

Madison shook her head and then shrugged. "I've been thinking the same thing about my mother and aunt Myra too. Olivia, don't you see? We couldn't have understood any of this until we experienced the thrill of falling in love in our own lives. It's a powerful emotion."

Olivia nodded firmly. "Here I've been trying to set up matches for everybody I know except for my very own father."

"Well, speaking of"—Madison arched an eyebrow—"it's a good thing you're sitting down because I have something to tell you."

"About my father?" Olivia's heart kicked it up a notch.

Madison nodded.

"Don't keep me in suspense!"

"Your father and my aunt Myra are over at Sully's having a mint julep."

"Together?"

"Yep."

"Wait—a mint *julep*?" Olivia blinked at Madison and then glanced up at the clock. "At four in the afternoon?"

"Your father decided it was five o'clock somewhere."

"My father said that?"

"Uh-huh, and Aunt Myra was wearing a skirt and carrying a bunch of mint like a bouquet. It was priceless."

Olivia smacked her hands to her cheeks.

"I know!" Madison continued. "They were bantering with each other as they headed out the door. They make such an odd but cute couple. I think they have potential."

"Truthfully, I had recently wondered the same thing." Olivia could only shake her head in amazement. "So you really think so?"

Madison took a swallow of tea, then opened a bag of chips. "She had him laughing so hard he had to grab the counter."

"Oh . . . my." Olivia felt her eyes fill with tears again.

"And when Aunt Myra sashayed in here with her hair down and wearing a skirt, Owen couldn't take his eyes off of her. I'll tell you, Olivia, I was overcome with emotion." She crossed her arms over her chest. "It was a beautiful thing. Now I know why you enjoy matchmaking. Meddling is so satisfying."

Olivia snagged a potato chip from the bag but shook it at Madison instead of popping it in her mouth. "Your Southern roots are showing, you so-called city girl. You just might belong here more than you think."

Madison munched on a chip and then said, "Well, now that I know I can get a perfect dirty martini, I might just have to reconsider."

"See, there's more here to offer than you even know," Olivia said in a light tone, though they both knew that Madison's dilemma was a real issue. There weren't many opportunities in Cricket Creek for playwrights.

"I do like my condo overlooking the river," she admitted. "Water just seems to get my creative juices flowing. It's a shame that beautiful building is basically empty. In Chicago waterfront property goes for big bucks."

Olivia reached for another potato chip and sighed. "The project came to a screeching halt when the economy tanked. The marina just isn't enough of a draw to keep it going. We need something more."

Madison dusted salt off her fingers and said, "It's a shame. The view is fantastic and it's some prime real estate."

"Well, if you come up with any brilliant ideas let me know," Olivia said with a shake of her head but then swiveled in her seat when the bell over the door jingled. Her pulse quickened when Noah entered, still looking way too amazing in his Cricket Creek baseball jersey. His butt was built for baseball pants.

Noah gave them a rather perplexed grin. "Guess what I just witnessed."

"What?" Olivia asked and Madison angled her head expectantly.

"Your father and your aunt singing karaoke over at Sully's."

"They don't have karaoke over at Sully's," Olivia said.

Noah raised his eyebrows and grinned. "They do now."

Olivia tried to picture this in her head, but she simply could not wrap her brain around her father singing in front of a crowd.

Madison clapped her hands. "I love it. What were they singing?"

"'Islands in the Stream.'"

"Dolly Parton and Kenny Rogers?" Olivia said softly, more to herself than to them.

Noah nodded. "Yes, but as I was leaving someone shouted for them to do some Johnny and June."

"Priceless," Madison said once more with a chuckle. "I would love to be a fly on the wall. I would suggest heading over there to watch, but it might make them feel self-conscious and quit."

"I don't know about that," Noah commented. "They

seemed to be on a roll with no stopping them. Of course the crowd was egging them on."

"Were they any good?" Olivia had to ask.

"No, not at all," Noah admitted with a grin. "But highly entertaining."

"Mercy me," Olivia mumbled. "Somebody put some crazy in the Cricket Creek water tower and we've all been drinking it." She gazed up at Noah.

"Hey, don't look at me." He raised both palms in the air. "I'm afraid of heights."

"Maybe." Olivia glanced at Madison and then gave Noah a pointed look. "But nothing has been quite the same since you roared into town in that little red Corvette."

Noah took his baseball cap off and ran his fingers through his hair. "So you're blaming me?"

"No," Olivia said, "I'm giving you credit."

When Noah tipped his head back and laughed, Olivia had to smile. "Hey, I'll take all the credit I can get. So, are you ladies ready for some baseball?"

"You two go on without me," Madison said. "I have to wait for my mom to come back before I can leave. Save me a spot in the bleachers. And tell Jason I'll be there as soon as I can scoot out of here."

"Will do," Noah said and then extended his arm toward Olivia. "Ready?"

"Yes," Olivia said and put two dollars down on the counter for her tea. She shook her head when Madison opened her mouth to protest her paying. "See you in a little bit," she said and slipped her hand into Noah's warm, firm grip. It was beginning to feel so natural to be at his side that she wondered how she could possibly cope with not having him in her life. Madison's question about what if Noah asked her to leave Cricket Creek entered her head. While she couldn't fathom moving away from her home, the thought of life without Noah seemed pretty doggone bleak.

"Whoa there," Noah said and tugged on her hand. "It might be the only traffic light on Main Street, but it's red."

"Sorry—my mind was elsewhere," she admitted with a short laugh.

Noah frowned at her. "Hey, you're not upset about your dad and Myra getting a little crazy over at Sully's, are you?"

"Oh, no, not in the least. In fact, I'm thrilled to hear that they're having a good time. They both deserve it. I'd pop on over there, but like I said, I don't want to ruin their revelry."

Noah responded, "It would be worth it to don a disguise. They were really singing up a storm."

"I would never have believed it."

He gave her a crooked grin and then squeezed her hand. "Life is full of surprises."

"It sure is," Olivia agreed and laughed when he took his baseball cap off and put it on her head. When she started to take it off he shook his head.

"No, it looks sexy on you. Keep it on."

"A baseball cap? Sexy?"

"On you." Noah leaned over and said, "Then again, everything looks sexy on you. Or even better yet, nothing at all."

"Oh . . . *right*!" Olivia hoped that the bill of the hat hid her blush, but she felt a feminine thrill at his comment.

After they crossed the street, Noah drew her to a halt. "I hope you know I was serious."

Olivia looked at him and then nodded. "The feeling is reciprocal," she replied in her best teacher tone, knowing it would make him laugh.

"Ah . . . Olivia, what am I going to do with you?"

"Everything," she answered this time in a slow Southern drawl, but then she giggled.

"Oh, just what you needed to say while I'm wearing tight baseball pants!"

"Are you complaining?"

"Hell, no!" he told her. "You continue to keep me completely off-balance. But just so you know, I'm going to hold you to it."

Olivia laughed, but she wondered what she would do if she were truly faced with making a choice of losing him or leaving Cricket Creek.

16
Play Ball!

After sitting down on the bleachers directly behind the backstop, Noah turned to Olivia and smiled. He loved the aroma of hot dogs, the smack of the baseball hitting the catcher's mitt, and a perfect pitch breaking over the plate. The chatter of the players and the shouts of the coaches took him back to a place and time that he truly treasured. Major-league baseball had been an amazing ride, but playing here had simply been for the love of the game.

"You miss it, don't you?" Olivia asked with a soft smile.

"Yeah, I do." Noah hadn't realized just how very much until now. Olivia was right. He had lived and breathed baseball for so long that the game was a part of who he was, and without it in his life something was missing. He smiled back at her, and as if reading his thoughts, she put her hand on his thigh and squeezed. She looked so damned cute in the baseball cap, and it suddenly occurred to him that Olivia filled another void in his life. It felt good having her by his side. He wondered how he could go on without her.

That's easy—take her with you when you go. She can teach school anywhere.

"Hi, Miss Lawson!" Chrissie shouted with a wild wave in their direction. She and her posse of giggling girls hurried over to the side of the bleachers. "Would you just look at you in your cap?" She looked at her friends and they all nodded in agreement. "Isn't this just exciting! Oh, I wanna beat those Morgan County Colonels so bad!"

"Me too," Olivia replied, so hotly that Noah grinned. So his sweet little schoolteacher had a competitive streak. Nice.

"Thanks for extending the deadline for the essay."

"Shh!" Olivia leaned forward. "Don't want to ruin my reputation," she added softly.

Chrissie's eyes widened. "Right—we'll keep it on the down low." All the ponytails swung back and forth when the girls nodded. "But it was very cool of you," she whispered.

"Just remember to turn in some excellent work and we'll all be happy."

"Yeah, as long as we win," Chrissie muttered.

Noah leaned sideways past Olivia and winked. "You got that right," he commented and reached over and gave Chrissie a high five. Olivia was so well liked and respected, and he had to admire her dedication to her school and students. Taking her away from here would be a real loss to the community.

"Oh, hey, Mr. Falcon. It was so awesome of you to show up at school today and get people to come to the game. It's gonna be packed. Thanks for coming, too!"

"Wouldn't miss it."

"That is so cool of you!" Chrissie continued and her friends nodded. Their ponytails swung back and forth again, but the blushes on their faces shown they still thought of him as the celebrity outsider, and all of them except Chrissie were hesitant to approach him. While Noah would always remember the thrill of signing his first autograph, right now he wished that he could simply be one of the crowd watching the game with his girl.

His girl . . .

Noah's heart beat faster at the thought, but then he wondered why he *wouldn't* consider her his girlfriend since she was constantly on his mind.

"Mr. Turner is heading this way!" Chrissie whispered in a high-pitched squeak. "Oh, my gosh, I can't *take* it," she said and fanned her face. "Let's bounce. See ya!" She wiggled her fingers and then hurried off with her friends.

"What was that all about?" Noah asked Olivia.

"Brandon Turner is our new hottie high school principal. All of the girls and some of the teachers have a huge crush on him."

"Including you?" Noah asked in a teasing tone but watched her closely.

"Oh, pul-ease," she scoffed. "He's kinda cute, but whatever . . ."

Noah felt a surge of relief and realized that he was jealous! And when the hottie high school principal came toward them Noah suddenly felt the need to slip his arm around Olivia's waist.

"Hello, Olivia," Brandon the hottie said with a warm smile that set Noah on edge.

Noah sat up a little straighter. *Miss Lawson.* Shouldn't she be Miss Lawson to him? And damn, the man looked as if he belonged in high school himself, not being the principal!

"Mr. Turner," Olivia greeted him with a smile of her own. "Have you met Noah Falcon?"

"We haven't met, although I understand you have been helping out the baseball team in many ways, including rounding up enthusiasm for the game today." He extended his hand. "Thanks so much."

"My pleasure," Noah replied and had to remove the arm around Olivia to shake his hand.

"I was a big fan of yours growing up."

Great. Noah ground his teeth together, feeling about a hundred years old, but he smiled. "Thanks." He gripped Mr. Turner's hand a bit more tightly than necessary and was rewarded with a slight wince.

"And we're so thrilled that you're starring in the community play. And we're also so proud that the play was written by one of our own. Olivia does such a wonderful job as the drama teacher. It's one of the reasons Cricket Creek has a reputation for excellence at the theater."

"Why, thank you," Olivia responded primly.

"And lucky you to get to be her leading man," Brandon said to Noah with a little sigh.

"Mr. Turner!" Olivia said and then blushed.

"I'm just making an observation," he said with a small shrug but a big smile.

"I'm honored. Olivia is very talented," Noah answered and wanted to wipe the smile off of Brandon Turner's face.

"That's what I meant," he said, but his gaze lingered on Olivia a little too long for Noah's comfort.

"Hey, Mr. Falcon, would you sign this baseball?" a student asked and Noah felt childishly glad.

"Sure," he answered.

Brandon had to step back to allow the student to come closer. "I'll see you around," he said with a wave and a nod at Noah. "Thanks again, Mr. Falcon."

"Sure thing, but you can call me Noah," Noah answered firmly as he reached for the kid's baseball. He signed it and handed it back to the student.

"Thanks. I'm president of student council and we'll auction it off to raise some money for the after-prom."

"No problem," Noah answered. When they were basically alone once again, he leaned closer to Olivia and said, "I always liked going to the prom. I'm glad it's a high school tradition that's still around, aren't you?" He raised his eyebrows at Olivia.

She shrugged and a shadow fell across her face. "I was never asked, so I don't know. The closest I've gotten is being a chaperone, and I'm one again this year."

"What?" Noah sat up straighter. "You're kidding. Why didn't I ask you?"

"Um, maybe because I was a geek and you were a jock."

"Well, I'm asking you now."

"Excuse me?"

"You just said that you're a chaperone. Do you get dressed up?"

"Yes."

"Well, I want to be your date," he said close to her ear. "Unless Brandon the hottie high school principal has already beaten me to the punch."

She put a hand to her chest and looked at him from beneath the bill of her cap. "Why, Noah Falcon, are you jealous?"

"Damned straight."

Olivia laughed. "He isn't into me."

"You're wrong, but will you allow me to be your date? I'll even wear a tux and bring you flowers."

She inclined her head. "I would be honored," she answered but then pressed her lips together.

"What?"

"Nothing."

"Olivia . . ."

She swallowed hard. "You just fulfilled a fantasy of mine."

"To be asked to the prom?"

She shook her head slowly. "To be asked to the prom by you."

There was something about her honest admission

that touched Noah. "Wait. Beneath that cap brim I see a *but* in your eyes."

"It wasn't because you were Noah Falcon, Big Man on Campus. All that sports stuff didn't impress me much. Geeks are funny like that."

"What, then?"

She gave him a slight shrug. "It bugged the daylights out of me because as the quintessential geek I frowned on everything you represented. But to put it simply, I liked you. You made me laugh when you weren't looking, and I fully admit that I thought you were hot stuff."

"As I recall, you acted differently."

She tilted her head up to look at him. "Geeks have their pride too."

Noah laughed. "I was a stupid jock."

Olivia shook her head no. "I told you there is no such thing. Haven't you seen *High School Musical*?"

"No."

"Glee?"

"No again."

"I'm going to have to broaden your horizons."

"Believe me, Olivia, you already have. Hey, want a hot dog before the game gets under way?"

"I'd love one. Mustard and just a bit of relish. And could I have some nachos with extra jalapeños, please?"

"Just the way I like them," he said as he climbed down from the bleachers, but then he came around to the side and said, "Don't be giving my spot to that high school principal."

"Then you better hurry back."

"Will do," Noah promised, but he was stopped by at least half a dozen people in his quest for a hot dog. Instead of autographs, though, it was for how-ya-doin', great-day-for-a-game, and various other friendly small talk. Just like when he was a kid, dads grilled while moms pushed cupcakes and candy at the concession stand. Everybody knew everybody and wore their Cricket Creek Tiger blue with hometown pride. The rivalry created a buzz of excitement in the air. And the idea that had begun to form in the back of his mind started to take flight.

"Hey, Noah!"

Noah turned around to see Jason heading his way. "What's up, Jason? Madison with you?"

"She'll be here soon," Jason answered before ordering a Coke. "I wanted to get a seat so she didn't have to stand. She's been on her feet all day helpin' out over at the diner in between working on the play. The girl works too much."

"Funny, but she says the same thing about you. I just think here in Cricket Creek people work hard."

Jason grinned. "Yeah, and play harder."

Noah reached over and gave him a knuckle bump. "It's nice to see that some things never change." Noah took the tray of hot dogs, nachos, and drinks from a smiling mom and then fell in step with Jason as they made their way back to the bleachers.

"Speaking of playing hard, I stopped at Sully's for a cold one before heading over here and guess what I saw."

"Myra and Owen sippin' on mint juleps while singing a duet?"

"Now how the hell did you ever guess that?"

"I was over there earlier when they were singing 'Islands in the Stream.' Like to have blown my mind seeing those two up there belting out that song. Now Myra I could have guessed, but Olivia's father?" Noah shook his head. "He doesn't seem the type."

"You're right about that. I've worked with him, and he's usually a man of few words and keeps to himself." Jason chuckled. "Ya know, it's good to see people out havin' a good ol' time, especially Owen and Myra. Everyone tries to keep their head up, but it hasn't been easy. Those wore-out dugouts are just one example of how budget cuts have hurt the athletic programs. It's a damned shame. These kids deserve better."

"I've seen your work, Jason. How are you doing?"

He took a swallow of Coke and then shrugged. "I'm doin' all right. I just hope things turn around here this summer." As they approached the bleachers he said, "Wow, it's really packed today. But then, we've always loved our baseball here, as you well know."

"You got that right," Noah agreed. When his cell phone rang he recognized the ringtone and frowned. "Hey, Jason, will you take this food to Olivia? I've got to return this call."

"Sure thing," Jason replied and took the tray.

"Thanks. I'll be there in a few minutes," he promised and headed over to the edge of the parking lot to redial the missed call from his agent. He pushed CALL BACK and waited.

"Falcon!" boomed the voice of Vince Bell. "Man, do I have good news for you."

"Shoot," Noah said, anxious to get back to the game.

"Since they killed you off, the ratings for *Love in the Afternoon* have fallen off sharply."

"Because of me?"

"Apparently, but regardless, that's the angle that I've been pushing hard. And since afternoon soaps are struggling anyway, this is big for you. They need ratings bad. They want you back."

Noah fell into shocked silence.

"Uh, I worked my ass off on this. You can thank me anytime now."

"I appreciate your efforts."

"Wow, that sure was heartfelt. I'm touched. Wait. Let me wipe away a tear. Falcon, don't you get it? They're talking about a media blitz—tags at the end of the show, promo ads. Your part will be expanded with a kick-ass story line."

"For real? But I was blown to bits."

"Falcon, it's a soap opera. Leave that to the writers. And of course this means you can leave that poky little hometown of yours and head on back to New York."

Noah felt a flash of annoyance. "Vince, I've been rehearsing for weeks. This play means a lot to the economy of Cricket Creek. I can't just leave them high and dry."

"You're not under any real contract. I made sure you had an out."

Noah gripped the phone tighter. "That's not the point. They need me."

"Really? Well they need you on *Love in the Afternoon*, and the pay is a helluva lot better."

"I'm doing this for free."

"Exactly."

"The play can't go on without me."

"What, no understudy?"

"Well, yeah, but—"

"Falcon, seriously, have you lost your mind? The reason you headed to Cricket Creek was to hone your acting skills in order to land a part. Dude, you've just done that and then some. Come on, it's community theater for a few weeks, not a run on Broadway. What the hell's holding you there?"

"I told you. They need me," Noah insisted. He stared out into a parking lot full of pickup trucks and older-model cars. These hardworking people were depending upon him. Olivia would never forgive him . . .

"Wait—is this about a chick?"

"Why would you say that?"

"In my experience things are always about money or a chick. Sometimes both."

Noah looked up at the blue sky and shook his head at the puffy clouds. Most of the time he found Vince amusing. Not today. "It's about doing the right thing."

"Falcon, come on! This opportunity won't last long.

Don't be stupid. Your parents are gone from Cricket Creek. After the play ends you're not likely to ever go back there again. You've done enough already. Get your ass back here to New York, where you belong."

Noah closed his eyes and inhaled deeply. He wasn't sure he belonged in New York anymore. "I won't do it."

Vince sighed at the other end of the line. "Listen, I'll hold them off for as long as I can. I hope you'll come to your senses. Don't throw away this opportunity. You'll regret it later."

"Just tell them I'll return for the fall schedule."

"That won't fly. They want to beef up the ratings for the summer."

"Okay, I'll get back to you," Noah answered, simply for the sake of no more arguing. He did feel a little guilty that Vince had worked so hard on getting exactly what he had wanted and then some. By rights he should be over the moon. But he wasn't. The thought of disappointing Olivia, Madison, and his hometown made his stomach sink. Why in the world did life have to be so complicated? He hated letting anyone down, Vince included.

Noah stood there for a moment longer, allowing the cool spring breeze to clear his head. But then the scent of popcorn and hot dogs drifted his way, reminding him that the game was about to begin. With a sigh he started to walk in the direction of the field just as his phone rang again. He didn't recognize the ringtone and squinted at the screen to see who was calling.

"No way!" Noah had to grin when he read the name Ty McKenna. "What's up, Triple Threat?" he answered, using the nickname the famous center fielder had earned during his major-league career. If Ty didn't hurt the opposing team with his bat, he would rob them of hits with diving catches or gun down a runner with his cannon of an arm.

Ty laughed at the other end of the line. "About the only threat I am these days is to myself."

Noah leaned against a big oak tree and braced his foot against the trunk. "What do you mean?" he asked with a measure of concern. Ty was about the most up-beat guy he knew.

"Falcon, I miss the damned game. Spring training always brings me down," his friend answered glumly.

"I hear ya."

"You too? I thought you had moved on to acting."

"Didn't you hear? I was killed off of *Love in the Afternoon.*"

Ty snorted. "Falcon, do ya think I watch soap operas? But seriously?"

"Seriously."

"So, you gonna be on another show?"

"Um, apparently my lack of real acting skills is an issue."

Ty laughed. "Kinda like your curveball?"

"Hey, I'll pitch to your sorry ass anytime you want. See if you can hit my curve or my fastball."

"Bring it on. Hey, where are you again?"

"You're not gonna believe it." Noah gazed out into the parking lot and grinned. "I'm in my hometown of Cricket Creek, Kentucky, starring in a community-theater production and boning up on my acting skills with the leading lady. Crazy, huh?"

"Not at all. Is she hot?"

"What?"

"Didn't you just say you were boning the leading lady?"

Noah shook his head. "Ty, will you ever change?"

"Funny you should ask. My girlfriend just screamed that at me last night."

"And what was your answer?"

"Hell, no."

Noah had to chuckle. "And will you be seeing her again?"

"I asked her the same question."

"Let me guess—she said 'Hell, no.'"

Ty sighed. "Screamed it, actually. Threw a valuable baseball at me and smacked me in the damned head."

"You don't seem too upset."

"Didn't really hurt all that much. She threw like a girl. Kinda like you."

Noah rolled his eyes. "Ty, I meant about breaking up with her."

"Easy come, easy go," Ty replied lightly, but this time Noah failed to chuckle and instead felt a touch of sadness. Now that he had someone special in his life, he realized what he had been missing all these years. Getting back to Olivia was his priority, not watching the game. That pretty much said it all . . .

Noah asked, "What's going on besides your love life?" Ty never called just for idle chitchat.

"I ran into Mitch Monroe over at Chicago Blue Bistro the other night."

"One of your favorite haunts, as I recall."

"Used to be. Since that hot little chef left, the food isn't the same."

Noah chuckled.

"What?"

"That hot little chef is Jessica Robinson, and you're not going to believe it, but she's from Cricket Creek and came back here to update her aunt's diner."

"Seriously?"

"I kid you not. And her daughter wrote the play I'm in. Small world."

"And a smaller town," Ty said.

"It's a nice place to live, McKenna," Noah said a bit defensively.

"Wait. Hold the phone. You're not thinking of settling down there, are you?"

Noah inhaled deeply and hesitated. The smells of fresh country air laced with the scent of a charcoal grill filled his head. Two little boys ran by him laughing as they chased each other, and he could hear the chatter of the excited crowd in the background. A sense of peace unlike anything he had felt in a long time washed over him. "I don't know," he finally answered.

"Wow," Ty said. "I don't think I could leave the city for a one-horse town. But hey, man, who says you can't go home again? Anyway, the reason for my call was to tell you that Mitch Monroe is thinking about investing in a baseball team. He was picking my brain, but he got me sort of wound up about the whole idea and wanted to know if I knew anybody else who might want in. I didn't say anything, but I thought of you."

Noah felt a spark of interest. "Major league?"

"He wasn't sure. He's just in the thinking stages. But like I said, I sure as hell miss the game, don't you?"

As if on cue, Noah heard the crack of the bat hitting the ball, followed by the roar of the crowd. "Hell, yeah," he admitted. "Listen, I do have some interest."

"Awesome," Ty said, sounding more like his old self. They had played minor-league ball together and had been friends ever since.

"Listen, I'll give you a shout when I have some time and we can discuss it further. Right now I've got a Cricket Creek game to watch. Catch ya later?"

"Sure. Have fun."

Noah smiled after he ended the call. New York might be calling him back, but baseball was calling him home.

17

Take Me Out to the Ball Game!

"I just told Jason that I was going to eat your hot dog," Olivia informed Noah as he squeezed in next to her on the bleachers. She handed him the silver-wrapped package. "You got back just in the nick of time."

"You know what they say," Noah said as he took the hot dog. "Timing is everything."

"I told her not to eat it," Jason said from the other side of Olivia.

"Thanks for lookin' out for me, Jason," Noah replied and then turned to Olivia. "Sorry—I got a phone call I had to take," he explained while unwrapping his hot dog. "Hey, there's a bite taken out of it!" He narrowed his eyes at Olivia and laughed, but she just shrugged.

She put her nachos in her lap and said, "Don't look at me."

He leaned close to her ear and whispered, "Impossible."

Olivia felt a hot shiver slide down her spine. The sexy sound of his low voice coupled with the feeling of his muscled thigh pressed against hers was enough to make her slide out of her seat and slither between the metal bleachers. "Chip?" She swallowed hard and tried to sound normal, though she felt like tossing her nachos out of the way and pulling Noah in for a steamy kiss. It was probably not the thing to do at a high school baseball game, though, and so she held the plastic container up toward him. "Be careful—the jalapeños are very hot and spicy."

"I like hot and spicy." He scooped a jalapeño-laden chip in the cheese and winked at her. "Game started yet?"

"No, just infield practice. There was a delay."

"Waiting for me?" he asked with a teasing grin.

"You are such a diva," Olivia said. "They're waiting on an umpire to arrive."

Noah laughed, but his eyes watered when he chewed his chip. "Holy . . ."

"Cow?" she finished for him and reached for Jason's cup. "Here, take a drink," she offered and then added, "wimp."

Noah took a long slug of the Coke and handed it back to Jason. "First I'm a diva and now a wimp? What next?"

"I'll think of something . . ."

"Speaking of divas," Jason commented as he saw Madison approaching them. "Here comes the queen."

"I prefer princess," Madison said, sitting down next to him and offering him some of her popcorn.

"As you wish . . ." Jason replied with a little bow and a roll of his hand.

"*The Princess Bride!* I love that movie," Noah announced and got raised eyebrows from them all. "What?" He shrugged. "I can't like a good romantic comedy?"

"Of course you can," Madison said but grinned at Olivia. "You two *are* a romantic comedy."

"This day has been full of surprises," Olivia admitted.

"And that's a good thing, right?" Noah's voice was teasing, but there was a look of hope in his eyes that touched Olivia.

"Yes." She felt unexpected emotion and leaned her shoulder into his. When she looked at him from beneath her baseball cap, he gave her a crooked, vulnerable smile and then took her hand.

And she lost her heart completely.

It wasn't until the announcer asked them to stand for the National Anthem that the spell was broken between them. "Oh!" Olivia put her nachos down before standing, but Noah's fingers remained entwined with hers. His voice was true and strong, and she had to wonder how many times he had sung "The Star-Spangled Banner" in his lifetime. She was proud of the fact that spectators stopped in their tracks and sang with pride, and she dearly hoped that Noah was beginning to understand the value of life in a small town. She couldn't imagine being surrounded by concrete and swallowed up in a big city.

When the song ended, the crowd applauded and the umpire shouted, "Play ball!"

Excitement crackled in the air and Noah squeezed her hand. "Takes me back to my high school glory days right here on this field. Good times."

Jason leaned over and said, "You got that right, Noah. Lots of schools concentrate mainly on football, but we still love our baseball. The high school season here is too short. If we want summer baseball we have to go to watch the Lexington Legends or the Louisville Bats play minor-league ball or head up to Cincinnati to take in a Reds game."

"That's gotta suck," Noah acknowledged.

The first batter for the Colonels got on with a base on balls. "Well, fudge," Olivia muttered darkly.

"Walks come back to haunt," Noah said as he polished off his hot dog.

"I thought that last pitch was a strike," Jason complained with a slap to his knee.

"I hope Casey guns him down trying to steal second!" Olivia leaned forward and cupped her hands around her mouth. "Don't let him have second, Casey!"

Noah raised his eyebrows. "You know more than I thought you did about baseball."

"I guess I have a few surprises of my own," she replied with a proud little lift of her chin.

"Oh, I know." He leaned close to her ear once again. "And I want to discover them all."

Olivia felt heat steal into her cheeks and wondered how she was going to last nine innings with the spicy scent of his cologne filling her head and his thigh pressed against hers.

At the clink of a metal bat connecting with a baseball, they turned their attention back to the field. A high pop-up to shallow center field had the hometown fans holding their collective breath, but the ball was caught in a diving catch that brought them to their feet. Madison's popcorn flew up in the air like confetti and they all laughed when Jason caught some in his mouth.

"Way to go, Jimmy!" Olivia bounced up and down, clapping wildly. She turned and gave Noah a high five. "That was amazing!"

"Reminds me of your catch in the park," Noah said with a grin.

Olivia nodded firmly. "Yeah, maybe I shouldn't have always been the last one picked for teams in gym class," she boasted but then shrieked and ducked when a foul tip clanked against the backstop.

Madison tilted her head in Olivia's direction. "Guess that ruined *that* theory."

"Really?" Jason said. "Like you're an athlete?"

"Sure I am." Madison threw a kernel of popcorn at him but missed at point-blank range. "Okay, academic team four years, first chair flute, and glee club." She laughed but then raised her hands in the air. "Of course now it's hip to be a geek." She bopped her head back and forth. "And to have wild, curly, Taylor Swift hair." She sighed. "Go figure—not that I'd want to go back to high school," she added in a low tone.

"Me neither," Olivia agreed with a groan. "No real glory days for me."

"I wish I had gotten to know you better back when you tutored me," he said and meant it. Back then, he had been all about baseball and being cool. "Damn, I was shallow."

"We didn't run in the same circles," she said breezily, but there was some pain behind her answer. "Well, I didn't run in any circle," she joked, but her laughter felt a little bit forced. It wasn't easy being the last to be chosen and not having a date for the prom. It was during those days that she most missed having a mom to confide in.

"I was a bonehead. You were cute and smart and sweet," Noah stated firmly. "I'm glad I'm getting a second chance to take you to the prom."

Olivia looked up at Noah with a smile that wobbled at the corners, and it tore him up thinking that he had ever caused her any kind of pain. "Me too," she answered softly, and Noah decided that he was going to go all out with a stretch limo and the whole nine yards.

The roar of the crowd had them giving their attention back to the game. They came to their feet and cheered when Casey the catcher gunned down the runner at second base.

"Way to go, Casey!" Olivia shouted and then did a little butt wiggle that made Noah laugh. He loved the way she got into the game and cut loose.

"Heads up!" Jason shouted when a foul pop-up sailed over the backstop. Olivia and Madison both ducked and popcorn once again went flying, but Jason caught the ball barehanded and tossed it back to the umpire.

"Shouldn't they say 'duck' instead of 'heads up'?" Madison grumbled. "That must have hurt like"—she paused and glanced at Olivia before adding—"the dickens."

Jason flexed his hand. "Anything for you, baby."

Madison crossed her hands over her chest and cooed, "My hero!"

Olivia laughed. "Oh, she's not a queen anymore, Jason. Now she's a Southern diva."

"Well, I declare!" Madison batted her eyes. "I rather like it."

Noah joined in the laughter and tried to remember when he had felt so relaxed in the company he was with. As the game progressed, the feeling became stronger. In the fifth inning the teams were locked in a pitchers' duel.

"We need to set them down one, two, three, and then get some base runners!" Jason declared with a shake of his fist.

"You got that right," Noah agreed. "We've got the top of the lineup coming up, and I saw signs of fatigue from the Colonels' pitcher. We need to take advantage of the situation." When he noticed that Olivia was on the edge of her seat, he smiled and then squeezed her hand.

"My heart can't take this," she said. "I am so nervous for our boys!"

"I'm telling ya, we're going to rock the Colonels' pitcher next inning," he assured her, but instead of smiling she frowned. "What, Olivia?"

"I want to win, but I hate that too," she admitted. "They're just kids, you know?"

"Yeah." Noah gave her a soft smile. He knew the pressure even at this young age. She was such a caring person. "I know." He tipped the bill of her cap up so he could give her a quick kiss. "You are so adorable."

Olivia rolled her eyes. "Yeah, I get that a lot."

"Livie, I'm not handing you a line," he insisted and

was a bit hurt that she still thought he was playing her or putting on a show. He also knew that even though the focus was on the game, people were watching with continued interest in the budding romance between the local schoolteacher and the ballplayer. It was the Cricket Creek version of a reality show, and as much as he was the hometown hero, Olivia was loved and respected in this small town, and opinion would likely change about him if he ever hurt her in any way.

The conversion with Vince popped into his mind and he took a long look around. No way was he going to let this town down. He simply couldn't.

"Noah, you were right," Jason said. A walk followed by a base hit and then a home run put Cricket Creek up by three runs before a relief pitcher was brought in and struck out the next two batters. "I know Jordan is pitching a shutout, but he's tired too. Do you think we need a reliever next inning?"

Noah lifted one shoulder. "I would relieve him, but at his age I was a starter and would have begged to stay in the game. I'm not sure what the pitch count is, but I'd take him out."

"I agree," Jason nodded and then slipped his arm around Madison.

"Okay," Madison said, "would someone please tell me why people yell 'Good eye'? Seriously, what the hel—heck does that mean?"

Jason replied, "It's when the batter resists swinging at a ball."

Madison angled her head. "But isn't that the point? To swing at the baseball?"

"Not the baseball. A ball. You know—not a strike."

Madison frowned for a moment and then raised her eyebrows. "Oh! Like if it's too high or low or whatever and so it's smart not to swing at a crappy pitch."

"Yeah, baby. You got it," Jason said and gave her a kiss.

"It's so cool to learn the lingo. I love lingo." She cupped her hands around her mouth. "Good eye!" she yelled, but then put a hand over her mouth after the umpire bellowed "Strike three," ending the inning. "Oops. I guess timing is everything. Should I yell 'Bad eye'?"

"No!" Jason warned, clearly horrified.

"I was kidding," Madison muttered and rolled her eyes at Olivia and Noah.

"Sure you were." When Jason laughed, Madison punched him in the shoulder. "Ouch! For such a girlie girl you pack quite a wallop." He rubbed his arm.

"I'm not a girlie girl! I'm a tough bit—er, cookie."

"Olivia, have you finally cured Madison of her potty mouth?" Noah asked.

"Hell, yeah," Olivia answered in such a deadpan tone that it took Noah a second before he burst into laughter. His mirth faded with the heavy clink of a Morgan County Colonels bat smacking a ball to deep center field. "Oh, no!" Olivia jumped up so fast that she toppled sideways and Noah had to catch her to keep her from falling. She clung to him and stomped her foot when the three-run homer sailed over the fence, tying up the game. "Doggone it," she grumbled and smacked her leg.

"You were right, Noah," Jason said. "We should have brought in a relief pitcher."

Noah nodded his agreement and watched the Tigers' coach head out to the mound and signal the bull pen.

"Why did the coach skip over the chalk line?" Madison asked Noah with a puzzled expression.

Noah grinned. "Luck. Not stepping on foul lines is a pretty general superstition, but there are probably more idiosyncrasies, superstitions, and good luck charms in baseball than in any other sport."

"Really?" Madison asked. "Like what?"

Noah thought for a moment. "Well, for example, Yankees outfielder Nick Swisher keeps a broken Yankees gnome in his locker."

"For real?" Jason asked.

"True story," Noah answered with raised hands. "He found it broken in the hallway and said it needed a home. Let's see . . . Wade Boggs ate fried chicken before every single game."

"Silly," Madison said with a shake of her head.

Noah shrugged. "He won five batting titles, two gold gloves, a World Series, and collected over three thousand hits."

"Damn." Jason laughed. "I would have eaten chicken too."

"Sounds pretty OCD to me." Madison rolled her eyes but then said, "Tell us some more. This is crazy, but I love all things crazy."

"Cubs pitcher Turk Wendell would wave to the center fielder before starting an inning and would brush his teeth between innings. And here's a weird one—Kevin Rhomberg of the Cleveland Indians had to touch a person back if they touched him."

"No way." Olivia shook her head. "What if he was tagged out?"

"He would wait until after the inning to touch him back," Noah replied. "My friend Ty McKenna wore black underwear every game."

"Triple Threat Ty?" Jason asked and Noah nodded.

"Why?" Madison asked.

"In baseball, players like things to stay the same if it works. It can even be people sitting in the same place in the stands. Not changing lucky socks. I never shaved before a game."

"It's trying to control something that can't be controlled," Madison commented, but Noah could see that she was clearly interested in the conversation.

"Well, we could use a good luck charm right about now," Olivia grumbled as the game approached the bottom of the ninth with the score tied.

"Put on your rally cap," Noah instructed.

Olivia grinned and turned her baseball cap inside out and around.

"Wow, you knew what that meant?" Madison asked with wide eyes. "Cool!" Her eyes got wider when others in the stands followed suit. It was a ripple effect, and soon most of the Tigers fans did the same thing. "Oh, I hope it works!" she said and linked her arm through Jason's.

Jimmy Walters, the first batter up, looked at three straight balls, drawing boos from the Colonels fans. "He's afraid to swing!" someone shouted.

"That was mean-spirited," Madison muttered.

"Don't let them get into your head," Noah said. As an athlete he knew how tough it was to keep from getting rattled.

"Make him pitch to ya!" Jason shouted. "A walk is as good as a hit right now," he explained to Madison, who nodded firmly.

"I get it!" she said with an excited little squeal. "Who knew sports could be such fun?" she commented, drawing a chuckle from Jason.

"My heart is beating a million miles a minute!" Olivia said, and when Jimmy got a base hit straight up the middle she jumped to her feet, almost losing her rally cap. "Woo-hoo! Way to go, Jimmy!"

Noah held on to her once again so she didn't tip over. He had to laugh—he couldn't imagine any of the other women he had dated having so much fun at a high school baseball game, and certainly never donning a too-big baseball cap inside out and backward. When she looked at him and caught him staring, she laughed.

"I know I look ridiculous," she said with a shrug and then plopped back down on the metal seat with a little clank. "I'm just so excited."

"Are you serious?" Noah asked.

"Well, I always thought so, but you're bringing out the crazy in me."

"Among other things, if you recall," he reminded her in her ear. "Your kind of crazy is cute, and getting into the game does it for me, Livie. Let's win this thing and hurry home." He kissed her on top of her rally cap. "A kiss for luck."

"Hope it works!" she said with a grin.

"Me too. That would mean I would have to kiss you whenever we need runs," he said. His head snapped up when he heard the bat connecting with a ball. "Another base hit!" He kissed her head again. "Runners on first and second. We need a sacrifice fly."

"Okay, explain the lingo," Madison requested. "I'm guessing it's not capturing a fly and sacrificing it in some crazy baseball ritual."

"When a fly ball is hit, the runner can advance once the ball is caught. You have to tag up and then run like hell!" Jason explained. "You essentially give up a hit, so it's a sacrifice for the batter."

"Oh . . ." Madison nodded slowly, as if trying to grasp the concept, but before she could ask any more questions a long fly ball to left field had them all on their feet. The runner at second tagged up and safely advanced to third.

"We need a hit! Kiss my head, Noah! You forgot to last time or that could have been a home run!"

Noah laughed and kissed her head.

"Steee-riii-ke!" the umpire bellowed.

When Olivia inhaled a sharp breath, Noah took her

hand. "Oh, poor Freddy Jansen under all this pressure! I hope he doesn't strike out. Noah, how did you stand it?" She squeezed his hand. "With all eyes on you?"

"It's part of the game. The rush," he said smoothly, but in fact there had been plenty of times when his knees were knocking.

"Never let 'em see you sweat?" Jason leaned over and asked.

"Exactly."

Freddy smacked the next pitch, bringing the entire Cricket Creek crowd to their feet, shading their hands over their rally caps. The ball sailed high in the air over the second baseman's head and looked as if it was going to be caught by the center fielder, but he suddenly started backpedaling while holding his glove over his head.

"Omigosh!" Olivia clung to Noah's arm.

"He's lost it in the sun," Noah told her.

The left fielder came running over to help, but a second later the ball tumbled to the ground, and all three outfielders scrambled to make the play. The Tiger on third ran for home just as the center fielder located the ball.

"There's going to be a play at the plate!" Jason said and they watched the runner gunning for home as the baseball sailed like a rocket toward the catcher.

18

The Games People Play

Olivia didn't realize she had been holding her breath until the umpire spread his arms like wings, signaling that the runner was safe. "Yes!" She bounced up and down while clinging to Noah's arm. A roar went up from the Tigers fans and rally caps were tossed into the air.

"Now that's the way to start the season," Noah said and turned so he could hug her, but Olivia surprised him with a chest bump so hard that they almost toppled over. "Whoa!" He laughed and wrapped his arms around her, picking her up for a bear hug.

"That was amazing!" Madison shouted, doing some jumping up and down of her own. "Who knew baseball could be so much fun?" she asked, drawing an eye roll from Jason and Noah. "Just teasing," she assured them. "Sort of . . ."

"Y'all want to head over to Sully's for a cold one?" Jason asked and Olivia was about to agree when Noah jumped in.

"We're heading back to Olivia's to rehearse." His deep voice sounded like all business, but he gave Olivia's hand a squeeze and an I-can't-wait-to-have-you-in-my-arms look. "With opening night right around the corner, we want to have the script down pat. Right, Olivia?"

"Yes, absolutely," she answered briskly, but when Noah rubbed his hand in slow circles over her back she all but melted like butter in a hot skillet. "Rr-iii-ght. In fact, we really need to get going."

"I understand and I applaud your dedication," Madison said seriously, but the humor in her big eyes let Olivia know that she knew exactly what was going on. "In fact, I think you should pull an all-nighter. You know, to get it right."

"That's what I was thinking," Noah said, but then one look at Madison's expression had him laughing.

"Come on, you two are positively giddy and it's pretty difficult to take Olivia seriously with her . . ." She pointed to Olivia's head. "What's it called?"

"Rally cap." With a giggle Olivia reached up and took it off her head to fix it.

"Hey, it worked," Noah reminded Madison.

"Maybe there is something to be said for all of those crazy superstitions," Madison agreed with a nod. "The theater has some as well." She shooed Noah and Olivia with her fingers. "Okay, you two go on and *rehearse*."

"Well, then, we'll see y'all later," Jason joined in and put his arm around Madison. Apparently, they weren't fooling anybody, and that was just fine with Olivia.

"See you tomorrow at the theater," Madison called over her shoulder.

"I want to get going." Noah assisted Olivia down from the bleachers. "But first I want to go over to the dugout and congratulate the team."

"Good idea. They'll love that, Noah." Olivia walked with him toward the dugout, but hugs and high fives made it a slow process. When they weren't greeting people, he held her hand and stayed by her side. Although he was stopped here and there for a quick autograph, Olivia noticed that Noah was treated more and more like he lived in Cricket Creek. She could only hope that he felt as if he belonged here as well.

"Congratulations, Coach," Noah said as he shook hands with Rick Randall. "Nice way to start the season."

"Thanks, Noah. But I have to give you some credit for the win. Having you work out with the team has really made a difference, hasn't it, guys?" He turned to the team and was met with cheers and whistles, but as usual Noah shrugged it off.

"Thanks, but I wasn't the one playing out there today. You guys were. And you made me proud to be wearing this Tiger jersey!" He jabbed his thumb toward his chest and was met with more cheers. "But as you guys know, I'm going to be starring with Miss Lawson in the summer play. I hope to see you all there. It took me a while, but I've found my inner artsy-fartsy."

His comment drew laughter, but Coach Randall held up a hand for silence. "Trust me, we will all be there."

"Just don't bring tomatoes," Noah said and nodded his head sideways at Olivia. "Miss Lawson's tried hard to make me into a better actor, but I've got a ways to go, so we have to go rehearse. See ya at the next game. Go, Tigers!"

Olivia waved at the team and felt all eyes upon them as they turned away. It still felt funny to be the talk of the town when she had always flown under the radar. She thought of her father singing over at Sully's and had to chuckle.

"What's so amusing?" Noah asked as they walked hand in hand toward her house.

Olivia shook her head slowly and then looked up at him. "I was just thinking about my dad and Myra singing together over at Sully's. And of course everyone is still buzzing about you and me."

Noah paused at her doorstep and tucked his finger beneath her chin. "Does that bother you?"

"Which one?"

"Either . . . both?"

Olivia was touched by the concern in his eyes. "No," she answered honestly. "It's about time Dad and I started living our lives . . ." She paused while searching for the right words.

"With gusto?"

Olivia snapped her fingers. "Yes, I like that. With gusto!" She tilted her head back and laughed.

"Now what are you thinking?"

Olivia gripped his hand tightly and tugged him up the front steps and into the house. "I want to kiss you with gusto." She tossed her rally cap to the side, not caring where it landed, and then wrapped her arms around him.

"I like your attitude, Miss Lawson," Noah said and pulled her closer against the length of his body.

"Me too!" Olivia declared, but before kissing him she looked into his eyes and saw nothing but sincerity. "Oh, Noah . . ." she breathed, and her heart pounded when he lowered his head and captured her mouth with his.

His mouth felt warm, soft . . . gentle, but when she opened her mouth for more, passion took over. "Livie, baby, you are driving me wild." With a groan he pushed her up against the smooth, cool wall in the living room and deepened the kiss to a hot fever pitch. He threaded his long fingers through her hair, massaging her scalp while he explored her mouth. He tugged gently on her hair, but with enough force that her head tilted sideways so he could have access to her neck. "You smell amazing, so sweet and yet sultry just like you. Livie, I wanted to do this the entire game." He eased his hands beneath her blouse and oh, so slowly slid them up her sides just shy of her breasts. "Ahhh, your skin is so soft." His touch sent a hot shiver down her spine and had her clinging to his shoulders for support. "If I'm being too bold, too rough, tell me."

"Babe, when will you learn that I won't break?"

"Damn, that was hot."

"What?" It was difficult to concentrate with his mouth on her skin.

"Calling me 'babe.'"

Olivia laughed. "My inner sexpot has a mind of her own," she joked, but her heart pounded when Noah suddenly cupped her chin in the palm of his hand and held her gaze.

"Let go tonight, Livie. Don't worry. Don't think. Just be with me. Will you do that?"

Olivia swallowed hard and then nodded. "Yes."

"Trust me."

"I will," she said, with a smile that was filled with emotion and yet didn't tremble this time. "Noah, I do trust you."

"Good. I know it sounds like a line, but I've never felt this way before." His eyes held hers for a moment longer and he searched her face as if wanting to be sure that she believed him.

"Me neither," she admitted and waited for the fear to grip her heart. In previous relationships she had always held back, afraid to give her heart only to have someone trample on it, like her mother did to her loving, trusting father.

For a second Olivia thought he was going to say more, but then he dipped his head and kissed her once again. She could feel the emotion behind the desire, and it swept her away. For the first time in her life, she loved without holding back. She wrapped her arms around him and when he picked her up she laughed and hooked her legs around his waist. She kissed him with heat, with such passion that she trembled from the intensity.

They kissed all the way to the bedroom and tried to keep kissing while undressing. Fingers fumbled, hands tugged, and shoes were toed off and went flying across the room. They laughed, groaned when he paused to slip on protection, and then sighed when they finally tumbled to the bed in a heap of tangled legs and white-hot passion.

When Noah scooted up and leaned against the mound of pillows, Olivia swung one long leg over and straddled him. She boldly let him look his fill while he cupped her breasts in his big hands.

"You are gorgeous."

Olivia wanted to thank him, but all she could manage was a gasp when he rubbed his thumbs over her nipples. She caught her bottom lip between her teeth but couldn't hold back a throaty cry of pleasure when his warm tongue replaced his thumbs. He licked, sucked, and when he lightly nipped with his teeth Olivia arched her back and wantonly, brazenly offered him more. "Noah . . ." She threaded her fingers through his hair, and when she rocked suggestively against him a muscle jumped in his jaw.

"I need you now," he said in a low, husky voice that felt like a physical caress. When his hands slid down to span her waist, Olivia came up to her knees and then slowly eased down onto the hard length of his penis. Her breath caught at the exquisite feeling and she gripped his shoulders while she moved at a slow, sensual pace. "Ah, Livie . . ." His eyes closed, but Olivia watched his handsome face, loving the play of emotion and the stark masculine beauty. Warm pleasure started to build and her heart raced. She moved faster and faster with a passion that felt wild and free. His strong hands guided her, helped her when her thighs quivered. "Noah!" Her breasts brushed against his chest and when he thrust upward deeply, his throaty cry of pleasure carried Olivia over the edge with him.

He wrapped his arms around her, holding her close, and then kissed her neck, her shoulders, before pulling her mouth to his for a hot, sweet kiss. Olivia leaned against him and enjoyed the feeling of being skin to skin, heart to heart. For a moment they were silent and simply remained entwined. Finally, Noah swept her hair over her shoulder and said, "That was incredible. You blow me away, Olivia."

Olivia cupped his cheeks between the palms of her hands and kissed him softly before saying, "The feeling is mutual."

"I know you have school in the morning, but I want to stay with you tonight."

"I want you to," Olivia told him. Sleeping in his arms all night was something she would never pass up. "I'm going to slip into my pajamas," she said and then kissed him lightly before easing off the bed. "There's a new toothbrush in the hall bathroom if you want to use it," she offered with a smile.

"Thanks. I will," he said, but then shook his head. "But I have one request."

Olivia raised her eyebrows.

"Forget the pajamas."

"You're right. Pajamas are overrated." Olivia laughed as she headed into the bathroom. After flicking on the light, she stared at her reflection and put her hands to her cheeks, thinking that she was glowing with happiness. It felt so good to love, to trust, and to allow the luxury of believing that somehow they would make this last beyond the summer.

After brushing her teeth and quickly washing her

face, she looked at her pajamas hanging on the hook on the back of the door and giggled. She had never slept in the buff before, but then again in the past few weeks she had done quite a few things that were out of character for her. "Oh, inner sexpot, I do love you," she whispered and for some reason felt compelled to tiptoe into the bedroom. She tossed the pillows to the floor and then slid beneath the cool sheet and waited for Noah to return to her.

When the BlackBerry on the nightstand vibrated, she picked it up, thinking that the phone was hers, and looked at the text message. What she read made her stomach plummet. The message from someone named Laney O. read:

Noah, you need to ditch that silly little play in that one-horse town and come home where you belong. I know you must still be angry, but I made a huge mistake and I will do whatever it takes to get you back. Love isn't the same without you. Call me.

Love isn't the same without you? Olivia put a trembling hand over her mouth and then set the phone back on the nightstand. When she heard footsteps coming down the hallway, she scooted down and pressed her head into the feather pillow, pretending to be asleep.

When Noah eased beneath the covers and wrapped his arms around her, pulling her close, Olivia tried not to stiffen. She swallowed a sob and wondered if she should confront him about Laney, but the pain of his betrayal cut too deep. No wonder her father had hurt so badly for so many years. A hollow ache settled in her chest, and she couldn't find the courage to address the situation. She wondered how she could even go on with the play, but she was going to have to dig deep and act the part. Madison and Cricket Creek were counting on the success of the play, and damned if she would let Noah Falcon ruin it.

When Noah kissed her bare shoulder a hot tear slid down her cheek, but she vowed never to let him see her pain. For her father's sake, she had learned a long time ago to mask the hurt of her mother's absence. She was a good actress. She could do this. The game was far from over.

19

Once More with Feeling

"Okay, find your marks and let's try this scene from the beginning," Madison directed with a frown. "This time kiss with some emotion!" She plopped down on her chair and crossed her arms over her chest. For the past few days something had been wrong with Olivia, and Madison didn't understand, but with opening night just two weeks away she was sweating bullets. They were down to final rehearsals and up until now lines were memorized, blocking felt just right, and lighting seemed perfect. After four weeks of rehearsals the stage crew had set changes down like clockwork. In fact, Madison had hoped to allow the stage manager to take over while she observed a run-through, but she just couldn't keep from breaking in with direction.

Olivia looked as if she had just sucked on a lemon and Noah appeared just plain confused. "Again!" Madison said sharply and rolled her fingertips to her temple as she observed Olivia's wooden performance. "Okay, you know what? Let's call it a night," she shouted to the cast and crew. She shoved her script into her leather case. "I'll see everyone at six thirty tomorrow. Olivia, may I see you, please?"

Olivia nodded and walked in front of the orchestra pit to where Madison leaned against the back of a folding table. "Are you going to tell me what's going on with you and Noah?"

"Nothing," Olivia said but swallowed hard. "I'm just tired from grading exams, that's all. School is over at the end of the week, so I'll be fine. I'm sorry, Madison."

"Yeah, right. Like I'm buying that line of bull? Noah just stormed off the stage and you don't seem to care."

"I care deeply about this play," Olivia assured her in a shaky voice. "I'll be fine." She pressed her palms downward toward the floor. "Just let me catch my breath. Tomorrow will be better."

"Better? Olivia, I don't want *better*. I need what you already had up there! Passion! Feeling! Emotion!" She pointed to the stage and then put a hand over her heart. "Come on, tell me what's got the bur up your butt," she demanded, but when Olivia's mouth trembled and her eyes misted over, Madison shook her head and then grabbed Olivia's arm. "Let's go to Sully's and slug down a dirty martini."

Olivia wrinkled up her nose.

"Okay, a glass of wimpy wine . . . whatever. You have to tell me what in the world is going on."

Olivia inhaled a deep breath. "Madison, I'm just burning the candle at both ends and I haven't been sleeping well. I truly just need a good night's rest, that's all."

"You are such a crappy liar," Madison responded tightly, but then her voice softened when Olivia's eyes filled with tears. She put a hand on her friend's arm and squeezed. "Listen, I'm going to Sully's. If you need someone to talk to, we can snag a booth and chat, okay?"

Olivia hesitated but then shook her head. "I'll be fine, and the play will go off without a hitch. I promise. The stress is just getting to me."

"Okay," Madison sighed as she slung her leather

satchel over her shoulder. "If you change your mind, just call me."

"Thanks, Madison. I will."

Madison nodded but shook her head slowly as she watched Olivia walk out the door. Something had happened between Olivia and Noah Falcon. Noah seemed frustrated but clueless and Olivia was acting just plain weird! Madison looked around the theater. Thanks to Jason and the art department at Cricket Creek High School, the set was beautiful. The lighting had been perfected over the past few weeks, and everyone had their lines down pat. Posters were placed everywhere, and ticket sales were strong, with opening weekend sold out. Local hotels and inns were filling up, and Wine and Diner was almost ready for its grand opening. Everything was going as planned. Olivia Lawson was the last person Madison would have expected to have a meltdown.

"Go figure," Madison mumbled as she locked the front door. Suddenly a dirty martini sounded pretty darned good and maybe a bite to eat as well, so she hoofed it down the street to Sully's. But after opening the door her heart thudded and her eyes widened.

What the . . .

Jason Craig and a gorgeous brunette sat in a booth with their heads bent together. Madison stood there for a good minute, but he was so engrossed with what the woman was telling him that he didn't even notice her! Madison's first inclination was to stomp over and present her sorry self, but she was so stunned by the sight of Jason with another woman that she whirled around and all but flew out the door.

Madison stood outside for a moment and then suddenly felt angry with herself for not having the moxie to march back in there and confront him. But seeing Jason with someone else felt like a sucker punch to her gut, and she simply couldn't do it. Still, she fisted her hands and contemplated heading right back in and tossing a drink in his face—or whatever dramatic scene she could muster up. But the past few days had already been so stressful that she just kept on putting one foot in front of the other until she reached the high-rise where she lived.

Madison tugged the heavy front door open with a whoosh and then stomped her foot when she remembered that she had driven to the community center earlier. "Grrr!" she grumbled, but she didn't want to walk all the way back into town. Instead she punched the elevator button way too hard and then stood there tapping her foot while the numbers seemed to descend in slow motion and then stop. After another minute she pressed the button again.

"That won't make the elevator come any sooner."

"Eeek!" Madison whirled around to see Noah Falcon standing behind her. "No-ah!"

"Before you say anything, I did not sneak up on you. You were lost in your own little world of pissed-off-ness."

Madison blinked hard at him. She wasn't one to give in to tears easily, but when she did it was noisy. "You scared me!" She was precariously close to some serious bawling.

Noah's expression softened. "You want a drink?"

"Martini?" she asked in a small but hopeful voice.

"My bar has an extensive selection."

"So the answer is yes?"

"Yes."

"Dirty?"

"I showered."

Madison attempted to laugh but hiccuped instead. "This was one sucky day."

"Tell me about it." Noah stood back and allowed her to enter the elevator first and then with a long sigh leaned against the mirrored wall.

Madison thought that he appeared exhausted and put a hand on his forearm. "Am I pushing everyone too hard this week?"

Noah shifted his gaze to her in surprise. "Why do you ask that?"

"Because Olivia is one of the most levelheaded people I know and you have pitched in the World Series, for goodness' sakes!"

"And?"

"And you both seem ready to crack. Look, I realize that this play is mostly you two onstage with very few supporting characters and that the pressure is on, so what else am I to think?"

Noah shrugged and took his gaze away from the changing numbers. "I have no idea what I did to upset Olivia. I've tried to talk to her and she pretends like everything is okay." He sighed and when the elevator stopped on the eleventh floor, he held the door for her to step out. "I might be a dumb jock, but I'm not that stupid."

"If you ever call yourself that again, I'm going to kick your ass, Noah." She jutted her chin out and dared him.

His laughter seemed a bit forced. "I'll remember that. Hey, drop your stuff off in your condo and I'll have a very cold, very dirty martini waiting for you. I'll be on the balcony, but I'll leave the door open."

"Sounds heavenly. I'll be there in just a few minutes."

She unlocked her door and dumped her purse and leather satchel on the kitchen island with a sad clunk. "Well, this day has really been a winner." She looked around and then sighed. The condo was small, but the open floor plan made it seem bigger. What she really loved was the long sliding glass doors that opened to a double balcony overlooking the river. She walked over and gazed out. The sunrises and sunsets were amazing, and the sight of the winding river usually calmed her nerves.

But not today.

She opted to change into sweats and flip-flops. She grabbed some sliced Cheddar from the fridge and a sleeve of crackers from her top cabinet. In her experience bachelors had an extensive liquor cabinet but were usually lacking in the snacks and chocolate department. She might not be a great cook like her aunt and mother, but she excelled in all things munchy and crunchy. Writers tended to graze rather than take the time for actual meals, and Madison was no exception.

Her flip-flops slapped against the bottoms of her feet as she made her way down the marble-tiled hallway. An antique-looking cherry table with a lovely floral arrangement made the space elegant, and Madison once again thought it a crying shame that the building was mostly vacant. When she reached Noah's condo, his door was unlocked as promised and she entered. "Hello?"

"Out here," Noah called from the balcony. The sliding doors were open, allowing the evening breeze to cool the space, which was larger than Madison's more modest quarters. Used as a model unit, Noah's condo had furnishings that were a gorgeous mix of deep chocolate leather and mahogany with splashes of crimson accents here and there.

Noah had changed to cargo shorts and a University of Kentucky T-shirt that read UK2K.

"What does that mean?" She pointed to his shirt.

He angled his head at her. "Two thousand wins," he boasted with a nod.

She shook her head. "With all of the baseball talk I had forgotten how crazy this town was for basketball."

"Wildcat basketball," he corrected with a chuckle. "Yeah, I bought this shirt at the mall last week." He lounged in a cushioned chair and pointed to the one next to his. A round table held a tray of mixed fruit, a wedge of Brie, and some water crackers. "Have a seat," he offered and then handed her a martini glass.

"Wow, I'm impressed," she admitted as she took the wide glass from him and cradled it in her hand. "I brought Cheddar and Ritz crackers, thinking that as a bachelor you'd probably have some stick pretzels."

"You'd be right. This feast was left over from when Olivia was here, before she decided to hate me."

Madison sat down and shook her head at Noah. "What's up with you and Olivia? Everything seemed so great between you two at the baseball game."

"Tell me about it." Noah shrugged his wide shoulders. "You got me."

"Something has to have happened, Noah." Madison took a sip of her martini and looked at him expectantly. "Can you think of anything that might have upset her?"

Noah took a swig of his beer and then eased back in the chair and crossed his long legs in front of him. "Damned if I know." He let the longneck dangle from his fingertips and stared out at the river below. "Has she said anything to you, Madison?" He turned and looked at her with such pain and confusion in his eyes that she reached over and patted his arm.

"No, only that grading exams and lack of sleep have gotten the best of her. She promised me that she would get her act together for the play, if you'll pardon the pun."

"And do you believe that?"

Madison looked at him for a long, measuring moment. "She might be able to muster a good performance, but I'm not buying her excuses for one minute," she answered quietly.

"Me neither." He tilted his beer bottle up to his mouth.

"Have you asked her what's wrong, Noah?"

He swallowed and then nodded slowly. "Sure. I got the same sort of noncommittal response from her as you did. I don't get it."

"That makes two of us," she said with a long, shaky sigh and another sip of the cold martini. "Any of it."

"Hey." Noah sat up straighter. "What else is wrong?" he asked gently, and when he gave her his full attention Madison realized that Noah Falcon might be a big strong athlete but he had a soft and tender side that most people didn't know. Her newly acquired and highly enjoyed matchmaking radar went on full alert. They might be on the outs for whatever reason, but Noah and Olivia were meant to be together and she was going to do everything in her power to make it happen. "Madison? You can talk to me and it won't go anywhere."

"Thank you." Madison nodded when his voice brought her back to her own romantic issues. She took a bigger sip of her drink and then bristled. "Well, I was walking into Sully's for a drink and guess who I saw."

"Myra and Owen singing again? Apparently they've made karaoke so popular that Pete bought a real sound system."

"No," Madison replied and stuck her bottom lip out. "I saw Jason and some hot brunette getting all cozy in a corner booth." She sucked her bottom lip back in and bit down.

"Did you check the situation out?"

She shook her head back and forth with quick jerky movements.

"Madison, why the hell not? It might have been perfectly innocent."

"They were, like, *intense*." Her eyes widened.

"But—"

"And he *smiled* at her."

"But—"

"And it wasn't a little ol' polite smile. It was a big one." She pointed both index fingers to her mouth and demonstrated.

"Stop—that smile was creepy."

Madison laughed, but her lips suddenly trembled. "Oh, Noah." She set her glass down, flopped back in the chair, and stared up at the sky. The sun was setting in a burst of orange and pink, and normally she would stop to admire the beauty, but tonight she barely noticed. "I thought he was different, you know? Small town, big heart. Sincere! But I guess dudes are all the same no matter where you live." She tilted her head down and looked up at him. "Sorry, no offense—I know you're a dude. But still . . . dudes royally suck."

Noah laughed. "Judging from that statement, no one would ever think you were an award-winning play-wright."

"Pffft." She rolled her eyes. "I'm just a girl, Noah."

The scrape of the screen door opening caught their attention. "Not hardly," said a deep voice edged with a sexy Southern drawl.

Madison looked around to see Jason coming out onto the balcony.

"An uppity, nerdy . . . idiot girl, maybe." He walked over pretty as you please and leaned against the railing.

Madison gasped and then whirled on Noah. "Did you call him?"

Noah raised his hands in the air. "No, I swear."

"Yeah, well . . ." Madison narrowed her eyes at Jason. "You're a small-town, redneck, stupid boy!" She crossed her arms over her chest. "And that hat is ridiculous."

Jason tilted his head and adjusted his vintage-style John Deere cap sideways. "Yes, yes . . . mmm"—he scratched his chin—"*yes*, and no, it is not!"

"At least you admit that you're stooo-pid." She leaned forward as she drew out the word and then felt pretty childish, but she could not stop herself. "So, if Noah didn't call you, why are you here?"

He leaned his back against the railing and said, "I'm beginning to ponder that very question. Madison, I didn't intend to come to Noah's condo. I was coming to see you and heard your voice all the way down in the parking lot."

"Really?"

Jason rolled his eyes. "You're my girlfriend, not Noah."

"Thank God for small favors," Noah commented.

"You get loud when you get riled up."

Madison frowned. "Then why . . ." She swallowed but couldn't quite get it out.

"Why what?" Jason waited for her to continue.

Madison raised her chin a notch. "Why were you in Sully's with that . . . that woman?"

"You were in Sully's?"

"Yes, and I caught your hand in the cookie jar," she sputtered, but judging by the smug look on his face she was about to be put in her place. She swallowed. "Didn't I?" she asked in a small voice.

"I'm not so big on cookies. I'm more partial to cup-cakes."

"Are you calling me a cupcake?"

"No, I'm calling you crazy." Jason flicked a glance at Noah. "Could you give us a moment?"

Noah looked at Madison in question, but she nodded. "It's okay, Noah." She thought it was sweet that he was looking out for her and thought once again that she was right about him. Noah Falcon was a good guy and Olivia ought to come to her senses and realize it. But first things first. She needed to get back to the task at hand. "Give us a minute."

20
Crazy Love

*N*oah headed to the fridge to snag another beer, but before he opened it he heard Madison shout, so he hurried back to the balcony. He was ready to kick some Jason ass but stopped in his tracks when he spotted him on bended knee with a velvet ring box extended upward. Madison had her hand over her mouth and didn't even realize Noah was standing there in the doorway. Noah didn't really think of himself as a romantic sort of guy, but the tiny patio lights on the balcony twinkled in the waning light and the indigo sky was still streaked with deep red, burnt orange, and purple. His forgotten beer dangled from his fingers and a lump formed in his throat. He wanted to turn around and give them their privacy, but he just couldn't look away, so he stood there quietly and waited for the scene to unfold.

"Madison, will you marry me?"

"Are you crazy?"

Her answer made Noah's heard plummet, but Jason didn't bat an eye.

"Hell, yes, or why else would I be doing this? You're bossy and you always have your nose in the air at the diner telling me how to do my own job."

"I have an eye for color and detail," she argued.

"And I had an eye for your cute little ass that you chose to give an extra wiggle to whenever you walked by me."

Madison gasped. "I did not!"

When Jason rolled his eyes, Noah wasn't sure where this was going, but he was riveted.

"Oh, like you didn't flex those muscles of yours to impress me?" Madison countered.

He grinned. "So were you impressed?"

"Yes, you've got some guns, Jason Craig. Now, what were you saying?" She glanced at the ring and then looked at him expectantly.

"I was saying that you're bossy and uppity and you might drag my sorry ass to live in the city where people would laugh at my accent and I might have to eat fancy food with nerdy writer types."

Noah swallowed hard. *This can't be good,* he thought, and watched Madison's reaction with held breath.

"Omigod." Madison put her hand to her chest and then gave Jason a slow smile. "You would do that for me?" She sliced her hand through the air in an arc. "Leave Cricket Creek?"

"Yes."

"Then you really are crazy."

"Crazy in love with you, Maddie. I'd follow your uppity ass to the ends of the damned earth."

"That was . . ." She pressed her lips together as if trying to maintain her composure.

"The best I could do."

"I was going to say 'beautiful in a Jason Craig kinda way,' but you didn't let me finish."

"This wasn't the proposal I had in mind." He grinned. "But I guess it's going the way I thought it might. You are not an easy chick."

"Nothing worthwhile is easy," she said, but then she

put a hand to her chest. "Oh, you had a plan? Like a speech?"

"Maddie Robinson, are you going to give me an answer?"

Jason looked up at Madison with hopeful eyes that made the lump in Noah's throat get bigger. *Wow, I am turning into such a softy.*

"Yes," Madison answered with a firm nod.

Jason looked at the solitaire sparkling in the box and then back up at her. "Yes, as in you're going to give me an answer or yes, as in you will marry me?"

"Y— Wait." She angled her head at him. "Just who was that girl in Sully's?"

Noah barely suppressed a groan.

"Not the girl I'm asking to marry me."

"Jason . . ."

He sighed. "She brought the rings to me."

"Rings?"

He gave her a lopsided grin. "I had three picked out and I couldn't make up my mind. As for Melissa, I knew her from school. Her daddy owns the jewelry store," he explained, but then pulled the ring back and snapped the case shut. "Wait—so you thought I was cheatin' on you?"

Noah audibly groaned this time, but neither of them paid him any heed.

"No," Madison insisted, but her cheeks turned pink. "Okay, perhaps the thought occurred to me."

Jason rocked back on his heels. "You've got to be kiddin' me."

"What was I supposed to think? You were in a bar with a beautiful woman. All cozylike."

"Cozylike?" His grin got bigger but then faded. "Don't you trust me, Maddie?"

"Omigod," Noah said, finally drawing their attention.

"I know!" Jason agreed. "She sure as hell should!"

But Madison tilted her head at Noah and arched one eyebrow in understanding. "You just had an aha moment, didn't you?"

Noah smiled. "About three slammed into my brain all at once. Now all I have to do is put the plan—no, make that *plans*—in motion." He shooed his hands toward them. "Sorry to interrupt. I'll give you some privacy," he offered, but as soon as Madison turned her attention back to Jason he couldn't help himself and stood there quietly and listened.

Jason took his baseball cap off and tossed it to the side. "Maddie, you know I'm true blue, right? Baby, I would never cheat on you."

"I know that. You're a good man, Jason Craig."

"No doubt?"

"None," Madison answered softly. She reached down and took his hand. "I don't know what was going through my fool head."

Jason grinned. "You're really starting to sound as if you belong here."

"Where I belong is with you," she answered and Noah almost shouted "Hallelujah!" but he managed to stay quiet and not intrude on their moment.

"Is that finally a yes?"

"Let me see the ring first," she said, but when he nodded and opened the box, Madison shook her head. "I was kidding, Jason. I'm sorry. I always joke when I'm emotional. It's stupid," she said, but then covered her mouth again. "I'm stupid! I was stupid for doubting you. Stupid for—"

"Hellfire, woman," Jason interrupted. He stood up, tugged her to her feet, and then kissed her soundly.

"What was that for? I haven't said yes yet."

"That was to shut you up. You are frustrating as all get out but certainly not stupid."

"Thank you—I think."

"For heaven's sake, would you just say yes? In a minute I'm gonna just say 'screw it' and propose to Noah."

"I'd have to take a few days to mull it over," Noah answered from the shadows.

"Yes!" Madison shouted and flung her arms around Jason. "Now I want the ring and the speech."

"On your balcony, not Noah's," Jason said with a glance toward Noah. "No offense, man."

"None taken," Noah said and stepped back out onto the balcony. He clapped Jason on the back and then hugged Madison. "Olivia was right. You two are meant for each other. Congratulations!" He winked at Madison. "Guess this day didn't suck so badly after all."

Madison gave him a pointed look and then hugged him hard. "That's why you should never give up," she said in his ear.

"Point taken," Noah replied before stepping back. "Now you two go celebrate. And don't worry. I won't breathe a word to anyone. I'll let you guys spread the good news."

"Thanks, Noah," Madison said and then linked her arm in Jason's. She leaned her head against his shoulder and gazed up at him adoringly while they walked away, and Noah felt another stab of emotion.

"Young love," he thought, and then sighed, remembering all the years that he'd thought he would never want or need a partner. "Shows just how damned wrong I can be. No, make that how damned arrogant," he muttered as he stepped out into the moonlight.

He braced his hands on the railing, and gazed out at the amazing view. He could barely see the river in the darkness, but he could hear water lapping against the shore. Lights from homes dotted the horizon, making him sigh. When was the last time he had felt as if he was truly home? Years of traveling with baseball and not coming back to a family had been what he'd thought he wanted—no responsibility, no guilt about being gone so much. But after spending time with Olivia he knew just how good it felt to love and to hold someone in his arms at night.

Someone to come home to.

His apartment in New York was nice, but it lacked any real warmth or comfort. In fact, this condo with furniture that wasn't even his felt more like home, but where he wanted to be more than anywhere else was in a certain little Cape Cod in the heart of town. Of course he knew why. It didn't matter where he laid his head . . . What mattered was who he was with.

Olivia.

Noah reached over and picked up his longneck from the table laden with the big tray of cheese and fruit. Just a few nights ago after rehearsal, he and Olivia had feasted on plump strawberries and sweet grapes, spread cheese and salami on crackers, and washed it down with red wine.

Noah took a swig of his beer and then chuckled softly at the vivid memory. They had been lounging out here when the sky had suddenly opened with a pop-up thundershower. While laughing, they hurried into the condo and stumbled into the bedroom, leaving the windows open. The cool, misty breeze and pitter-patter of the falling rain served as a backdrop while they had made lazy love for hours.

Noah inhaled a deep breath of pungent evening air that smelled of earth, river, and soil. He stared out into the darkness and shook his head slowly. Olivia didn't trust him. He didn't know what he had said or done to spook her, but if the pieces of his plan came together as he hoped, he would be able to prove to her without a doubt that his intentions were true. All he had to do now was make it happen. With that in mind he headed into the condo, located his laptop, and plopped down on his bed to do some research.

Hours later, his eyes were burning with fatigue, but excitement wouldn't allow him to even think about going to sleep. Instead he began working on a PowerPoint presentation to e-mail to Ty McKenna, with a copy to Mitch Monroe.

"Wow!" Excitement escalated as his fingers clicked rapidly over the keyboard. When he finished he rubbed a hand down his face and yawned. After reading through the data once more, he sent the document to Ty and copied Mitch.

Noah folded his hands behind his head and smiled slowly. With a little bit of luck this venture just might work.

21

Hit Me with Your Best Shot

Olivia used a tape gun to secure the last box of books in her classroom. With a groan she stood up and pressed her hand against the small of her back. "Done!" She dusted off her hands but then gazed at the shelves for any stray items. Except for grading the final exam and going to the prom on Saturday her duties for the school year were over. Normally, a carefree feeling that summer break was about to start would wash over her, but ever since she had read the text message on Noah's phone, all she felt was a heavy sense of sadness.

Olivia sighed as she blew an errant lock of hair out of her eyes. She had brought back her tight bun in an odd effort to regain control of her life, but during her packing it had degenerated into a sloppy ponytail. In the mood she was in she didn't care.

Olivia closed her eyes and fisted her hands at her sides. Not only was Noah leaving at the end of the production, but evidently he had a girlfriend that he had never told her about. "I am such an idiot," she muttered. She inhaled a deep breath and willed herself not to cry, which was a skill she had perfected over the years. Her ability to act had surfaced at a very young age.

Olivia inhaled another shaky gulp of air, but when chalk dust invaded her nostrils she tilted her head back, put her index finger beneath her nose, and tried to suppress a sneeze—without success. "Ah-ah-ah-*choo!* Ah-choo! Achoo!" As usual, her high-pitched sneezes exploded in a silly little series of three that never failed to amuse her students.

"God bless you."

With a little cry of alarm Olivia whirled around and almost tripped over a box of books. One flip-flop went flying through the air and she had to right herself by grabbing her desk. "Oh, Mr. Turner!" She put a hand to her chest and tried to sound professional. "Good afternoon," she said and somehow managed to muster up a smile.

He stepped into the classroom. "Sorry to startle you, Olivia."

"It wasn't your fault. I was in a world of my own."

"Hey, school is over except for prom and graduation, so I'm not really your principal until next year," he reminded her with a smile of his own. "That means you can call me Brandon." He walked over next to her and casually leaned his hip against the desk. "Okay?"

"Okay, Brandon," Olivia answered, not really sure where this was going, but she had an inkling. His neatly pressed khakis and blue polo made Olivia feel grungy in her ancient Garth Brooks concert T-shirt and well-worn jeans.

He cleared his throat and said, "So, I was wondering if you might like to have lunch with me today."

"Um . . ." She searched her brain for a reason not to and came up with, "Brandon, as you can see, I'm a mess." *In more ways than you even know.*

"You look perfectly beau—uh, fine to me. We could head over to the diner for a quick bite. They have construction going on, but they are still open for business."

Olivia hesitated. She knew that rumors had been flying since she and Noah were no longer being seen around town together. In fact, at the last couple of baseball games she had sat in a stadium chair instead of anywhere near him in the bleachers.

"We could discuss your suggestion of adding a glee club next year," he added as an extra incentive. She wondered if Brandon was really into her like Noah had suggested and was making his move. "I think it has some merit and I'm prepared to support you with the school board."

Olivia mustered up a half smile. "You're not playing fair, Mr.— I mean, Brandon."

"Is that a yes?" His boyishly charming smile had her nodding in spite of her appearance and her mood.

"Sure . . . yes," she replied, thinking that a nice quiet lunch just might cheer her up. Mooning over a man who had toyed with her affections was insanity. And after all, Brandon was handsome, *charming*, and he was . . . She tried to think of something else and came up with *he was here and here to stay*. A better mood would make for a more productive rehearsal and put to rest poor Madison's fears that the play was going to end up a flop.

"Great. I'll pick you up, or we can walk if you prefer," Brandon said, and to Olivia's surprise he leaned over and gave her a quick kiss on the cheek just as Noah Falcon walked into the room.

For a second Noah appeared shaken. Then he masked his expression with a sardonic arch of one dark eyebrow. "Sorry—am I interrupting?"

"Hi, Mr. Falcon. No, I was just leaving," Brandon answered lightly but then turned to Olivia. "See you in a little while."

Olivia nodded absently at Brandon but turned her attention to Noah. Her heart lurched in her chest when she noticed that he appeared rumpled and bone-tired, although he still managed to look sexy in low-slung faded jeans and a plain white V-neck shirt that stretched across his wide shoulders. "Are you okay, Noah?"

"Didn't get any sleep last night."

"Any sleep?" Olivia leaned back against the desk for support. She tried not to be concerned but failed. "Why?"

"Are you dating him, Olivia?"

His direct question took her by surprise. Olivia wasn't sure if she wanted to deny it or play it up. "No. I mean, we're having lunch, but—"

"He just kissed you."

"On the cheek and it was unexpected! Not that it's any of your concern."

"You're right." He placed a stack of papers on her desk and folded his arms across his chest. "I know that comment was my cue to leave, but unfortunately I've never been one to take a hint. Plus I have to ask, are you ever going to explain what I did that turned you against me?"

Olivia gripped the edge of the desk. She didn't want to get into this here and now.

"Oh, come on. I at least deserve to know what I did."

"You lied to me," she announced and raised her chin a notch.

"Lied to you?" A muscle jumped in his jaw. "I've been a lot of things in my life, but a liar isn't one of them."

"Well, misled by omission, then."

Noah angled his head. "What did I supposedly omit?"

"That you had a girlfriend."

"A girlfriend?" He reached up and stroked his chin. "Really, now?"

Olivia nodded, but suddenly she felt a bit less sure of her knowledge. "I . . . and I didn't mean to, but I picked up your phone thinking it was mine after we . . . we . . ."

"Made love?"

Olivia's eyes widened and she went over on shaky legs and closed the door.

"Wouldn't want *Mr. Turner* to know, now, would we?" Noah asked tightly.

Olivia leaned back against the desk once more. "Our conversation is nobody's business, Brandon included."

He shrugged. "Go on."

Olivia nervously licked her lips. "Like I said, I read the message by mistake. I would never snoop. Well, not for something like that," she amended with a barely there smile. It was the kind of thing that Noah usually laughed at, but when he remained stoic she knew she was in real trouble. She cleared her throat and went on. "But someone named Laney said that she was wrong to let you go and something about love not being the same without you," she explained in a rush and then nibbled on the inside of her lip while she looked at him expectantly.

Noah nodded slowly. "Laney was absolutely right."

"Oh." Olivia's stomach did some really weird things while she waited for him to go on, but he didn't. "Okay."

Finally he said, "Laney Gordon is a producer for *Love in the Afternoon*."

"Really . . ." Olivia felt a sense of elation, but then heat crept into her cheeks. "Oh, it makes sense now. I didn't know."

"All you had to do was ask. Instead, you assumed the worst."

Olivia closed her eyes and swallowed hard. "I'm sorry."

"Sorry? That's all you have to say for believing me to be a total jerk and giving me the cold shoulder all week?"

She opened her eyes and nodded slowly. The pain etched on his face went straight to her heart and it started thumping with a dull ache. "Truly sorry. I . . . I don't know what else to say," she added and it was true. How could she begin to apologize for accusing him of something so horrid?

"I don't know if there is anything you could say." Noah looked at her for a moment as if he were going to add something more, but then he glanced away. "Yeah, apparently ratings have dropped since my untimely demise and Vince, my agent, negotiated a sweet deal with them if I would come back to the show."

Olivia pointed to the papers he'd set down on her desk. "Is that what these are all about?"

Noah raked his fingers through his already tousled hair. "No, Olivia," he replied in a tired voice.

"Then what is it?" Her aching heart began to race.

"A friend of mine wants to invest in a baseball team. This is just the beginning stages, but if all goes well, and I think it will, I want to build a stadium here in Cricket Creek."

"If you build it they will come?" she asked in a small voice and was rewarded with a ghost of a smile. But when hope blossomed, his frown returned.

"Yeah, I hope so. Cricket Creek is a baseball town without a franchise anywhere near here. With the playhouse and the marina all in the quaint river setting, a baseball stadium and team could breathe life back into the economy. I could see a future with restaurants and shops along the riverbank drawing both locals and tourists. Of course, that kind of growth would depend on the success of the baseball venture, but it would be a solid beginning."

"And the condo complex is already built. Maybe it would finally sell out." Olivia felt a surge of excitement. "Are you thinking minor league?"

"No, not really." Noah shook his head. "Being here in this small town reminded me that so many good players get passed over. This league would be all about guys who never got a good look from scouts and minor-league players who got cut. Granted, only a select few will make the climb or get noticed, but it's an opportunity for a second chance." He paused. "That's something not too many people are lucky enough to get." He gave her a pointed look that she wasn't sure she understood.

"And that's what you're getting on *Love in the Afternoon*? A second chance?"

Noah scrubbed a hand down his face. "Olivia, I turned it down. So you really thought I would leave you and Madison high and dry? Disappoint everyone in the town where I grew up?" He pushed away from the desk. "Damn, do you even know me at all?"

"I—"

He raised a hand to stop her. "I knew you thought I might not stay here after the summer, and we were going to have to work through that. But, Olivia, your total lack of trust flat-out floors me. You thought I lied to you and you believed I would up and leave the play without a lead this close to opening night?"

"This is community theater, Noah, and we have an understudy. You were just handed what you came here to accomplish. I'm sure it's an offer that won't last long. How can you turn it down?"

He blew out a sigh and then took a step backward. "Wow." He laughed without humor. "Maybe because I care?"

"Oh, Noah . . ." She reached out to him, but he took another step away. She felt panic rise in her throat. She knew now that she had been so very wrong! She wanted to fix it, but she didn't know where to begin. "I'm sorry," she repeated, but it sounded lame even to her own ears.

Noah gave her a long look and then said, "You know, coming back here made me realize how much I miss baseball. You made me see that, Olivia. You were right. Baseball is a part of who I am and so is this town." He patted his chest. "You helped me remember the value in a lot of simple things that I had forgotten were so special. An ice-cream cone on a warm summer evening. A high school baseball game." He smiled slightly. "Butter cookies. Walking hand in hand with someone you care for. The list goes on and on."

Olivia pressed her trembling lips together in an effort not to cry.

After inhaling deeply, he said, "And you know what? I realized that my career was never about the money or even the fame." He paused as if gathering his thoughts and emotions. "I get a bigger kick out of the welcome sign to Cricket Creek than just about anything."

Olivia wanted to pull him into her arms, but she was terrified that he would push her away. "I understand more than you think. It was about the love of the game, not all the trimmings. Noah, Madison writes her plays because she has to express herself through her words or not feel complete. Jessica cooks with her hands, but it comes from her heart. I teach, but it's not just a job—it's a part of who I am. It is such a blessing to have that feeling. To have what you do be an extension of who you are, and yet not be confined or defined by it."

"It is," he agreed. Then he glanced around the classroom. "But lately my life has been focused on something very different," he began but then stopped.

"What, Noah?" she softly prompted.

"Happiness." He jammed his hands in his jeans pockets and looked down at the green-speckled tile floor.

"And did you find it?"

His eyes locked with hers. "For a brief and shining moment I sure thought so."

Her heart skipped a beat. "What changed?"

"You. You see, just like you just said, I thought you saw things in me that others didn't. Valued me for who I am and not what I do. The whole package," he admitted quietly. "Believed in me for something other than my batting average or television ratings and that I am more than baseball and beefcake. For the first time in my life I wasn't trying so damned hard to please everyone . . . my father, my coach, my agent, the fans." He sliced his hand through the air and then shook his head. "I was waking up each morning and simply feeling . . . happy."

"Noah, I do believe in you. Entirely."

"Really?" He looked over at her. "Olivia, you thought I lied to you." He put one hand up. "Okay, wait—no, *misled*. Sounds more polite that way, doesn't it? Then you thought I was going to skip out of town and head back to said girlfriend and continue on with my life pretty as you please." He tilted his head sideways. "How could I look at myself in the mirror?" He snapped his fingers. "Oh, right, to admire my reflection."

"I don't think that about you! I'm sorry. I guess I was just . . . just scared."

"Yes, I guess you were scared because when it came down to brass tacks you didn't trust me as far as you could throw me."

"Seeing the text message threw me for a loop. Noah, I guess I thought that this little town wouldn't be enough to hold you. That I wouldn't be enough." *I wasn't enough for my own mother, so how could I be enough for you?* screamed inside her head, but she couldn't bring herself to voice her worst fear: *I will love you and you will leave me.* Would she ever get past that? She'd thought she could, but one little text message and it all went flying out the window. Her fear way beyond jealousy. But how could she explain something that was so frightening and yet sounded so shallow when voiced?

"Because I'm an arrogant, unfeeling athlete and you're so far above that?"

Olivia gasped. "How could you say such a thing?"

He took a step closer this time, crowding her space,

making her want to kiss him and slap him at the same time. "About you or about me?"

"Both!" Anger such as she had never felt bubbled up inside of her. Or perhaps it was anger that was bottled up inside of her. White-hot and sizzling, it made her head feel as if her head would explode at any moment. When he took a step closer, she fisted her hands and stood her ground. "Neither of those things is true."

"Really? Your holier-than-thou attitude is pretty hard to swallow."

Olivia inhaled sharply and then sputtered, so livid that words would not even come out of her mouth. She wondered if he even knew how deeply his words cut. She'd always tried to be perfect, better than everyone else—otherwise perhaps her father would leave her too. Silly, she *knew*, but the fear was buried deep within her, and for Noah to have reached in and found her darkest fear made her want to kick and scream. Her heart pounded hard and her breath came in shallow gasps. She became light-headed and leaned back against the desk for support.

"You don't understand," she protested tightly.

"No, I sure don't!" he responded with just as much heat.

"Go to hell, Noah Falcon."

He laughed harshly but remained silent.

She closed her eyes and clenched her teeth. She had never said such a thing before and it was on the tip of her tongue to apologize, but she was so angry with him for making her feel like that lost little girl who stood by the window praying for her mother to return. She had never cried, just stood there dry-eyed and waiting. Hoping until all hope was lost. Loving meant risking losing. And she didn't know how to ever get past that feeling that haunted her still.

22

Let's Get the Party Started

*N*oah took one look at her pale downturned face and wanted to drag her into his arms and hold her close. Hurting her felt like a rubber band snapping at his heart, and he seriously wanted to kick his own ass. Causing her pain was the last thing he wanted to do, and he had promised himself that he wouldn't! Even though her lack of trust cut him to the core, he shouldn't have lashed out. "Olivia . . ."

When she looked up, another lock of hair fell over her forehead, loosened from the tight bun that had given up the fight a while ago. She brushed at her face with trembling fingers and swallowed hard. She looked so sweet and so vulnerable and when he noticed she was wearing only one flip-flop it was so Olivia that he nearly smiled. "Yes, Noah?"

Oh, to hell with it. "Listen, I need to tell you—" he began just as the door swung open. The *how I really feel about you* died on his lips when he saw who entered.

"Olivia, are you ready?" Brandon took a step into the room, appearing young and chipper, but his smile faltered when he looked from Olivia to Noah. "Oh, Mr. Falcon," he said politely, but he clearly wasn't pleased to

see Noah. "Um, is everything okay here?" he asked ten-
tatively. Noah supposed that he could feel the tension
hanging thickly in the room.

"Don't you believe in knocking?" Noah demanded.

"I don't normally knock when I enter classrooms,"
Brandon answered and then turned to Olivia. "But I do
apologize. Shall we?" he asked and waved a hand toward the door.

"Shall we"? Was he serious? Who says "Shall we"?
Noah nearly snickered. But then he thought that Olivia probably said "Shall we?" and he suddenly felt big
and clunky next to the natty high school principal. He
looked at Olivia and tried to get a bead on what she was
thinking.

"Unless I was interrupting something?" Brandon
flicked a got-you-back glance at Noah, who had a hard
time not scowling.

"N-no," Olivia stammered.

"We're going to discuss some important school matters," Brandon explained in what felt like a condescend-
ing tone. "Olivia had been hoping for a glee club next
year, and I think she just might get it." He smiled indul-
gently at Olivia and when Noah refused to budge, Brandon said, "Um, I think the baseball team is warming up
if you want to head on over there."

"Right," Noah commented and brushed his hands
against his thighs. He was tempted to remind Brandon
that he was starring in a play with Olivia, so he wasn't as
much as a caveman as Brandon was trying to make him
out to be, but he didn't want to go that route. "Sometimes I'm not so good at taking a hint," he commented
and gave Olivia a pointed look. He hoped she might
tell Brandon to take a flying leap, but she just stood
there looking confused. Then he remembered that this
was her boss. He didn't want to put her in any kind of
predicament, and he seriously needed to leave before

he punched Brandon Turner in the mouth. "I believe I *shall*." He gave them a brief salute and then concentrated hard on not stomping out of the room like an angry child.

Noah's cowboy boots clicked down the hallway, and he gave the double doors a hard shove. Once outside, he blinked in the bright sunshine and slipped on his silver aviators. But instead of leaving, he braced one bent leg against the concrete and leaned his shoulders against the rough brick. The heat of the sun-warmed building seeped through his cotton shirt, but he barely noticed.

"Dear God!" Noah shook his head and gazed up at the clear blue sky dotted with puffy clouds, and then it hit him. He was totally hurt and thoroughly pissed, and oddly enough, this confirmed that he loved Livie Lawson beyond all reason. Why else would he feel this way? And her silly ass might be scared to believe in him for reasons he couldn't fathom, but he'd be damned if he was going to give up. He hadn't been kidding when he had told her he wasn't a liar, but there was something else he sure wasn't either—and that was a quitter.

Noah sighed. He was a complete novice at having to prove himself to a woman, but he knew just who to turn to for assistance. He pushed away from the wall and reached into his pocket for his phone, then grinned when he spotted a yellow flip-flop lying in the green grass. He looked up and saw that the window to her classroom was open; it must have flipped out the window and flopped into the grass. He shook his head, thinking that only Olivia could have managed to do that. He walked over and picked it up. "I even have a prop," he murmured. "Madison is going to love this."

Noah tossed the flip-flop into his Corvette and slid in behind the wheel. He shoved the car into gear and headed over to Myra's Diner, hoping to catch Madison there. He could have called to find out, but he thought he'd grab a bite to eat there regardless. It had nothing to do with Olivia possibly being there with Brandon Turner. Okay, perhaps it had a little bit to do with that, Noah admitted to himself—and then grinned. *Or maybe a lot.*

Even though he was still angry with Olivia, he wasn't prepared not to forgive her for her mistake. After all, it made more sense to be happy than to be right. And he certainly knew the irrational feeling of being jealous. He sure hadn't felt passionate enough to want to punch a man over a woman until now.

He was prepared to pull out all of the stops and knock her socks—okay, make that her flip-flops—off. "Oh, yeah . . ." An excellent plan was forming in his head. All he needed was a little help from his friends and he could hopefully pull it off. When he was finished wooing Livie Lawson, there would be no doubt in her mind that he loved her and wasn't going to leave Cricket Creek. Well, he hoped, anyway. One thing she sure had accomplished was taking him down a notch or two—and perhaps that was a good thing. "Get over your damned self, Noah Falcon." While waiting at the stoplight, he shook his head. Maybe it was the schoolteacher in her, but the woman certainly knew how to make a person work for it.

Noah snagged a spot across from the diner and headed inside. The lunch rush was beginning to thin down, and he was glad to see Madison and Jessica behind the front counter. He glanced around discreetly and was actually relieved that Olivia and the pesky Brandon, who seriously needed to be punched, were nowhere to be found.

"Hey, Noah," Madison said and hurried over to where he sat down. She waved her hand beneath his nose. "Isn't it gorgeous?"

"If you'd stop waving it around, I'd be able to see it," he said, drawing a chuckle from Jessica. Noah grabbed Madison's hand and gazed at the diamond solitaire. The diamond wasn't huge, but he could tell that the quality was excellent, and the simplicity of it suited her. "It's beautiful," Noah commented and was surprised at the emotion he felt. He stood up and came around the counter and pulled her in for a big hug. "Sweetie, I am so happy for you," he said gruffly. "Don't know about Jason, though," he joked and was rewarded with a hard shove. But when he looked down at her, he saw that she was swiping at the corner of her eyes. He turned to Jessica and opened his arms for another hug, and then she was swiping at her eyes too. It occurred to him that Jessica had never gotten to experience this joy when she found out she was pregnant. "Congratulations to you too, Mama."

Jessica sniffed hard. "Yeah, the years have flown by, haven't they? Seems like just yesterday..." she began and then put a hand over her mouth and blinked. "Ah ... I'm getting soft in my old age." She shook her head and then laughed.

"Old?" Noah tilted his head. "Well, I know someone who thinks you're hot."

"Who?" Jessica asked with a frown.

"Ty McKenna."

Jessica's eyes widened and she exchanged a glance with Madison. "The baseball player?"

"Triple Threat himself." Noah walked back around the counter and sat down. "Yeah, we played some minor-league ball together. But, anyway, I was talking to him on the phone and he mentioned, and I quote, that Chicago Blue, his favorite restaurant, wasn't the same since the hot little chef left."

"Way to go, Mom!" Madison said, but Jessica rolled her eyes.

"There's not a bigger player on the planet, and I don't mean baseball. He was with a different woman every time he walked into Chicago Blue Bistro."

"Oh, so you noticed," Madison commented with a sly smile.

Jessica's cheeks took on some color, but she shrugged. "The man always made an entrance. It was hard not to notice him."

Noah took a swig of the tea that Madison placed in front of him. "I'm just sayin' . . ."

"Whatever," Jessica muttered and reached for a menu to hand to him.

"Ty will be coming in for the play," Noah added and watched for her reaction.

"Really?" Jessica asked breezily. "That's nice of him."

"Said he wouldn't miss it. By the way, he couldn't believe that you lived here. You must have made quite an impression on him."

"Maybe it's your turn for some romance, Mom. Hey, if Aunt Myra can hook up with Owen Lawson, anything can happen. They're fishing together right now. Isn't that so cute?" She looked at Noah. "And who would have thought I'd be engaged to Jason? Not many people would have taken that bet." She angled her head at her mother. "You just never know when love is going to jump up and getcha."

"I think you mean bite you." Jessica refilled Noah's iced tea glass from a big metal pitcher.

"Mom!" Madison protested.

"Oh, not you and Jason!"

"Of course not!" Madison said and then turned back to Noah. "What's this about Mom making an impression on Ty McKenna? Really?"

"More like my food made an impression on Mr. Triple Threat. Believe me, I'm not Ty McKenna's type. As I recall, he went for big boobs and long legs. I am lacking in both categories. Know what you want?" she asked, and Noah wondered why she wanted to change the subject so quickly.

He didn't even have to look at the menu. "Chicken-fried steak, mashed potatoes, and green beans."

Madison shook her head. "How on God's green earth do you eat that stuff and not get huge?" She circled her arms out to her sides.

"I've eaten my way through Cricket Creek—that's for sure." He patted his stomach. "It helps that I've been working out with the baseball team. It sucks that the high school season is almost over, but I told them I'd like to help out with the summer camp."

Jessica and Madison both stopped in their tracks, and Madison leaned in close so that onlookers couldn't hear. "So, are you thinking of moving here, Noah?"

"If I can get a certain pesky little schoolteacher to come to her senses and quit doubting me," he answered darkly.

Madison put her hands on the counter and leaned even closer. "I see a plan in those eyes of yours. Are you going to let me in on it?"

"Absolutely. And I'm going to need your help to pull it off. Are you in?"

"Of course!" Madison gave him an excited little jerky nod. She turned to Jessica. "Mom, are you going to help too?"

"Nope." Jessica gave them a negative shake of her head and busied herself wiping down the counter. "I don't mess in other people's business, unlike you and Olivia."

"Where's the fun in that?" Madison wrinkled her nose at her mother and then turned her attention back to Noah. "Okay, spill."

Noah explained his plan of action to Madison, and although Jessica was straightening things up, he knew she was listening with one ear. When he was finished he asked, "Well, do you think I can pull this off?"

Madison tapped his chest and shook her head no.

"You can't. But we can. And stop pretending you weren't listening, Mom. You are totally helping out and Aunt Myra too. Oh, and Mabel. And Chrissie and her posse. The whole damned town if we need them! The trick is going to be keeping Olivia in the dark."

"And here's the important question." Noah inhaled a deep breath. "Do you think it will finally win her over?"

Madison grinned. "It will be a grand . . . What do you call it . . . ? Hammer?"

"Grand slam," Jessica corrected, drawing their attention. "All right already. I'm in! The two of you will need all the help you can get." She pulled out a notepad. "Now let's get started."

23

No Doubt

*M*adison opened the door to her condo and after tossing her keys and purse onto the table she headed straight to the fridge for a cold bottle of water. She was halfway through gulping it down when strong arms encircled her waist from behind and warm lips nuzzled her neck. With a groan she absently set the bottle on the counter and tilted her head to the side. "Mmm, you smell like coconut," she said with a low chuckle.

"That's the downside of showering at your girlfriend's place."

Madison lifted her left hand in the air and wiggled her ring finger. "Fiancée," she reminded him.

"I stand corrected," he said and eased his hands beneath her pink peasant blouse.

"That's better." Madison leaned back against his damp bare chest and reached up to run her fingers through his wet hair. "And is there an upside?" she asked breathlessly. Her knees nearly buckled when he slid his callused hands up her smooth skin and then cupped her breasts. He rubbed his thumbs over the satin demibra, and her nipples instantly reacted.

"Oh, no doubt." Jason pressed intimately against her.

"There's your upside, babe," he said and then turned her around to face him. While looking into her eyes he guided her hand down to his erection, poking against the towel slung low around his waist.

"Mmmm . . . I like it." Madison parted the soft terry cloth. She slipped her hand in and found him aroused and ready.

Jason sucked in a breath. "Damn . . . girl," he said and when she circled the tip of her finger over his smooth head he gasped and grabbed the edge of the counter. A silky drop of moisture appeared and he groaned. "Ahhh, Maddie." His hazel eyes dilated, making the golden flecks stand out. With his hair slicked back, his prominent cheekbones and full mouth created such stark masculine beauty that Madison sighed. The dark blond stubble shadowing his chin gave him a dangerous bad-boy edge that had her all but melting.

"How does that feel?" she asked with a slight smile.

"Amazing."

She tugged the towel off, grasped his steely-hard shaft, and began to stroke him lightly. "And this?"

"More amazing. God . . ." His muscles tensed, showing off his ripcord strength that came from hard physical labor.

"I love touching you," she said as she slid her palms over the sculpted contours of his chest. "Tasting you." She pressed her mouth against his shoulder and began a trail of kisses up his neck, letting her tongue dart out and swirl over his skin. She licked the rough stubble on his jawbone and then ran her tongue across his warm, soft bottom lip before sliding it into his mouth.

Madison moaned when Jason threaded his fingers into her mass of curls and kissed her back with silky heat that made her toes curl. He tasted like mint and man, and she suddenly needed to have her bare skin next to his.

"I want you naked," he said in her ear before sucking her earlobe into his mouth and causing a slow tingle to travel down her spine.

"You were reading my mind," she replied and then took a step back. He watched her slowly untie the bow at the top of her blouse and then unbutton the tiny pearls one by one. She shrugged her shoulders slightly so that the soft pink cotton slithered down her arms and pooled onto the white tile floor. After popping open the snap on her jean skirt, she tugged the zipper down inch by inch and then let the skirt join her blouse on the floor, leaving her standing before him in her barely there nude bra and matching lace thong.

Jason sucked in a breath. Madison knew she was pretty in a cute, petite way, but the desire in his eyes made her feel absolutely gorgeous. She watched him while she reached around her back and unhooked her bra. Her breasts weren't big, but they were high and firm, with dusky pink nipples that were taut and begging for his warm mouth, soft tongue. But when she reached down to take off her panties Jason shook his head.

"No, let me." His husky plea felt like a physical caress and Madison could only nod. "Baby, turn around and lean up against the counter," he said and then changed positions while nuzzling her neck. Again she could only nod but did as he asked. When he slipped one finger beneath the top of her thong, her breath caught and she had to grip the edge of the counter for support. He oh, so slowly moved his finger back and forth, lightly grazing the top of her mound. Her stomach quivered and heat pooled between her thighs. And when he dipped his head and swirled his wet tongue over one nipple, her grip on the counter tightened.

He teased with his tongue and his finger, applying just enough pressure to have her begging for more.

Madison's eyes fluttered shut and she thrust her chest upward as an invitation for more and more . . .

"Oh!" she gasped when he suddenly dropped to his knees and then slid her thong down to her ankles. He kissed his way up her calf, her thigh. She could feel his warm breath getting closer and closer to where she wanted him and when he cupped her ass and buried his head between her thighs she instinctively spread her legs. When his warm tongue licked her sensitive spot she threaded her fingers through his damp, shaggy hair and urged him on.

"God!" Achingly sweet pleasure spread through her veins like thick, warm honey, and when she tried to pull his head back he was relentless until she arched against his mouth and cried out his name. When she collapsed against him, he picked her up and while she was still reeling with heart-pounding aftershocks he eased her up onto the edge of the counter.

"Baby, wrap your legs around me."

"Mmm," was all she could muster as she hooked her ankles at the small of his back. "That was amazing," she murmured with her head resting against his shoulder.

"We've just begun," he said and then tilted her head up.

"Making love?"

"No . . . our life together," he said and then captured her mouth in a searing kiss.

Madison clung to him, savoring the taste of her body on his mouth, the silky sensation of his skin rubbing against hers, and the scent of coconut mixed with musk. He had a hard body and a soft heart, small-town values and big-city dreams. He was kick-ass crazy with a Southern voice, but most of all . . . he was hers.

Madison pulled his head back hard and placed her hands on either side of his cheeks. She looked into those beautiful eyes flecked with gold and said, "Jason Craig, I love you."

"Ah, Maddie, I love you too. I couldn't get you out of my mind from the moment you scowled at me and said that the color of the trim I was painting looked like pigeon poop."

She giggled and then rolled her eyes. "I am such a little shit."

"You're my little shit, and I wouldn't have it any other way," he said, drawing a chuckle from her.

"Your romantic sentiments steal my breath," she teased, but then he truly took her breath away when he entered her with one sure stroke.

"God, you feel good." He made love to her slow and easy at first, bringing her back to full arousal before white-hot passion took over. She clung to his wide shoulders and matched his rhythm, giving her heart and her body to him fully without holding anything back. He was so strong and yet managed to be tender at the same time, making her climax with a sweet explosion that rocked her to the very core of her being.

Madison kissed him deeply while the words of her play rang out in her head . . . *If you could choose just one thing to have in this life, love would win every single time.*

She had no doubt.

Later, after feasting on Papa Vito's pizza, they headed to her bedroom to relax. "Aren't you going to put on some sexy little nightie?" Jason asked with a bit of a pout.

"I like wearing your T-shirt. It smells like you."

"But I'm right here," he reminded her as he turned back the frilly comforter. He wore gray boxer briefs but shimmied out of them before slipping beneath the covers.

"I like the intimacy of your shirt." Madison grabbed a book from the pile on her nightstand and handed him the remote.

"And I like silky little frilly things."

She opened the book and gave him a glance. "Well, get over it," she said with a lift of her chin, but she was fighting back a smile.

He pointed the remote at the television and turned it on. "Are you always going to be this hard to live with?"

She lifted one shoulder and concentrated on her book. "Maybe."

"You do know that the book is turned upside down."

"I can totally read upside down."

"Sure you can."

Madison looked up at the television and said, "And you do know that you turned on the Disney Channel."

"What, don't you like Hannah Montana?" He laughed. She tossed the book to the floor and he clicked the television off and they rolled into each other's arms.

Jason slid a hand up her leg and under the hem of the T-shirt. "Oh, no panties."

Madison laughed and slid her hand up his thigh and wrapped her hand around his erection. "Um, well, now, are *you* always going to be this hard to live with?"

"You'd better believe it," he said and then pulled her on top to straddle him.

"I believe it." Madison moved suggestively against him. "As my aunt Myra would say, a hard man is good to find." Then she held his face in her hands and gazed at him with serious eyes. "I've been writing about love for a long time, but you've made me a true believer, Jason." He swallowed hard and the emotion shining in his eyes touched her heart. Without speaking, she came up to her knees and then slowly sank down onto his erection. She sat there very still simply loving the feeling of him buried deep and connected intimately. "I've been searching and I've finally found my place in this world."

"In Cricket Creek, Kentucky?"

"With you . . ."

"I'll move to the city, you know. Whatever makes you happy, Maddie."

She smiled and then leaned in to kiss him tenderly. "Thank you, but I have to admit that I love it here. Noah has big plans for this town, and I want to be a part of the development."

"Speaking of Noah, are he and Olivia on good terms?"

Madison threaded her fingers together as if in prayer. "Not exactly, but he and I are working on it." She pressed her lips together and said, "We have a plan."

"Do I want to know about it?"

Madison angled her head. "Well, let's just say it's going to take a village . . ." she admitted with a small smile. "You in?"

"Do I have a choice?"

"Mmmm, no."

"Then I guess I'm in."

"That's my boy," she said and then started moving slowly against him. "I'll give you the details, but first things first . . ."

24

Love on the Rocks

$\mathcal{I}$t happened again. As soon as Olivia entered Grammar's Bakery for a much-needed chocolate brownie fix, everyone stopped talking and then tried to cover it up by doing something busy. Mabel almost pulled it off by wiping down the counter, but Chrissie's attempt to rearrange cupcakes so that white icing and chocolate were in separate rows was a dead giveaway. They had been talking about her. She could just feel it. The same thing had been happening all over town.

"You missed one." Olivia pointed to a chocolate-topped cupcake sitting side by side with a vanilla-iced one.

"Well, look at that. You're right." She reached inside the shelf and fixed the situation. "I know it's an OBC kinda thing," Chrissie explained with a wave of her hand.

"Right," Olivia said and almost rolled her eyes. This was coming from a girl whose locker had been a disaster. "Your French manicure looks great. Do the purple tips match your prom dress?"

"P-prom?"

Olivia frowned. "Um, yes, you know, that big dance in the gym tomorrow night?"

Chrissie gave her a nervous chuckle and put the heel of her hand to her forehead. "Oh, the prom . . ." She shrugged. "I guess my mind was on the cupcakes. You're still chaperoning, right?"

Olivia inhaled a deep breath. "I don't know. I might ask Madison to do it for me. Rehearsals have worn me out this week." Yeah, her acting skills were being put to the test each night. First, she had to pretend that being with Noah and having to play his love interest onstage didn't bother her. She still felt terrible that she had misjudged him, but she didn't know how to makes things right. "I don't know if I'm up to it." She had been so excited when Noah had asked her to go, but now everything had changed.

Olivia sighed as she gazed into the nearly empty glass cases. She really needed chocolate! While Noah hadn't been flat-out unfriendly, he had seemed preoccupied all week, and she had heard that he had flown out of town several times, making it back just in time for rehearsal. In fact, yesterday he had rushed out of the community center as if the hounds of hell were nipping at his heels, and they'd had to cancel rehearsal today when he failed to make it back to town. Not that it mattered. They knew the script backward and forward. But still . . . she wondered if it had something to do with going back to the soap opera. Did he change his mind? Not that she could blame him. He had every right to be angry with her, but she hated that Cricket Creek might suffer the loss at her hands. The thought made her stomach hurt, but she didn't have the courage to go to him. Rejection wasn't something she could handle right now. But she would eventually have to confront him, for the sake of Cricket Creek.

"Miss Lawson, the prom wouldn't be the same without you," Chrissie protested, bringing Olivia back to the present. She looked at Mabel for help. "Don't you think so, Miss Mabel?"

Mabel nodded so hard that all of her chins shook. "Olivia, I made an extra-special sheet cake this year and little pastel petit fours that are to die for. Sugar, you know you'll be sorry if you don't go."

"Oh, seriously, I don't think I would be missed, and I know Madison would get a kick out of going with Jason."

Chrissie shook her head and stomped her foot for good measure. "But it's my senior year and I want you there."

Olivia shrugged. "We'll see. Do you have any brownies left? I'm in serious need of some chocolate in the form of one of your soft, fudgy brownies."

"Oh, sweetie, we're out," Mabel informed her. "I wish I had known—I would have saved you one."

"That's okay. I know you're about ready to close," Olivia said glumly. "Maybe Myra made some over at the diner. I'll head over there. See y'all later." She turned to go with a small wave and a forced smile. Just as she reached the front door, Adam and his father came into the bakery. Little Adam's baseball cap was tilted slightly to the side and he was holding his father's hand. For some reason seeing them together made Olivia imagine Noah holding the hand of his child . . . their child.

"Hey, remember us? Dan Forman and my son, Adam?"

Adam tugged on his father's hand and looked up at him. "Is this the lady we hit with the baseball?"

Dan nodded at Adam and then gave her a sheepish look. "Hey, tell Noah it was great of him to show up at Adam's game. We thought you might be with him." He raised his eyebrows in question.

Olivia felt heat creep into her cheeks. "Oh, Noah led you to believe that we were married, but he was just teasing. We're starring in the play together, but we're just ... friends." She felt Chrissie's and Mabel's eyes upon her but was too embarrassed to turn around.

Dan tilted his head. "Wow, you could have fooled me." He grinned. "Well, you *did* fool me. You two make a cute couple. He was so worried about you, and you dived to save him from getting hit."

"You did?" Mabel asked with wide eyes. "Oh, I would have loved to have seen that."

"Oh, Miss Lawson, that's so romantic!" Chrissie gushed, and Olivia finally turned around.

"It was merely instinct," she explained, hoping her face wasn't beet red. Then she turned back to Adam and Dan. "Well, it was nice to see you guys." She patted Adam on the head. "Good luck with your baseball."

"Thank you very much!" Adam said with a big grin. "Noah is gonna help teach me to pitch! Will you come with him to watch?"

Olivia forced another smile. "I'll try," she promised. Then with one last wave she hurried out the door.

Once she was outside she inhaled a shaky breath, and although she headed toward Myra's Diner, when she arrived at the doorstep she paused and then decided to keep on walking and go home. She wasn't in the mood for small talk. Perhaps she had a hidden stash of chocolate somewhere in her house. One could only hope.

As she headed down Oak Street, a sense of hometown pride washed over her. Although hard times had befallen Cricket Creek, lush green lawns were meticulously manicured, with an abundance of blooming flowers adding both color and the sweet scent of summer. Stately trees reached toward the sky, and you'd be hard-pressed to find so much as a cigarette butt littering the sidewalk. The aroma of charcoal grills and the sounds of music and laughter filtered toward Olivia, and she smiled in spite of her sad mood. Neighbors both young and old paused and waved as she strolled by, but she merely wiggled her fingers in return and kept on walking, though it was normally in her nature to stop and chat.

But not tonight.

Tonight she wanted a piece of dark chocolate, some bourbon on the rocks, and then she just might indulge in a rare good old-fashioned cry. But when she got to her house she was surprised to see her father sitting on her front stoop. "Dad!" she called and willed her emotions to stay in check. "What brings you here?" she asked with a smile that she barely managed to keep from trembling at the corners.

"Just wanted to come over and see my lovely daughter." Owen stood up and gave her a hug. "I would have let myself in, but the spare key beneath the rock over there was missing."

"Oh," Olivia said with a nod. "Sorry." She didn't want to tell him that she had given the key to Noah, and hoped that he didn't guess. "I'll have to put it back." She had begun locking her door at Noah's insistence.

He stooped and picked up a bag. "Brought you some brownies from the diner. Myra sent them to you," he said and then blushed just a bit.

Olivia accepted the bag from him. "Oh, you were reading my mind!"

Owen smiled before leaning down to kiss her on the forehead. "I can still do that once in a while."

"Thank you so much!" Olivia felt emotion clog her throat. In his quiet way her father always knew how to cheer her up. There'd been countless times when he brought her home a treat or called just when she needed it most. "I stopped at the bakery, but Mabel was out of just about everything." She walked past him and opened the door. "Come on in."

"Feels good in here," Owen said as he followed her into the kitchen. "It's gettin' kinda sticky outside."

Olivia nodded. "I think we might get some much-needed rain tonight, but at least it's supposed to be nice for the prom tomorrow." She set her purse on the kitchen table and then reached into the cabinet for a glass. "Want something to drink?"

"Whatcha got?"

Olivia pulled a bottle of Buffalo Trace bourbon out of the bottom cabinet. "Want a little nip?"

Owen arched one eyebrow. "Oh, why not?" he said with a grin.

Olivia nodded and reached for another glass. "Coming right up." Neither of them was a big drinker, but Olivia was in a restless mood and dearly wanted to relax. She pushed the crushed-ice button on her fridge door and filled both glasses, then added a generous shot of bourbon followed by a splash of water. She handed her father his drink and joined him at the table.

For a moment they sipped in silence. Olivia could feel that something was on his mind, but instead of pushing she gave him the time to put his thoughts together. He took another sip and then ran his fingertip over the edge of his glass before looking across the table at her.

"I'm sorry, Olivia."

"Whatever for?" she asked softly. She hoped he wasn't feeling any guilt over his blossoming relationship with Myra.

"For not bringing more joy into your life."

Olivia put her hand over his. "Dad . . . it's not your fault that she deserted us." Olivia refused to use the word "mother."

He had to clear his throat before continuing. "Nor is it yours, and I was remiss for not making damned sure that you knew that."

"Oh, Dad . . ." She squeezed his hand. "We did the best we could. And it was pretty damned good."

"'Damned'?" He chuckled softly, but then brushed

a tear away. "You're cussin' and I'm cryin'. What's up with that?"

"Maybe we're finally learning to deal with our emotions . . . or at least to let them show. But, Dad, I was serious. You did a good job."

"Ahh, sweetie. Always the perfect little girl." He sniffed hard and then rubbed his eyes with the heels of his hands. "Ahh, Olivia, I never told you, but your mother was pregnant with you when we got married. I insisted that we marry." He shook his head. "I was terrified that she would give you up for adoption if we didn't tie the knot and I couldn't live with that. But I was wrong for trying to force her into living a life she never wanted and wasn't cut out for."

"Dad, you sent her off and paid for her dream to come true! She was wrong to desert us! To . . . to cheat on you!"

Owen nodded. "That she was, and someday she will have to answer to a higher power for her actions. But, Livie, she would have been miserable in the long run. I understand that now."

"You do? Why?"

"I know now how it feels to truly be in love." He chuckled. "Myra makes me laugh. Lights up my life."

Olivia felt elation at his admission. "Oh, Dad, I am so happy for you! Myra too. She is a gem."

"She is somethin' else, that one. I'm enjoying life in a way I had never been able to do . . . or maybe allow myself to do." He patted his chest. "Livie, I've become a new man."

Olivia smiled. It was the first time he had called her that in a long time. "You are both hardworking, good people. You deserve happiness and so does she."

He angled his head and swallowed hard once more. "It has made me finally forgive your mother." He paused and added, "I dearly hope you can do the same."

She pulled her hand back and took a sip of her drink. The cold bourbon chilled and burned at the same time. "You're asking too much of me."

"Forgiving her will open your heart, Olivia. Set you free to live and love without fear."

Olivia put her hand to her mouth while hot tears slid down her cheeks. "Oh, Dad, I think it might be too late."

"No"—Owen shook his head and brushed tears from her cheeks—"Livie, honey, it's never too late. I don't know what happened between you and Noah, but you surely glowed when you were with him."

"I love him, Dad. I really do. But I don't know how to fix what I did." She let out a sob. "I hurt him terribly. I accused him of being a liar and a cheat!"

"Did you apologize for what you did?"

"Of course! But I don't know if it could ever be enough. Trust is the foundation for any relationship. I failed to believe in him—the one thing he truly wanted."

"Livie, does he know why?"

She shook her head slowly.

"Then tell him."

"Oh, Dad, he's been going out of town. I think he's moving back to New York!"

"Let me ask you something. Would you go with him if he asked you?"

"Leave Cricket Creek?" Her eyes rounded. "Leave you?"

"Olivia, I can drive a car. Fly on an airplane. In fact, Myra and I are thinking of doing some traveling. Jessica is pretty much going to take over the renovated diner, and except for snowplowin' and a bit of wood choppin' my business is slow in the winter. We've been discussing wintering somewhere south."

"Really?"

He smiled. "You and I have been lying low for a long

time. It's time for us to soar. If you love Noah, go with him."

"But I love it here."

Owen smiled. "Girlie, Myra and I sat in on your play rehearsal the other night."

"You did?"

He nodded. "In the back where you couldn't see us. The two of you are magic together even during this rough patch that you've hit."

Olivia smiled through the tears.

"Have you forgotten the meaning behind Madison's story?" He patted her hand. "If you could choose *just one thing*?"

Olivia pressed her lips together and said softly, "Love would win every single time."

"Livie, we had a rough row to hoe, but don't let love slip through your fingers."

"I might have already done that," she said sadly.

"I don't think so . . ." He gave her a long look and then nibbled on the inside of his cheek.

Olivia's heart kicked it up a notch and she narrowed her eyes at her father. "I keep getting the impression that something's afoot and I'm the only one in this town who isn't in on it. Am I right?"

Owen took a sip of his drink but avoided her direct gaze.

"Dad?"

Owen inhaled a deep breath and then raised his gaze to look at her. "Oh, boy . . ."

Olivia leaned back in her chair. "So I am right. I knew it! Are you going to tell me what's going on?"

"Sweetie, I can't do that."

"Did you promise not to?"

"No, but—"

"Then tell me!"

He closed his eyes and swallowed.

"You know I'm not good with surprises. I'm a need-to-be-prepared kinda girl." She gazed at him imploringly.

Owen shook his head slowly. "No can do."

She covered his hand with hers and shook it back and forth. "I won't let on that you spilled the beans."

"Okay, I will tell you two things." He held up his index and middle fingers.

Olivia nodded eagerly.

"That boy loves you beyond reason." A slow grin spread across his face as if he was thinking about whatever was going down. "So does this whole damned town, for that matter."

"Oh . . . Dad." She felt tears spring into her eyes once more.

"Promise me this. Whatever you're asked to do tomorrow? Just do it. No matter how silly it seems."

"Daaaa-d!" Olivia put both palms on the table and leaned forward. "That's *all* you are going to tell me? Seriously?" she pleaded.

"Sweetie, it's called setting your fears aside and trusting. Something you and I have been lacking in for a long time. Well, no more." He held up his glass and with a nod coaxed her to do the same. He clicked his glass with hers. "To trusting our gut . . . our heart." He drained his glass and then scooted his chair back. "I'd better get goin'."

Olivia pushed her own chair back and stood up with him. "I'm not going to squeeze any more information out of you, am I?"

"Nope." He kissed her on top of her head. "But I suggest you get yourself a good night's sleep." He reached down and took both of her hands in his.

"Right." She rolled her eyes. "Now just how am I going to do that?"

Owen chuckled and then tilted his head toward the

bottle of bourbon. "One more little hit of that should do ya just right."

Olivia sighed, then nodded. "Okay, Dad. Dang, you're a tough nut to crack." She walked him to the door, and when he'd gone, she took his suggestion, adding some ice and topping off her drink. After getting ready for bed, she propped herself up against the pillows and nursed her bourbon. She racked her brain for what could possibly be going on but came up with a big goose egg. She considered calling Madison, but she didn't want anyone to know that her father had alerted her to whatever surprise was in store for her. "I guess I'll just have to wait and find out," she whispered as she leaned over and turned off the light.

Olivia snuggled into the feather pillow thinking that sleep would evade her, but the soft cotton felt heavenly and the bourbon had her relaxed. Or maybe it was her father's insistence that Noah loved her that eased some of her earlier tension. But whatever the reason, she felt more at peace and more hopeful that she had felt in days, and after a few moments she drifted off into slumberland ... Mmmm, make that Noah-land. His face drifted into her dreams and she sighed.

25

Oh, What a Night!

"*N*oah, for heaven's sake, would you just chill?" Madison fisted her hands on her hips and shook her head at him. "Don't ask me how we pulled it off, but everything is falling into place nicely."

"What if—"

"Stop saying that!" Madison cut him off by stomping her foot. "This is fun. We have every detail covered. Now you can stop worrying and enjoy it." She waved her hand in an arc around the gym. "Just look! It's simply perfect!"

"Yeah, it is." When Noah followed her hand he just had to smile. "But—"

"No-ah!" Madison quelled him with a pointed look, but then gave him a reassuring smile. "Look, I just got a text message from Chrissie. She and her friends have the vintage dress that Mom and Aunt Myra found last week. They're going to tell Olivia that they bought it just for her and guilt her into wearing it. It is so nineteen nineties sparkle with a slit up the side, but Olivia won't be able to refuse her students. Chrissie is prepared to cry."

"What if it doesn't fit?"

"Mom is an expert shopper. It will fit."

Noah shoved his fingers through his hair. "I'm trying to maintain my composure, but I don't think I'll be this damned nervous on opening night."

"Noah." Madison raised her hands and put them on his shoulders. She had to look up to make eye contact. "Olivia isn't going to turn you away from her doorstep. She's the one who screwed up here, remember? You're just knocking some sense into the girl."

"True. I've never worked so hard for a woman in my life."

"Then it must be love."

He felt a swift kick of emotion. "It is. Damn, why am I so afraid?"

Madison tilted her head at him. "Because nothing makes us feel more vulnerable than love. But she's going to be blown away when she sees the effort you've gone through to re-create the prom night that she never had. Of course, *this* is going to be better, since you're spending piles of money on decorations and food." Madison put her hand to her mouth. "I get choked up just thinking about it!" She took a deep breath and said, "Okay, I gave the deejay the playlist and it's chock-full of nineties music. Chrissie and her friends even know how to do the Macarena. Isn't that cool?"

"No, the Macarena is stupid."

She laughed. "Hey, babe, it's your era, not mine."

"We gave you *The Simpsons* and *South Park*. Reality TV."

"Thank you so much!" she said with a roll of her eyes.

"Oh, and hmm, let me see ... cell phones." He snapped his fingers. "Oh, and a little thing called the Internet."

"Invented by Al Gore, right?"

Noah laughed and began to feel a little bit more relaxed.

"Look, we have posters up everywhere of everything popular in the nineties, like Madonna, the Backstreet

Boys, and *NSYNC. Oh, and the Teenage Mutant Ninja Turtles."

"Cowabunga, dude."

"What?"

Noah grinned. "Nothing."

"The nineties slide show that the drama club put together is great." She arched an eyebrow. "And there's one big surprise that you don't even know about."

"I don't like surprises."

Madison lifted one shoulder. "Too bad," she said, and they both turned when Mabel came into the gym pushing a cart laden with a huge cake and other goodies. Madison looked at the script and clapped her hands. "'Prom Night Nineteen Ninety-six!' I love it."

"Thanks!" Mabel said but then shook her head at Noah. "What are you still doing here? You need to go get gussied up, young man."

"Don't forget the corsage," Madison reminded him and then looked to where a disco ball was being installed in the middle of the ceiling. "Oh, this is so much fun!"

A moment later Jessica hurried into the building. "I just passed the caterer and the florist on the way in. This gym is about to be transformed. I'm going to stick around to oversee things so you two can go and get ready."

"Mom, I want you to come tonight, too."

She flipped her hair over her shoulder. "I will. I'm going to take tons of pictures."

"No, I mean, wear the amazing dress you bought with Aunt Myra and have some fun."

Her eyes widened slightly. "No . . . thanks. I'm not a prom kind of girl," she added, and it suddenly occurred to Noah that at sixteen and pregnant . . . Wow, she never made it to prom night either. Damn . . .

"Mom, Aunt Myra and Owen are coming, for goodness' sakes. This isn't going to be your run-of-the-mill prom night. Plus, you love to dance and you never get the chance."

"Madison, I don't have a date," she protested. "Not that I want one," she added firmly.

Noah looked down at the cell phone that was vibrating in his hand and grinned when he saw who was calling. He flicked a glance at Jessica. "Hey, I think I might have you covered."

Jessica's eyes widened for real this time. "What?" she sputtered, but Noah shushed her by holding up his index finger.

"What's up, Ty? You in town yet? Just got here? Great! Hey, listen, you want to go to the Cricket Creek High School prom tonight? No, I'm not kidding, and yes, I have a date for you. No, you perve, she's legal. Yeah, she's a chaperone."

Jessica shook her head violently and mouthed, "No!"

"No, not a seventy-year-old. Would I do that to you? Okay, I would, but, no, she is gorgeous." He decided not to let on that Jessica was the former chef at Chicago Blue Bistro, so he avoided telling him her name.

"Noah!" Jessica verbalized and tried to jump up and grab his phone without success.

"Hey, Ty, I'll explain the situation. See ya at my place in a few. You have directions, right? Cool. Yeah, we'll hook you up with a tux when I get mine."

When Noah ended the call, he was met with an if-looks-could-kill-glare from Jessica. "I'm not going to the prom with Ty McKenna."

"Mom, are you out of your ever-lovin' mind?" Madison sputtered. "He was in *People* magazine's Most Beautiful issue a few years back. The man is hotter than a two-dollar pistol on a Saturday night."

Noah looked at Madison and chuckled. "You have embraced your inner redneck."

"I know, and I like it," she answered with a grin, then turned her attention back to her mother. "Mom, you need to embrace Ty McKenna."

"I already told you that he is not my type."

"Mom, do you have a type?"

Her chin came up a notch. "Yes, and it's not him!"

"You don't really know Ty McKenna, Jessica," Noah calmly pointed out.

"I've seen him in action at Chicago Blue Bistro, remember? He is a womanizer. He invented 'Hit it and quit it' . . . Sorry, earmuffs, Madison."

"Mom, I'm almost twenty-four. Get real."

"Jessica." Noah arched one eyebrow. "You seem like a woman who can hold her own. Or maybe you think you can't handle Triple Threat?"

"Pffft," Jessica protested with a flick of her hand.

"Then what do you have to lose, Mom?" Madison challenged. "Seems like perfect timing to me."

"Speaking of . . ." Jessica turned to Noah. "Why is Ty McKenna here in Cricket Creek already? The play isn't until next weekend."

"Business," Noah answered. "He could make a real difference in a project we're looking into."

"Mom, it sounds like you need to be nice to Ty. Really nice." She gave her mother a sly wink.

"Madison!"

"I'm just sayin'. You might have to take one for the team."

"Maaa-di-*son*! Dear God, you have way too much of your aunt Myra in you!"

"Mom, I'm just teasing. Sheesh, y'all need to chill."

Noah chuckled. "Y'all?"

"Hey." She wiggled her ring finger. "I'm back home again and here to stay. I'll start writing some Southern-bent plays. I always did like Tennessee Williams."

Jessica closed her eyes and shook her head. "Noah Falcon, I could wring your doggone neck!"

Madison clapped her hands. "So that's a yes?"

"A very reluctant one," Jessica muttered, but Noah sensed a bit of breathless excitement in her tone that she tried to mask.

"I knew you bought that amazing dress for a reason. You just didn't know it at the time." Madison did a little tap dance. "Isn't that just the way life is? Oh, this is going to be a good night. This is going to be a good, *good* night!" Madison sang and did another little jig that had Noah laughing in spite of his jitters. "A fairy-tale night."

Jessica shook her head slowly. "You and your imagination."

Madison laughed with pure delight. "Oh, you just wait and see!"

Madison's mood was infectious. She seemed so happy, and he knew the reason. For a second Noah thought Jessica might have actually started to smile, but then she seemed to catch herself. "Lay off the caffeine, would ya, Madison? Or is it another dirty martini?" Noah asked.

Madison refused to be subdued. "I am drunk on life!" she announced with a little spin, but she had to catch herself on the edge of a table. "Oh . . . that made me dizzy."

"You *are* dizzy," Jessica said, but this time she had to grin at her Madison's antics. The transformation in moody little Madison was amazing, and Noah could tell that Jessica was happy for her daughter. But now that Myra and Madison each had someone special in their life, Jessica must be feeling lonely.

"Are y'all gonna get dressed at Aunt Myra's place?" Noah asked.

"Yes," Madison answered.

"Okay, I'll have a limo pick Ty up at my condo

and then swing by and scoop you guys up. How's that sound?"

"Peachy," Jessica muttered. "Do we seriously need a limo? That must have cost an arm and a leg."

"Mom!" Madison demanded. "Just kick back and have some fun for a change." She looked at a crew that was stringing hundreds of twinkling lights and then back at her mother. "This is truly going to be a night to remember. I just know it."

26

If the Flip-flop Fits

"Coming!" Olivia shouted when her doorbell chimed again. After tossing the towel she had been drying her legs with into the bathtub, she reached for her robe. While knotting the sash she hurried to the front door, wondering who could be calling on her just a couple of hours before the prom started. At the door she stopped and put a hand to her chest. Perhaps this was a clue to what her father had alluded to yesterday? So far her day had been boringly normal.

With a wildly beating heart she pushed back the frilly yellow curtain and peeked outside. What? Chrissie, Allie, and Jackie stood on her porch and the three of them held a plastic garment bag. With a frown, Olivia tugged the door open. "Hello, girls. Shouldn't y'all be primping for the prom?"

"We will, but first we have something for you," Chrissie replied. "May we come in?"

"Sure." Olivia stepped aside for them to enter.

Chrissie glanced at Jackie, the bubbly cheerleader, who became the spokesperson for the trio. "Well," Jackie began, "we were shopping at Chloe's Closet yesterday."

"The vintage clothing store on Main?" Olivia asked. These girls were mall shoppers.

Jackie nodded firmly. "I read in *Glamour* that you can find some sweet stuff in these kinda stores. Retro is totally in right now," she explained and shoved her hand beneath Olivia's nose. "Check out this amazing ring."

Olivia looked at the gigantic flower-shaped design and nodded. "It's . . . interesting."

"Thanks," Jackie said. "Well, we saw this dress on the mannequin and decided it was soooo you."

Chrissie and Allie's heads bobbed in agreement.

"You bought a dress for me?"

"You totally need to wear this to the prom tonight," Jackie said and then nodded for the girls to unveil their treasure.

They fumbled with the plastic bag and finally revealed a midnight blue evening gown shimmering with threads of silver. But the halter neck and a pretty revealing slit up the side gave Olivia pause. "I—Uh," she stammered, "it's lovely, *truly*, but I already have a dress picked out to wear." She gestured toward her bedroom.

The three of them pulled a collective pout and then Jackie spoke up. "This style is meant for someone tall and slender just like you! It skims your body and flares out at your calves . . . so perfect for dancing."

"Girls, I'm merely a chaperone. I won't be doing much dancing." Since she'd blown off Brandon Turner, she doubted that even he would ask her to dance.

"You might want to bust a move," said shy little Allie.

Olivia tilted her head at the dress. "I just might bust a seam in that dress," she said, but Jackie shook her head firmly.

"No way. This material is totally soft and stretchy. Feel it." The girls thrust the dress closer to her. "Go ahead." Jackie encouraged her with a nod. "Touch it."

Olivia nibbled on the inside of her lip and then

reached out and gingerly touched the dress. "Oh!" The material was indeed soft, and she suddenly wondered what it would look like on her. She had never worn something so sexy.

But then she pulled her hand back. "Girls, I really appreciate your gift, but I can't wear it."

"It's just a prom dress," logical Allie pointed out.

Olivia opened her mouth to protest again, but Chrissie's bottom lip started to quiver and she said, "Miss Lawson you are my favorite teacher of all time. Please wear this in honor of our graduating class." She blinked at her hopefully and the other girls nodded.

"I . . ." Olivia hesitated just long enough for the trio to pounce.

"Oh, thank you!" Jackie said. "You won't be sorry! This is going to be an amazing night. Make sure you have your picture taken with us, okay?"

"Yes, but—" Olivia began, but suddenly she was holding the dress and the girls were scampering out the door. After they were gone she stood there, blinking out the bay window.

Finally, she looked down at the evening gown draped over her forearms. Fingers of sunlight reached through the glass and made the dress shimmer. "Oh, dear God, what have I just agreed to?"

She walked on shaky legs into her bedroom and laid the dress on her bed next to her much more conservative black sheath. "Oh, what the heck?" She untied her robe and slipped into the midnight blue gown. After taking a deep breath, she turned and looked into her full-length mirror. "Oh . . . my." She swallowed and then ran her hands down the soft material.

While the dress wasn't overly revealing, it was a lot sexier than anything she had ever worn, and when she took a step closer to the mirror the slit in front exposed one long leg all the way up to her thigh. She caught

her bottom lip between her teeth, then turned sideways to check out her bare back. "I can't wear this," she
whispered.

And yet the dress fit as if it had been made for her.

She turned back to face the mirror and lifted her hair
up from her neck, thinking that a simple French twist
would be perfect. She had silver sandals and a silver
clutch . . .

"No!"

But then she remembered her promise to her father
to go along with whatever was asked of her. "But what
could . . . Omigod." Her pulse raced and her eyes widened at her reflection. Could Noah be coming to get
her? To take her to the prom just as he had said he
would?

Her cell phone rang and she reached inside her purse
on her bed. Her fingers trembled as she wondered if it
might be *him*. Oh . . . "Hey, Madison. What's up?"

"I just wanted to know when you'll be ready. Jason
is backing out on me, but I still want to help chaperone.
Can I come with you?"

Olivia's heart sank, but she inhaled a deep breath
and tried to sound normal. "Sure." At least she wouldn't
be walking in by herself. "Hey, you won't believe it, but
some of my students bought me an amazing vintage
dress to wear."

"Wow, that's cool! Are you going to?"

She flicked a glance at the mirror. "I said I would, but
I don't think so."

"Oh, come on, Olivia. Don't be a wimp. You don't
want to disappoint them, do you?"

"No, but—"

"Then wear it. Mine is very promish. Spaghetti straps,
low back."

"But you're not a teacher at Cricket Creek."

"So what? Hey, did you try it on?"

"Yes . . ."

"And does it fit?"

Olivia nodded at her reflection. "Like a glove."

"Then wear it! Quit being a fuddy-dud. We won't be wallflowers. I'll dance with you!"

Olivia had to smile at her young friend's enthusiasm. Her life certainly had picked up the pace in the past few months. After inhaling deeply once again, she made her decision. "Okay, but when you get here you'll have to let me know if you think it's too revealing."

"I promise. See you in a little while. A lot of you," she added with a giggle that had Olivia rolling her eyes at her reflection.

"You can say that again."

"Oh, Olivia, this little town needs some more shaking up. Pour yourself a nip of Kentucky and get ready to have some fun, girl!"

Olivia laughed. "A nip of Kentucky?"

"Bourbon, sister. Hey, this is my state, my town now, Olivia."

"Well, you *were* born here, you know."

Madison chuckled. "And now I'm back and going to the prom! See you in a bit."

Olivia ended the call and then shook her head. Other than the dress, this prom was shaping up to be like all the other ones she had chaperoned over the years. As she headed to the bathroom to get ready, she wondered what her father was making such a big fuss about last night and actually felt a little stab of disappointment.

Even so, she took special pains with her hair and makeup since the dress was so pretty. She added some smoky drama to her eyes and used a darker shade of lipstick than normal. After giving her French twist one last shot of hair spray she tugged a lock of hair loose to fall forward and brush against her cheek. Tear-shaped faux-diamond earrings dripped from her earlobes and a matching necklace added a touch of sparkle between her breasts.

Olivia walked back into her bedroom and slipped her feet into the silver sandals. After taking a deep breath she stood in front of the full-length oval mirror for a moment. "Wow . . ." She gazed at her reflection with a sense of awe. Until recently she had never really thought about her appearance much except to focus on being neat and tidy. But being with Noah had changed all that. He made her feel beautiful. Desirable. She had to wonder what he would think of her in this dress, and a lump formed in her throat when she thought of that.

She put her fist to her mouth and whirled around, half tempted to take the dress off, pull on her sweats, and simply stay home. There would be plenty of people there to chaperone. But just when she reached up for the clasp at the nape of her neck her doorbell chimed. "Oh, get over your sorry self," she muttered and picked up the silver clutch. She hurried as fast as she could in her unaccustomed heels, giving herself a pep talk along the way. When the bell rang again she tugged the door open. "Hold your horses! I'm . . ." She faltered and her eyes widened. "Oh, my goodness!"

"As a matter of fact, the horses are being held," Noah said with a slow grin.

Olivia looked beyond him to the shiny white horse-drawn carriage waiting at the curb. "Where did you manage to get that?" she asked in a breathless voice, then realized that he was standing there looking positively delicious in a jet-black tux.

He shrugged his wide shoulders. "It was a pumpkin until just a few minutes ago. And that dude driving it was a mouse."

"Of course it was." She laughed softly. "So, you must be Prince Charming?"

He presented her with a deep bow. "I am the prince

of Cricket Creek," he announced in a deep voice that
sent a hot shiver down her spine. He had a pink corsage in one hand and a yellow flip-flop in his other hand.
"And I am here to see if this fits."

"Have you tried everyone else in Cricket Creek?"

"I have. You are my last hope, although Mabel tried
really hard to squeeze her foot in," he answered with a
grin. "May I come in?"

Olivia nodded. "You may." She stepped back and allowed him to enter. When she got a whiff of his spicy
aftershave she nearly swooned.

"Have a seat for me, please."

Olivia gratefully sat down on the sofa, as her legs
were about to give way. Her heart pounded when Noah
knelt in front of her and gently took her foot in his hand.
He eased the silver sandal off and then slipped the yellow flip-flop on.

"A perfect fit," he announced and then looked up into
her eyes. "I just knew it. So you have the other one?"

"Yes. Do you want me to wear them tonight?" Olivia's heart was pounding so hard that she thought surely
her teardrop necklace must be bouncing off her chest.

Noah shook his head slowly. "No," he said. He
reached inside his tux jacket, pulled out an envelope,
and handed it to her. "This is where I want you to wear
the flip-flops."

Olivia opened the envelope with trembling fingers
and then her eyes widened. "Hawaii?"

"I thought we would need some postplay recovery.
Are you interested?" he asked and looked at her with
such hope in his eyes that it touched her heart.

"Yes," she answered softly.

"Excellent," he said with a huge smile. "But first
we have a ball to attend." After he took the flip-flop
off, he slipped the sandal back onto her foot and then
reached for the cluster of tiny pink rosebuds accented

with white baby's breath and silver ribbon. "Your wrist, please."

"Certainly." Olivia smiled as she extended her arm and wondered when she was going to wake up from this dream.

Noah slid the corsage over her hand and up to her wrist. When his fingers brushed against her skin she felt a flutter in her stomach.

"Noah . . . I'm sorry that—" she began, but he put a fingertip to her lips.

"Livie, it's okay," he assured her, and when she shook her head in protest, he said, "No, *really*." He rubbed his thumb across her bottom lip and looked into her eyes. "Hey, listen," he continued softly, "you've always been about everyone else's needs and feelings. Your father. Your students. This town. But tonight?" He stopped as if trying to gather his emotions.

"Yes?"

Noah took her hands in his. "Tonight, my beautiful princess, it's all about you." He tugged her gently to her feet and pulled her into his arms. After kissing her softly, he said, "I love you, Olivia."

"Oh, Noah, I love you too." She put her palms on either side of his cheeks. "And I will go anywhere with you. New York . . . the ends of the earth. It doesn't matter. As long as I'm with you."

Noah leaned in and rested his forehead against hers. His shoulders moved up and down and she knew he was gathering his emotions. Finally, he pulled back and looked at her. "It means the world to me that you said that, Livie. But you won't have to leave Cricket Creek. I still have a few more surprises up my sleeve tonight. Are you ready?"

She gave him a soft, lingering kiss and then nodded. "I am ready."

But before they headed out the door he took a step

back and swept his gaze over her from head to toe. "You take my breath away in that dress."

"And you are absolutely stunning in that tux, Noah Falcon." She looked at the midnight blue piping on his shirt and the matching handkerchief tucked in his pocket. "You knew about the dress?" she asked and then raised her eyebrows. "Wait—you planned this entire thing, didn't you?"

"I had lots of help."

"Lots? Let me guess . . . Chrissie, Jackie, and Allie. Oh, and Madison! She set me up too."

He nodded slowly. "Um, but you set her up, remember? Guess it was payback." He gave her a sideways glance. "And I do have to admit to doing a bit of matchmaking of my own," he boasted, rocking back on his heels.

"Really?" Her eyebrows shot up. "Who?"

He crooked his elbow in invitation. "Come with me, Princess, and find out."

Olivia tucked her arm through his and they headed out the door to the awaiting carriage. But instead of going straight down the road to the high school, they took a scenic ride around town. She really did feel like royalty . . . well, Cricket Creek royalty anyway. People everywhere stopped and waved, prompting Olivia to ask, "Was I the only one in town who was in the dark about this?"

"Yep, that's a pretty safe bet. Good thing we had to put this together so quickly or I'm sure you would have found out, being the busybody that you are." Olivia laughed, but he looked at her with suddenly serious eyes. "This town loves you to pieces, Livie. Everybody jumped on the bandwagon."

"Bless their hearts!" She swallowed hard. "I told you Cricket Creek is a town worth saving," she added in a husky voice.

"And that's what we're going to do."

"How?" Her eyes widened. "With the baseball complex?"

"Just sit back and let the evening unfold."

Olivia smiled and tucked her arm through his. "Okay," she answered and she truly felt like a fairy tale princess as they *clip-clop*ped through town. Finally, just as the sun was setting, they ended up in front of the gym entrance at the school. Noah helped her down and then tipped the driver.

As they strolled down the sidewalk to the gym doors, Olivia felt a sense of anticipation. "We're late, so I guess everyone is inside," she commented when no one was in sight.

"Waiting your arrival," he replied, but then he paused at the double doors. "I do love you, Livie," he said, but before she could reply he pushed the door open with a soft *whoosh* ...

When they stepped inside it was pitch-black and silent.

Olivia's heart pounded and her hand in his trembled. He gave her a reassuring squeeze. A moment later the ceiling came alive with hundreds of twinkling lights against a dark background looking like a star-filled sky. Olivia sucked in a breath and was overcome with emotion. Round tables covered in white linen with matching high-backed bow-tied chairs were squeezed together for a bigger than normal crowd. Lovely floral arrangements topped the tables, along with tiny votive candles floating in water.

And all eyes were on them!

The audience remained silent while they made their entrance, but when Noah leaned over and gave her a kiss they burst into wild applause. Olivia's chest ached with emotion when it hit her that this had all been set up ... *for her*. She looked out over the crowd of grinning students and then spotted a table with her father, Myra, Madison, Jason, and . . . Wait—Jessica Robinson in an evening gown next to a handsome man that she didn't recognize. She looked up at Noah, and as if reading her mind he said close to her ear, "That's Ty McKenna sitting next to Madison's mother."

"The baseball player?"

Noah nodded. "My efforts at matchmaking. I guess you're rubbing off on me. Look!" With a big grin he pointed toward the stage, where a banner draped at the back read: CRICKET CREEK HIGH SCHOOL PROM 1996!

Olivia put a hand over her heart. "This is the prom night I never had!"

"From the fashion to the music, most of tonight will be a throwback to the nineteen nineties." Noah pointed to the walls. "There are posters of movies and pop culture. They thought of everything."

Olivia had to cling to his arm for support. "So much trouble for me?"

"It wasn't trouble, Olivia." He tilted her chin up. "More like so much love for a very deserving person."

Olivia couldn't keep a tear from sliding down her cheek. "I am blown away and the night has just begun."

Noah smiled as he chased away the tear with his thumb and when she heard the collective sigh from the crowd another tear escaped. "You're right," he agreed as he pulled her onto the dance floor. "Olivia, this is only the beginning . . ." and she knew he wasn't referring just to this night.

Noah led her to a microphone set up in the center of the dance floor and the lights went up. "Good evening, everyone!" he announced and his words were met with thunderous applause. "I want to thank everyone who pitched in and helped pull this off. It wasn't easy to fool Olivia Lawson. She tends to know everything that's going on in Cricket Creek." He gave her a sideways wink and grinned and was caught with an elbow jab that had everyone laughing. "I know y'all are eager to eat and start dancing, but first I have a little announcement to make." He glanced over at Ty and his grin got bigger. "Well, maybe I should say that I have a big announcement to make."

When a hush fell over the room, Noah took Olivia's hand but then had to pause when he was hit with an unexpected wave of emotion. Finally, he took the microphone in his hand and began.

"As most of y'all know, I came back here to my hometown when my character, Dr. Jesse Drake, was blown to smithereens on *Love in the Afternoon*. Well, the secret got out that my acting skills needed some serious sharpening, so I decided to come to Cricket Creek to try out for *Just One Thing*, the heartwarming and funny play written by our very own Madison Robinson." He looked over to Madison and raised his palm for her to stand. When she bowed, she was met with another round of thunderous applause.

Noah grinned. "She took a chance on giving me the lead, and with the help of Olivia the two of them managed to whip me into shape. Let me tell ya, it wasn't easy, but I am proud of our work and I'm excited that opening night is next week." When he paused and swallowed hard, Olivia gave his hand a squeeze. "When I arrived back in town, I was so thrilled to get cookies at Grammar's Bakery, an ice cream at the Dairy Hut, and pizza at Papa Vito's. There are so many memories here for me . . . I could go on all night. But I was saddened to see so many businesses struggling." He shook his head. "The marina is in trouble and the beautiful high-rise that I'm living in by the river is barely hanging on." When the audience fell silent, he inhaled a shaky breath and then smiled while raising his fist skyward. "But y'all refuse to give up!" His declaration was met with cheers and whistles. "Myra's Diner is being remodeled and turned into the upscale Wine and Diner. Madison's play is sold out."

He looked at Olivia and smiled. "Of course, I was told by someone I won't name that if I was going to be in this play I had better take it seriously or my butt would be kicked."

"Noah!" Olivia hissed, and when the mic picked up her voice the crowd erupted into laughter.

"I know." Noah nodded at the crowd and then angled his head at her. "I was pretty darned scared, so I thought I'd better take saving this town a step further and build a baseball complex down by the river," he announced and the crowd cheered like crazy. "With the help of my friend Tyler McKenna, who is here with us tonight, and Mitch Monroe, an investor friend, we hope to be breaking ground just as soon as we get through all of the permits and red tape. If all goes well—and so far it has—next summer we will have a professional baseball team in Cricket Creek, Kentucky!"

While the crowd cheered Noah looked at Olivia, who beamed back at him. The love shining in her eyes warmed him to his toes. He held up his hand for silence. "Olivia Lawson told me that this town needed saving. She said that Cricket Creek wasn't just buildings and businesses but a community and a way of life that needs to be preserved. I couldn't agree more!" The crowd cheered again, and he nodded to Madison, who reached under the table. When she walked toward him with a big metal sign, everyone quieted down and waited.

"Thanks, Madison," Noah said, keeping the sign turned away from the crowd. "I've always been thankful for the support I've gotten from Cricket Creek, and when I rode into town the welcome sign reading CRICKET CREEK, KENTUCKY, BIRTHPLACE OF NOAH FALCON made me grin with pride. But I have a new sign that I want erected," he said and after glancing at Olivia he flipped it around. "This isn't just where I was born. This is the home of Noah Falcon! So I changed the word "birth-place" to "home." It's official. I'm back!"

The crowd came to their feet. Noah handed the sign back to Madison and then pulled Olivia to his side. "Now let's get this party started!" he shouted. In the crazy cheering he didn't notice the arrival of Chrissie, Jackie, and Allie until Chrissie reached up and took the microphone.

Chrissie bounced her palms downward. "Would y'all please have a seat? Thanks!" she said and then smiled over at Noah and Olivia. "Just a few weeks ago Mr. Noah Falcon came roaring down Main Street in that flashy red convertible of his and woke up this sleepy little town. All I can say about that is that we sure needed it!"

Olivia joined in the laughter, but she looked over at her father and gave him a slight nod before putting her arm around Noah and hugging him closer.

Chrissie pointed at the banner behind her. "And while we are grateful to Noah Falcon for all he has done and what he is going to do, tonight's prom is in honor of Olivia Lawson, who has been dedicated to her profession and this town. No one works harder or cares more," Chrissie said, and once again everyone in the entire room came to their feet.

Olivia was glad to have Noah's strong arm around her because she was overcome with emotion. She brushed a tear away and waved to the crowd.

Chrissie put her hand up and then motioned Allie and Jackie to come forward. Jackie held a crown and Allie held a tiara. "The class of two thousand eleven has voted and the overwhelming response was to crown Noah Falcon and Olivia Lawson as prom king and queen!" Jackie placed the crown on Noah's head and Allie secured the tiara on top of Olivia's French twist. Wild applause, cheers, whistles, and camera flashes lasted a good ten minutes. Finally Chrissie subdued the crowd and said, "It is only fitting that they have the first dance. And of course after a heated discussion we have chosen the perfect song! Then we will have dinner before the rest of us join Noah and Olivia to dance the night away!" She swept her arm in an arc toward them. "And now may I present our two thousand eleven Cricket Creek High School prom king and queen!"

Olivia's heart pounded when the room went dark and then with the first line of LeAnn Rimes singing "You Light Up My Life," the twinkling lights lit up the night. Noah swept her into his arms and Olivia found herself floating across the dance floor feeling like a fairy-tale princess. And as she twirled past her father's table she saw Myra's head leaning against his shoulder and they were both crying. She caught a glimpse of Madison and Jason glowing with happiness. And when she spotted spitfire Jessica sitting next to superstar Tyler McKenna, her matchmaking radar went on full alert. Hmm ...

As she danced past all of the smiling young faces, it occurred to her that they would all have paths to take and choices to make. She suddenly thought of her mother, but instead of anger she felt only sorrow. And in that moment she forgave her. Ah ... who knew that forgiveness was such an uplifting, liberating feeling? It was as if a rubber band around her heart had been cut free.

"I didn't know you were such a good dancer," Noah whispered in her ear.

"Me neither," Olivia replied. "I feel like I'm in the middle of a dream. If I wake up in a minute, I'm going to be ticked to no end."

Noah tilted his head back and laughed but then looked into her eyes. "Me too, unless I wake up next to you. I love you, Livie." His voice was gruff and full of emotion.

"I love you too," she said in his ear and then kissed his cheek.

When the song ended Noah looked down at her and arched an eyebrow. "Well, we've already been upgraded from prince and princess to king and queen. What do you think will happen next?"

Olivia laughed. "I don't know, but I can't wait to find out." She tilted her head at him. "Oh, and Noah Falcon?"

"Yes, my queen?"

"Welcome home."

He looked into her eyes and smiled. "There's no place I'd rather be."

When he leaned in and gave her a sweet but lingering kiss, the lights and music faded into the background and for a moment Olivia closed her eyes and forgot that they were the center of attention in a crowded room. Wild applause and whistles brought them back to the present and Olivia opened her eyes to a standing ovation. She put her hand over her mouth and then looked up at Noah. "Let's hope we get this same reaction on opening night."

"Oh, we will," Noah assured her with a firm nod. "You can count on it."

27
Just One Thing

"I had forgotten how much I hate wearing makeup," Noah commented as they stood backstage. With a wince he gingerly scratched the tip of his nose. "This goop is even worse than the stuff they used on *Love in the Afternoon*. I look like a goon."

"Not to the audience," Olivia assured him with a hand on his arm. "I know it seems excessive, but it all works well with the lighting. I just peeked through the curtains. It's a packed house and you can just feel the excitement. Have you looked? Ty McKenna is out there. He's sitting next to Jessica."

"Let me guess. You orchestrated that little coincidence."

"Me?" She put a hand to her chest.

"Yeah, you."

"Okay, yes."

He shook his head and smiled but then swallowed hard. "Damn, Livie, I think I might throw up."

Olivia angled her head and almost chuckled, but then she realized that he was serious. When she reached down and took his hand, it was cold and clammy. "Listen, you know your lines inside out. In dress rehearsal you were perfect and didn't miss a beat." She squeezed his hand. "You'll do fine. No, I take that back. You're going to be amazing."

He responded with a groan. "I think I have to pee."

"You just did that."

"Oh . . . right. I think my entire system is on overload."

"Noah, remember that you're going to be telling a story with your voice and body. I know it isn't easy, but try to get rid of the tension. The audience will be able to see it. Feel it."

"Okay." He closed his eyes and inhaled a deep breath. "Damn, I wasn't this nervous when I pitched in the World Series."

"And why not?"

He shrugged. "I was confident."

"You should be confident right now. Remember our affirmation exercises?"

"Yes." With his eyes still closed he nodded slowly. Last-minute scurrying was going on everywhere, but Olivia stayed focused on Noah. She was having her own case of opening-night jitters, but she didn't let him see it.

"You can do this." She put her hands on his shoulders. "Say it."

Noah opened his eyes. "I can do this." He nodded slowly and then repeated, "I can do this."

"Feel better?"

"Yeah." Noah attempted a smile. "Wait. I can't remember my first line." He fisted his hands. "Livie, what is my first line?"

"Hi, Amy."

"Right."

"You were teasing, weren't you?" She gave his shoulder a shove.

"Yeah," he scoffed.

She eyed him closely.

"Okay, no."

"You're going to do fine."

"I know . . ."

"Say it like you mean it."

"I know!" He blew out a long sigh and then mustered up a real smile. "I love you."

Olivia felt her heart swell. Seeing the vulnerable side of this big, strong man made her melt. "I love you too. And love is what Ben and Amy are all about. Listen, forget about the footlights and the black hole and just live the part. Okay?"

He nodded more firmly this time.

"Come on, Noah, let's kick some . . ." She looked right and left and then whispered, "Ass."

Noah laughed and Olivia was relieved to see some of the tension leave his shoulders. "I don't think that particular expression fits our situation."

"You're starting to talk like me."

"And you're starting to talk like me. What's up with that?"

She raised her eyebrows. "Spending too much time together?"

He tucked a finger beneath her chin. "Never."

Olivia looked at him and felt a warm rush of happiness.

"Break a leg," Madison said as she rushed past Noah and Olivia.

"I always hated that expression," Noah complained. "Seriously, what does that mean?"

Olivia smiled. "Origins are heavily debated, but basically the superstition in theater is that it's bad luck to wish good luck, so it's an antonym theory."

"Makes sense in a weird way. But then again, baseball players understand superstitions."

"Places!" Madison shouted.

"Oh . . . God," Noah muttered and leaned over for a quick kiss. "Now that's gotta bring me some major good luck."

Olivia took her place on the park bench and picked up the newspaper she was supposed to be reading. She took a deep, calming breath and waited for the swishing sound of the curtain opening. The bright lights went on, bringing life to the stage as she assumed the role of Amy. She could feel the excitement, the energy from the audience, and when Noah made his entrance there was a round of applause. She glanced up from her paper and her heart pounded as he walked across the stage past the park bench, hesitated, and then backed up.

"Hi, Amy."

"Ben?" She widened her eyes, lowered the paper, and put a hand to her chest. "Ben Crawford?"

Ben walked over, raised one leg to rest his foot on the park bench, and propped his elbow on his thigh. "None other."

"What brings you back to town?" She looked up at him with hopeful eyes.

"Business. Just passing through."

"Oh." She lifted her chin a notch, but her voice sounded crestfallen. "I've heard you've done quite well for yourself over the years," Amy said with false brightness and gave her hair a who-cares flip. But her eyes told a different story to the audience.

Ben shrugged. "I guess you could say that." He looked away as if the admission made him uncomfortable. "And you? Still making jewelry?"

She nodded shyly. "I recently opened my own shop downtown."

"Well, congratulations!"

"Oh . . ." Amy waved a dismissive hand. "I barely make ends meet, but I seem to make my customers happy and I love what I'm doing."

"I'm glad for you. Where are you living?"

"I rent a tiny apartment above my shop. Where are you living these days, Ben?" She tilted her head to the side.

He shrugged again. Looked away. "Here and there."

"I heard you have houses on both coasts."

"I live mostly out of a suitcase."

She put a hand on his thigh but then quickly withdrew it when their eyes met. "That can't be easy."

"You always had a soft heart." He put his foot down on the ground and straightened up. "Well, it was nice to see you, Amy."

Amy nodded. "Same here." She watched Ben walk away with wistful eyes.

Olivia could feel the audience lean in and listen. They knew what was going on. Ben and Amy were long-lost lovers who went their separate ways. They were being given a chance to reconnect and they were blowing it!

Ben walked all the way to the other end of the stage, but then suddenly stopped and turned around. Amy quickly snapped her newspaper back in place and pretended not to notice until Ben was once again in front of the park bench. "Amy, would you like to go and grab some lunch?"

Amy took a moment to look up from her paper. "I thought you were just passing through?"

"I can spare a little time for an old . . . friend."

Amy let the seconds tick by and then nodded. "Okay—it will be interesting to catch up."

Olivia could hear the audience breathe a sigh of relief. The curtain closed and the stage crew scurried in to change the set to an outdoor café. Ben and Amy laughed over old times while the sun sank lower in the sky, and by the end of the scene it was quite clear that they still had deep feelings for one another.

The second act of the play involved an inventive split

stage showing Ben wheeling and dealing in his office while Amy works quietly in her shop. They talk on the phone, send e-mails, and long to see each other. When they do, sparks fly. Ben envies Amy's simple lifestyle and she resents his over-the-top financial success. They are worlds apart with neither of them willing to give in or compromise. But as the scene progresses, Ben misses meetings to be with Amy, and she neglects her jewelry to be with him.

Olivia could feel the audience connecting and pulling for them. They get it. For Ben and Amy it becomes less about money or success and more about simply being together. Getting a second chance. But by the third act Ben and Amy are faced with a series of choices that can either bring them together or drive them apart. Madison's play hammers home the theme that above all else there is just one thing that matters most in this life, and Ben and Amy finally choose it.

Love.

During tough times it was easy to lose faith and focus, and Olivia could sense the audience homing in on and grabbing a renewed sense of hope.

The house lights flashed on, and during the curtain call Olivia and Noah were met with a standing ovation and cheers and whistles that wouldn't die down. Jason was hugging Madison in the wings. Her father and aunt Myra were brushing tears from their eyes and bouncing with excitement. Olivia hadn't known her father could bounce, and she laughed with delight. Jessica Robinson dabbed at her eyes with a tissue. Ty kept glancing at her and finally pulled her in for a hug. *Yes!*

With a huge smile Olivia looked over at Noah. She knew that he could feel the energy, the excitement. As they took another bow she said, "You saved this town, Noah."

"No, Livie." He shook his head, then brought her

hand to his mouth for a tender kiss. "Cricket Creek saved me."

Olivia blinked back tears. "There's still a lot of work to be done."

Noah smiled. "That's the fun part, Olivia. We've only just begun. . . ."

Read on for an excerpt from
Luanne McLane's next
Cricket Creek novel,

CATCH OF THE DAY

Coming from Signet Eclipse in January 2012.

"Lordy, Lordy, Jessica Robinson is forty!" Madison announced in a singsong voice. "So, Mom, how does it feel to be turning the big four-o?"

"It's just a number, Madison," Jessica answered evenly and gave her daughter a little flip of her hand for good measure. Of course it was a big, fat lie.

"Well, you certainly don't look it—that's for sure." Madison plopped down on the sofa and patted her mother's leg.

"Thank you, sweetie." Jessica smiled but didn't look up and continued to flip through the *Modern Bride* magazine, knowing that her eyes would give her away. Madison had an uncanny way of reading people, which was one of the reasons her daughter was an amazing writer. Her sweet and poignant play, *Just One Thing*, had been a smash hit at the Cricket Creek local community theater last summer and had landed her a job teaching creative writing at Cooper College, a small but prestigious liberal arts school just outside of town.

"I just hope you've passed those good genes along to me," Madison added, making no mention of the father she never knew or the grandparents who were mortified when Jessica had ended up pregnant at sixteen. But when she had shown up on Aunt Myra's doorstep in Cricket Creek, Kentucky, her feisty, free-spirited aunt had welcomed her with open arms. "I want to be a cougar just like you."

"You can't be a cougar if you're married." Jessica flicked her daughter an amused glance. "Or at least you shouldn't be."

"A MYLF, then."

"Madison!" Jessica shook her head so hard that her golden blond ponytail shook from side to side. "Wait. What is that?"

"A mother you'd like to f—"

"Okay, I get it. I swear you've got more of your outrageous aunt Myra's genes than mine!"

"That's because her outrageous genes overpowered your calm ones. Like little gene sword fights." She made little swishing motions with her hand.

"You are truly crazy."

Madison lifted one shoulder and grinned. "I'm just sayin'. But really, Mom, I would never peg you as forty. You truly don't look it but . . ." Madison swallowed and then nibbled on the inside of her lip.

Jessica inhaled a deep breath and then had to prompt, "But what?"

"You need to get out more often."

Jessica drew her eyebrows together. "I *am* out." She sliced her hand through the air.

Madison tilted her head downward and rolled her eyes up. "Mom, coming over to my condo isn't going *out*. I mean going out . . . out."

Jessica tried not to squirm in her seat. "Madison, Monday is the only day Wine and Diner is closed. You know how demanding the restaurant business is. I like to kick back and relax during my time off. Oh . . . did you see this dress?" Jessica tapped the glossy page with her fingertip in an attempt to change the subject. "I love the simple yet elegant design, don't you?" she continued. "You should really say yes to a dress soon."

"Mom, Jason and I haven't even set a date yet."

"And you've been engaged for nearly nine months!"

Madison tilted her head and sighed. "With all of the riverfront construction going on, Jason barely has time to breathe, much less worry about a wedding. When things settle down with the baseball stadium, we'll set a date. We're thinking next spring. But anyway, about going out . . ."

"Madison," Jessica warned in a low tone.

"Mom, it's your birthday!"

"Just another day as far as I'm concerned, and I am so grateful that you didn't throw me one of those cheesy parties with droopy-boob gag gifts."

"You made your thoughts on the subject crystal clear." Madison leaned over and looked at the wedding dress. "But what do you say we head over to Sully's and grab a bite to eat and a martini? Celebrate just a little?" Madison held her thumb and index finger an inch apart.

Jessica scrunched up her nose. "I don't think so." She nonchalantly turned another page of the magazine but had to swallow a stupid lump forming in her throat. Flipping through the brides' magazine reminded her of the fact that at forty her chances of a fairy-tale wedding were getting slimmer and slimmer. She put out the vibe that she was as happy as pie with her single status and that she treasured her independence, but seeing her feisty aunt Myra blissfully in love and Madison happily engaged had Jessica suddenly getting hit with bouts of lonesomeness. It sure didn't help that sexy as sin Ty McKenna, manager of the Cricket Creek Cougars, ate at Wine and Diner several times a week. And he didn't simply eat the food—he savored and appreciated her culinary efforts, carefully choosing the perfect wine to go with his meals. For Jessica there wasn't a better turn-on. Ty McKenna had awakened a yearning she had thought long gone, but she knew him from his pro-baseball days when he'd frequent Chicago Blue Bistro, where she had been head chef. She had never seen the hotshot athlete with the same woman twice, so he could flirt until he turned blue in the face, but she wasn't about to let him break her heart.

"Earth to Mom? Are you getting hard of hearing in your old age?" Madison teased and gave her mother's arm a playful shove.

"What?" Jessica cupped her hand over her ear but then mustered up a chuckle. "Sorry. I was thinking about the summer menu," she fibbed.

"Well, give yourself a break! It's your birthday!"

"So you keep reminding me."

"Because you seem to keep forgetting, old lady."

Oh, she had not forgotten. "Madison, thanks so much for the lovely necklace. Nicolina Diamante makes such beautiful handmade jewelry. It was so sweet that you remembered how much I adore her creations." Jessica put the *Modern Bride* magazine on the glass coffee table and dusted her hands together. "Now, I really should get home and start working on the menu. Summer will be here before you know it. I'm thinking about adding a mango salsa, cold corn and black bean dip—"

"Come on, Mom! We should celebrate!" Madison pleaded firmly.

"Sweetie, I love my gift but it's no big deal."

Madison pressed her lips together, which was a sure sign she wasn't giving up. "Well, then, let's go out and celebrate my teaching position at Cooper. You promised to go out and clink glasses together, but we never did." Her chin came up in challenge.

Damn . . . Madison had her there.

"Besides, I'm hungry, and I don't have anything in the fridge to fix."

"Imagine that." Jessica cocked one eyebrow. "You really need to learn your way around the kitchen, Madison. Jason is a small-town boy used to home-cooked meals."

"I can't believe my ultra-independent modern mother just said that to me," Madison muttered.

"The boy's gotta eat . . . and so do you."

Madison bounced around on the sofa cushion to face her mother. "Okay, I'll make you a deal. Come with me to Sully's, and I'll find some time this week to come over to the diner for some cooking lessons."

"Oh . . ."

Madison really wasn't playing fair, and she pounced on her mother's slight wavering. "Come on, Mom. Jason is working at the baseball stadium. I'm bored. Hungry!"

Jessica rolled her eyes. "Girl, you want some cheese with that whine?" Jessica kept her voice light but she truly didn't want to celebrate. What she really wanted was to go home, get into her pajamas and wallow in a bottle of merlot. The fact that this milestone was hitting her hard took her by surprise! But deep down she knew the reason why.

Tyler McKenna.

Also available from
LuAnn McLane

He's No Prince Charming

At sixteen, Dakota Dunn was America's Pop Princess. Now twenty-five, she's all grown up—and definitely washed up. She decides to head to her family's lakefront retreat in Tennessee, planning to write songs and transform her image from squeaky clean to kickin' country.

Turns out there's a new manager at the marina, a sexy, if cranky, cowboy Trace Coleman—a former bull riding champion benched by injuries. He's none too happy about Dakota's arrival—and makes no secret of it. But though Trace is rough around the edges, Dakota feels a pull of attraction she can't quite shake. For all his brooding, Trace has an animal magnetism that may just lead Dakota to dig in her heels and hold on tight...

Available wherever books are sold or at penguin.com

LuAnn McLane

writes

"Endearing and sexy romances that
sparkle with Southern charm."
—*New York Times* bestselling author
Julia London

Redneck Cinderella

Raised by her widowed father, Jolie Russell could keep up
with any man—that is, until wealthy and sexy land
developer Cody Dean struts into her life.

Cody buys the Russell farm with an impossible-to-refuse
multimillion-dollar offer, then relocates Jolie and her dad
to the Copper Creek Estates. But the country club
atmosphere isn't ready for Jolie's kind of country. As
her two worlds collide, Jolie wonders how she can ever
hope to capture Cody's heart without giving up her grits.

**Available wherever books are sold or at
penguin.com**